CW01261730

Midnight Movie Monographs

SPIRITS OF THE DEAD

MIDNIGHT MOVIE MONOGRAPHS

SPIRITS OF THE DEAD
(Histoires Extraordinaires)

Including three stories by
EDGAR ALLAN POE

TIM LUCAS

MIDNIGHT MOVIE MONOGRAPHS
SPIRITS OF THE DEAD
Copyright © Tim Lucas 2018

COVER ART AND DESIGN
Copyright © Neil Snowdon 2018

SERIES EDITOR
Neil Snowdon

Published in July 2018 by Electric Dreamhouse, an imprint of PS Publishing Ltd. by arrangement with the author. All rights reserved by the author. The right of Tim Lucas to be identified as Author of this Work has been asserted by him in accordance with the Copyright, Designs and Patents Act 1988.

FIRST EDITION

ISBN
978-1-786364-08-1

Design & Layout by Michael Smith
Printed and bound in England by T.J. International

PS PUBLISHING
Grosvenor House
1 New Road
Hornsea, HU18 1PG
England

e-mail: editor@pspublishing.co.uk
Internet: www.pspublishing.co.uk

Contents

3....... Author's Note
7....... Mystery of Mysteries
13...... The Facts in the Case of *Histoires Extraordinaires*
31...... Metzengerstein
45...... "Metzengerstein" by Roger Vadim
77 ..... William Wilson
98...... "William Wilson" by Louis Malle
127..... Never Bet the Devil Your Head
139..... "Toby Damnit" by Federico Fellini
207..... Premiere and Distribution
215..... Afterlife
219..... Dead Reckoning
227..... *Selected Bibliography*

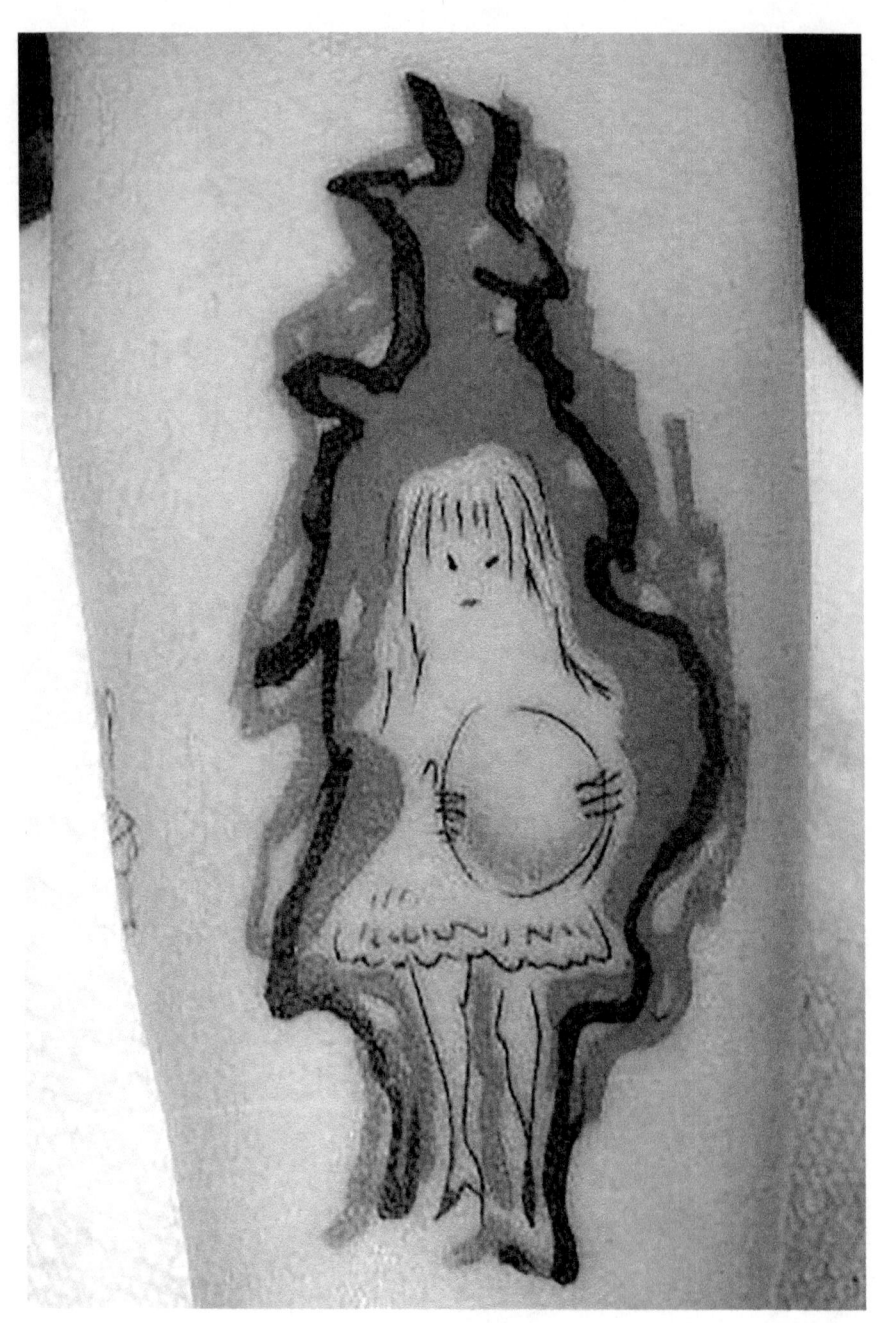

Gil Ray's arm, photo courtesy of Stacey Malone

In memory of GIL RAY
(1956—2017)

And, with love, to my *Bambina Diavola*.

"*Deep into that darkness peering, long I stood there, wondering, fearing, doubting, dreaming dreams no mortal ever dared to dream before.*"

—EDGAR ALLAN POE

Author's Note

THIS MONOGRAPH IS ABOUT *Spirits of the Dead (Histoires Extraordinaires)*, a French-Italian co-production made in 1967-68 that brought together three of Europe's most successful art house directors—Roger Vadim, Louis Malle, and Federico Fellini—to adapt, of their own choosing, three previously unfilmed stories by Edgar Allan Poe.

In order to relate the film's history with accuracy, I've had to take into account the inconvenient fact that it is not one film, but many—and I don't just mean the three individual works, but the film as a whole. The facts are messy. Although technically a French-Italian co-production, all versions of the film bear the copyright of Les Films Marceau and its French distributor, Cocinor, which indicates its French identity as dominant. This makes sense: after all, the project was conceived by Raymond Eger, a producer with Les Films Marceau, who subsequently selected and hired its three directors; however, two of the three stories were ultimately produced in Italy under the supervision of the film's Italian co-producer, Alberto Grimaldi of Produzione Europee Associati (PEA).

In France, the film is known as *Histoires Extraordinaires* ("Extraordinary Tales"), and for the greater part of this book, this will be my title of reference—though I believe the French version of the Fellini episode to be an atrocity. I give this title precedence partly because of the film's copyright but also because this was the title given to the first French collection of Poe stories by its translator, the decadent poet Charles Baudelaire, in 1856. One of the film's most notable qualities is that it is the first, and perhaps only, movie to evoke the flavor of Baudelaire in its adaptations of Poe. This version of the film includes the definitive version of Louis Malle's "William

SPIRITS OF THE DEAD

Wilson," and in Roger Vadim's "Metzengerstein," it contains unique footage of Jane and Peter Fonda giving their performances in French; this is the version of that story most flattering to it, though Peter's lines are dubbed by another actor, because Jane—a French resident since 1963— speaks her lines most persuasively in French, and she delivers most of them in live sound recording, which means that the performance we hear is the performance she gave. Unfortunately, the Vadim segment suffers in any version bearing the screen title *Tales of Mystery and Imagination* (such as the version presently shown by TCM and The Criterion Channel in America), which weds the French dialogue to the English visual track—a marriage not intended.

In Italy, the film is called *Tre passi nel delirio* ("Three Steps to Delirium"), a title I like—not only because it describes the film's narrative arc and ultimate arrival, but because it echoes the title of Mario Bava's *I tre volti della paura* ("The Three Faces of Fear," 1963; known in English as *Black Sabbath*)—the original Italian terror anthology, and a film that works in much the same way, serving up two period pieces and a stylized contemporary ringer. However, the Italian dubbing fails to serve the picture on any level.

It was always part of the film's design that it would be accessible to English-speaking audiences. Three of its five top-lined stars were American or English, while only two were French, and an American screenwriter was present on the set of both French segments. The English-dubbed export version of the film bears the aforementioned title *Tales of Mystery and Imagination*—a title which, like *Histoires Extraordinaires*, carries a literary association; in this case, to the first posthumous compilation of Poe's works (published in England by Grant Richard, 1902) to exclude his poetry, satires, criticism and essays to emphasize his attraction to the macabre. This version of the film preserves the English performances of Jane Fonda, Peter Fonda and Terence Stamp—the first two are helpful, and likewise complement footage unique to the this version, yet the third is absolutely essential to the film's best interests.

It is a tragedy of our times that many home video companies, entrusted with the preservation of vintage international cinema, have habitually suppressed the English-dubbed soundtracks recorded for such films. This is sometimes unavoidable, due to unresolvable clearance issues, but a prevailing bias against English dubs has arisen. Such tracks now tend to be seen as unnecessary and inauthentic, given the availability of original language soundtracks and English subtitles. However, we mustn't forget that subtitles are a deal-breaker for many viewers and that it was always the goal of such films to acquire large audiences, which have in fact diminished as more rights holders have chosen authenticity over accessibility. Once in a great while, an English track proves definitive. *Tales of Mystery and Imagination* is sometimes the onscreen title of a film sold on home video under the title *Spirits of the Dead*.

This, however, is not quite accurate. The title *Spirits of the Dead* only truly applies to a version of *Tales of Mystery and Imagination* that was recut and further post-produced for North American release through American International Pictures in the summer of 1969. *Spirits of the Dead* was, in fact, a *product* of American International Pictures. Exclusive to this version are two voice-over recitations by actor Vincent Price (a fixture of the company's earlier Poe productions) and a recut version of Federico Fellini's "Toby Dammit," supervised by the director himself, which removes approximately four minutes from its running time—and arguably improves it. Once the film was retired from theatrical circulation in 1972, the company's television branch AIP-TV made it available (minus its nudity and shots of graphic bloodletting) as part of a Poe syndication package from 1973 to 1982. It has since disappeared entirely from circulation, its rights having long since reverted to its producers. Though the Price recitations are included on the Arrow Academy Blu-ray disc as a supplementary item, their integration into the feature and the tighter "Toby Dammit" are no longer optional. As such, the true *Spirits of the Dead* has become something of a "lost picture."

The film was not released in the UK until April 1973, and then in a slightly cut (but still X certified) version that snubbed AIP's recut in favor of a return to *Tales of Mystery and Imagination*—a title trimmed for advertising purposes to *Tales of Mystery*.

There is one other alternative British release of the film—*Powers of Evil*, an early PAL VHS release on the Xtasy label, which runs only 77 minutes. It cuts out the Louis Malle segment and shows the Fellini and Roger Vadim segments in reverse order. I can't imagine this release was ever authorized.

I have chosen to include the three Poe stories adapted by the film to allow the reader convenient and annotated access to them. In writing about *Spirits of the Dead (Histoires Extraordinaires)* itself, I have approached the individual segments in the manner of one of my audio commentaries for DVDs and Blu-ray discs—that is, by describing their narrative development scene-by-scene, sometimes shot-by-shot, meanwhile inserting my observations, along with relevant quotes and production details, where appropriate.

Finally, I would like to express my thanks to Stephen R. Bissette, Ian Armer, Bill Pickard, Steve Saragossi, and Adrian Smith for their friendly assistance; to Dorothy Moskowitz Falarski and David Huckvale for their wise musical counsel; to Joe Busam for showing me the film on his nine-foot screen (very informative!), and especially to my good editor Neil Snowdon for his warm support and encouragement of this project. I should also mention that the late Gil Ray, to whom this book is dedicated, was a member of such respected bands as Game Theory and The Loud Family, a dear man, and the only person I've ever known who may have loved *Spirits of the Dead* more than I. He actually had Fellini's sketch of the *bambina diavola* tattooed on his arm, and I believe he was listening to Nino Rota's soundtrack when he crossed his own bridge, leaving his long battle with cancer behind him. The memory of Gil makes me wish I had written this book sooner.

—Tim Lucas

THE MYSTERY OF MYSTERIES

IT WAS A CHILL SUNDAY NIGHT in Norwood, Ohio. In 1970, Norwood was a small city within the city of Cincinnati, consisting of some 30,000 people, almost all of whom were white and who, every weekend without fail, drove back across the Ohio River to some more compelling form of home in our neighboring state of Kentucky. Most local men worked for the noxious, smoke-pumping Fisher Body automotive plant, and spent their off-hours drinking beer and smoking butts at Lutsch's Tavern near the train tracks, or tinkering with stubborn motors under the hoods of used cars they had picked up cheap or won in a card game. The local women were either extremely loud and abrasive, or totally sweet and completely withdrawn, or some third variety you just couldn't figure, but you could see them all sitting on their porches in rockers or lawn chairs, chain-smoking as they watched what they thought was the world going by.

I sure as hell didn't belong there. In later years, I would blame my geographic misplacement on a hard-of-hearing Guardian Angel, who had apparently heard my request to be assigned to Cinecittà as "Cincinnati." But, at this particular moment in time, with man newly landed on the Moon and the Beatles breaking up, I didn't yet know even this much about myself. I was already fourteen, but intellectual stimulation was rare in my world. Rare, but—as was beginning to dawn on me—not impossible.

As I say, it was a chill Sunday night. The air was charged with that anticipatory feeling that arises when the sun goes down on a school night. And where was I? I was standing under the illuminated marquee of my neighborhood movie theater, the Plaza Theater at 4720 Montgomery Road—a many-miles-long stretch of road that we locals called "the pike"—

SPIRITS OF THE DEAD

because a wisdom still beyond my ken told me there was no other place in town where I more belonged.

The day before, I had been knocked sideways. At a Saturday afternoon matinee, I had come to see *Spirits of the Dead* at this theater. And now, if I could not see *Spirits of the Dead* again, I at least had to be near it.

I wish I could be absolutely certain of the date. According to Cincinnati newspaper archives, *Spirits of the Dead* had its local premiere in the neighboring township of Oakley at the 20th Century Theater at the end of July 1969, when I was both too young and too far away to see it. It had a general re-release in November-December 1970, and played again as a supporting feature at drive-ins in March-April 1972. I can find no listings for an indoor showing at the Plaza, but their newspaper advertising was always spotty; even as a kid, I sometimes had to walk up to the pike to see what was playing on their marquee.

My most reliable guides to a correct timeframe are the newspaper listings for television showings of Mario Bava's *Kill, Baby... Kill!*, which I remember seeing first, when it ran on WXIX-TV, Channel 19, Cincinnati's premier independent station. These listings mention broadcasts taking place on Sunday, July 19 and Wednesday, July 22, 1970—and that Wednesday broadcast (11:30pm on a school night) sounds right. Another broadcast is noted on Sunday, March 19, 1972—only a couple of weeks before *Spirits'* last drive-in showings—but in 1972, the Plaza finally met the wrecking ball after a year or more of closure. So the night in question likely coincided with those November-December dates in 1970. If so, Sunday would have been November 29, a good candidate for a chilly evening. This would mean I saw *Spirits of the Dead* for the first time on Saturday, November 28th, 1970.

There was always some excitement and anticipation involved when a new Poe film came to my neighborhood theater, but in this case I had experienced trepidation as well. *Spirits of the Dead* was an R-rated film ("Persons Under 16 Not Admitted Unless Accompanied By A Parent Or Adult Guardian") promoted with the lurid tagline "Edgar Allan Poe's Ultimate Orgy!" Norwood was a very conservative town where I received warnings from school officials if the back of my hair was seen to be touching my collar. I was aware that attempting to buy a ticket to such a film at my age could very well lead to my public embarrassment, to an adult authority figure (say, a female box office cashier) denouncing me in front of others as delinquent, criminal, or worse. Fortunately, at fourteen I was tall and stocky and serious, all qualities that made me look older, so gaining admission turned out to be no problem at all.

Once my ticket was torn, what I witnessed over the next two hours took the top of my head clean off.

I staggered back out into the daylight afterwards, unable to process the parade of anachronism, eroticism, sadism, and kaleidoscopic delirium I had just seen. Adding to my disorientation, had I really seen once again the ghostly blonde-haired girl who had chilled me not so long before in that TV broadcast of *Kill, Baby...Kill!*, her spectral approach always signalled by a white bouncing ball? How was that possible? Where did she come from? And which movie was the first to introduce her?

I could literally think of nothing else for the next twenty-four hours, except how I might see and experience that disorienting deluge again.

The pen writing the story of my life chose to obsess me by denying me.

My monthly allowance was spent and my mother refused, or (quite possible) was unable, to advance me the dollar-fifty of an Adult admission to see a movie I had already seen. I begged. I called friends, offering to sell comics I knew they had coveted. Nothing worked. I looked at the clock with mounting hopelessness as the time approached when the final showing would begin. I had no money, no expectations, but as the hour approached when I knew those curtains were bound to open, I grabbed my jacket and walked up the street to the theater, leaning into the cold winds with the slim, mad hope that someone up there might see me, take pity on me, and let me pass inside.

When I got there, I could see a few people already buying tickets to the final show, but only a few. So there would be lots of empty seats. What damage could it possibly do to let me inside, to let me sit in one of the hundred or more seats going to waste? But I knew it was not my place to ask such questions, however reasonable. I took my place to the right of the box office, where a one-sheet poster for the film was mounted behind glass. My eyes drank it in.

As I held my post, I glanced at my wristwatch almost minute by minute until I knew it was *showtime*. At some point after the previews had run and the film had started, I saw the cashier leave and the box office darken. My watch advised me when the movie was most likely about to start, when the first story of the three was probably ending and the second beginning. The night air got colder and I zipped my jacket up to my chin.

A couple of men in their early-to-mid-20s, employed by the theater, came outside for a smoke. I hovered, smiling and trying to look friendly, as though taking part as they talked and joked between themselves. They sometimes shot a glance in my direction, but they never acknowledged or included me.

In my head, I rehearsed the way I might beg their indulgence. I could even imagine the way they might look around to see if the coast was clear and say, "Aw hell, go on in," but I found myself incapable of speaking up, of asking. Even now, I ask myself—why not? The worst they could have done was refuse me, to tell me it was against theater policy.

What held my tongue? Was it pride? Was it shame?

Soon, they finished their cigarettes and went back inside. Not long afterwards, one of them returned carrying a ladder. It was time to change the marquee.

The real pain set in when my watch finally told me that the third and final story, the one directed by Federico Fellini, was on the point of beginning. "Toby Dammit" was at the heart of all this madness, really. How could I begin to believe what I had seen until it dazzled me a second time? But those precious minutes also ticked away, as I watched the man unhang the plastic black letters that spelled out SPIRITS OF THE DEAD and replace them on the bright marquee with a title I forgot at the very moment it was spelled out.

I knew the movie had finally ended when the meager audience straggled back out through the front doors. I studied their faces. Not one of them looked as affected by the experience as I had been.

As I walked back home, my face burned against the brisk night air, burning because I felt so deeply ashamed of my inability to ask for what I so deeply desired.

I didn't know how or when I would ever see *Spirits of the Dead* again, but a railing voice I had welcomed inside me was adamant:

I am going to get across!

THE FACTS IN THE CASE OF
HISTOIRES EXTRAORDINAIRES

THE FILM I FIRST KNEW ONLY as *Spirits of the Dead* began its worldly adventures as *Histoires Extraordinaires*, which had its genesis in the mind of French producer Raymond Eger (1911–1982). Eger had been producing films since his twenties, when his company Les Films Véga—formed with fellow cinema enthusiasts Roger de Venloo, Francis Cosne and Alexandre Mnouchkine—backed a film called *Alerte en Mediterranée* (1938), directed by Léo Joannon and starring Nadine Vogel and Pierre Fresnay. After the war, Les Films Véga came into its own with such productions as Henri-Georges Clouzot's *Quai des orfèvres* (1947), which gave Eger the leverage to break away from his partners and form his own production company, Les Films EGE.

It was under this banner that Eger produced the final Laurel & Hardy film *Atoll K/Utopia* (1951) and the early French-Spanish co-production *Les Amants du Toléde* (1953), the latter groundbreaking in the sense that it was made simultaneously in distinct French and Spanish versions by directors Henrí Decoin and Fernando Palacíos. Eger produced several more films for Decoin and also Marc Allégret, whose *En effeuillant la marguerite/Plucking the Daisy* (1956)—a vehicle for sex starlet Brigitte Bardot—became an enormous success. It was written by Bardot's husband Roger Vadim (1928-2000), who had entered the business as Allégret's assistant, and its immense success gave Vadim the leverage to become a director with his next screenplay,...*et Dieu créa la femme/...And God Created Woman* (1956). Eger did not produce it, instead sticking with Allégret, whose next film *Sois belle et tais-toi/Be Beautiful But Shut Up*

(1958), introduced to the screen two young actors named Alain Delon and Jean-Claude Belmondo. He then renewed acquaintance with Vadim by producing his...*et mourir de plaisir/Blood and Roses*, which Paramount acquired for international release. In these early successes and ensuing friendships, the seeds of *Histoires Extraordinaires* were sown.

In the early winter of 1967, after producing Claude Chabrol's *Le scandale/The Champagne Murders*, Eger (who was then 55 years old) suffered a myocardial infarction. He was suddenly unable to work, and sent to a clinic for months of imposed rest. There, for the first month of his residency, he was forbidden absolutely anything that might excite him: visitors, conversations, television, even reading. Thus he embarked on a period of absolute isolation and loneliness in a colorless room. What began to take shape in his mind during those maddening weeks were memories from his adolescence—particularly cherished memories of the great pleasure he had experienced while discovering the stories of Edgar Allan Poe in a collection entitled *Histoires Extraordinaires*—the Charles Baudelaire translation of Poe's writings first published in 1856.[1] As Eger delighted in the scenes and passages he recalled, he began to consider the stories in cinematic terms. As day dissolved into day, he began to dream big: imagining an epic compendium of Poe stories interpreted by the greatest filmmakers on the continent. The moment his restrictions were lifted, Eger began re-reading Poe. He also had a telephone installed in his room and began conducting business from his bed.

One of the great ironies of cinema is that its decisions are often made by the people who seem to know least about it—which is to say that Eger's great sickbed eureka to produce a Poe anthology (a *"film à sketches,"* as such films were known in France) was by no means original. Even the title *Histoires Extraordinaires* had already been at least twice around the block.

In 1914, David Wark Griffith made what is generally considered to be the first great American horror film with *The Avenging Conscience, or "Thou Shalt Not Kill"*, an innovative film that told a single story wrought

---

[1] For the record, the Poe stories selected by Baudelaire for this influential but incomplete volume were: "Murders in the Rue Morgue," "The Purloined Letter," "The Gold Bug," "The Balloon Hoax," "The Unparalleled Adventure of One Hans Pfall," "Ms. Found in a Bottle," "A Descent Into the Maelstrom," "The Facts in the Case of M. Valdemar," "Mesmeric Revelation," "A Tale of the Ragged Mountains," "Morella," "Ligeia," and "Metzengerstein."

from elements taken from Poe's stories "The Pit and the Pendulum," "The Tell-Tale Heart," and the poem "Annabelle Lee."

In 1919, German director Richard Oswald made the first horror anthology film *Unheimliche Geschichten* (1919), whose title translated into French as *Histoires Extraordinaires*. It was a collection of five terror tales by different authors, including Poe's "The Black Cat." More than a decade later, in 1932, Oswald would direct a more comic sound remake of his silent classic, this time adding a second Poe story ("The System of Doctor Tarr and Professor Fether") to the mix.

Subsequent Poe anthologies include a 1949 BBC broadcast on the first centenary of Poe's death; Jean Faurez' *Histoires Extraordinaires à faire peur ou à faire rire…/Unusual Tales* (1949, which paired two Poe stories with two by Thomas de Quincey), and the Mexican *Obras Maestras del Terror* (1960) by Enrique Carreras—the first complete Poe anthology film, starring the great actor Narciso Ibañez Menta in effective black-and-white adaptations of "The Facts in the Case of M. Valdemar", "The Cask of Amontillado" and "The Tell-Tale Heart"—a list that notably includes two of the three stories that Richard Matheson would adapt within the same year for Roger Corman's anthology *Tales of Terror* (1961), which opens with the persistent beating of a human heart.[2]

M. Eger seems to have known nothing of any of this, or cared very little. If indeed he knew, his estimation of those other films must have been very low, not on the same scale as his wish to consign this great American master of the short story into the hands of his own generation's great masters, when the portmanteau format was still yielding such titles as *The Oldest Profession*, *Woman Times Seven* and *The Witches*, all released between 1966 and 1967.

It is worth noting that Eger's brainstorm roughly coincided with American International Pictures' (AIP's) apparent abandonment of their Edgar Allan Poe franchise, which had been highly profitable since its introduction in the fall of 1960. Since that time, Poe had been almost

---

[2] One would imagine the Carreras film would have been rushed into English language release. However, for obscure reasons, it was withheld from US distribution until it surfaced in 1965 through U.S. Films, a minor distributor whose actual distribution of prints was fulfilled by American International Pictures. It cannot be confirmed whether AIP acquired and then suppressed the film before advancing their own "remake," as it were, but it remained unissued until after Roger Corman announced in 1965 that he had made his last Poe picture.

exclusively the cinematic property of producer-director Roger Corman, whose reign had resulted in no fewer than eight Poe adaptations for AIP, nearly all of them starring Vincent Price: *The Fall of the House of Usher* aka *The House of Usher* (1960), *Pit and the Pendulum* (1961), *Premature Burial* (1962, with Ray Milland), *Tales of Terror* (1962), *The Raven* (1963), *The Haunted Palace* (1963, a Poe film in title only, actually based on H.P. Lovecraft's 1927 novella *The Case of Charles Dexter Ward*), *The Masque of the Red Death* (1964), and *The Tomb of Ligeia* (1965). The "Poe cycle," as it came to be known, had its starting point when Corman proposed that Arkoff and Nicholson take the $250,000 they were habitually spending to generate black-and-white double-features and produce a single, more prestigious, stand-alone feature in color and widescreen. This gamble resulted in reported profits of close to $1,500,000 in the film's first year of release, lifting AIP from its early status as a maker and distributor of black-and-white programmers to the status of a great independent. Of course, all of this was able to happen in no small part because the complete works of Edgar Allan Poe resided in the public domain.

During this period, Poe films continued to be made abroad, such as Antonio de Martino's *Horror/The Blancheville Monster* (1963) Antonio Margheriti's *Danza Macabra/Castle of Blood* (1964) and Dr. Harald Reinl's *Die Schlangengrube und das Pendel/The Torture Chamber of Dr. Sadism* (1967), but—in a rare expression of professional courtesy—their associations with Poe were not mentioned in their North American promotion.

Pit and the Pendulum may have been the biggest money-maker of the cycle, but the Poe cycle itself proved a perennial cash-cow for AIP, and commanded more respect than the company's second greatest success, the *Beach Party* series. However, someone with Corman's keen eye for economics could see that the Poe films' returns were gradually diminishing. He could also understand why: the audiences that once attended them at kiddie matinees were growing up—so Corman matured with them, abandoning the Poe cycle in 1966, in favor of motorcycles.

Before doing this, Corman signed a development deal with 20th Century Fox which gave him a modicum of office space on the studio lot where he could generate ideas for future projects. The first two such projects—*The Wild Angels* (1966) and the LSD-themed *The Trip* (1967), both "Recommended for Mature Audiences"—were considered too exploitative by the major and ended up sending him back into the yoke at AIP. At this point, as various parent groups began complaining about violence and promiscuity in films made for young people, Arkoff and Nicholson began meddling with the actual content of Corman's work, cutting and reworking scenes from *The Trip* and adding a *Dragnet*-like disclaimer at the beginning, which incensed Corman as well as the film's screenwriter, Jack Nicholson—and at the same time led to the first-ever condemnation of an AIP film by the Catholic Legion of Decency. Corman once again withdrew from the company and his next proposal to Fox, *The St. Valentine's Day Massacre*, was finally approved for production; the film was made and released later in 1967. In the meantime, AIP repackaged different combinations of reddening Corman prints as "Dusk to Dawn" Poe-A-Thons for the drive-in market while moving tentatively forward by claiming that their Jules Verne knock-off *War-Gods of the Deep* (1965) was "from Edgar Allan Poe's 'City in the Sea.'"

If anyone brought any of this information to Raymond Eger's attention, it would have surely occurred to him that, if AIP were interested in preserving their proprietary rights over the Poe brand, they were free to do so—by acquiring the American rights to the film he had every intention of making.

Roger Vadim

When Raymond Eger was ready to begin recruiting talent it was natural—considering their history together—that his first call would go to Roger Vadim. As the writer-director would remember, following the completion of *Histoires Extraordinaires*, "A year and a half ago, when I was still nervous about his health, I went to see Raymond Eger at his clinic. Instead of the sick friend I was expecting, I found an enthusiastic producer inviting me to film a story by Poe—any one of my choosing. No other director had yet been approached. I was completely free from any constraint of circumstance."[3]

---

[3] Vadim, "Perché ho scelto *Metzengerstein*" in *Tre passi nel delirio* (Bologna: Cappelli, April 1968), pp. 177. Translated by the author.

Vadim was very pleased by the invitation—"I am *always* ready to make a fantasy film!" he enthused—but he was also concerned about the possibility of conflict with *Barbarella*, his adaptation of Jean-Claude Forest's adult comic strip for Dino De Laurentiis, which was then in pre-production. Budgeted at $9,000,000 and attached to a world-wide Paramount distribution deal, it was Vadim's biggest professional break and he was obliged to begin shooting as soon as the set constructions were completed at Dinocittà. However, Eger assured him that he was flexible and that he would allow him to make his Poe story in his free time, around the timetable dictated by *Barbarella*. So Vadim agreed.

He described his process of selecting the story, which included a measure of personal identification: "As I have already demonstrated several times—I do not mind at all the idea of freely adapting a literary text for the screen if the author interests me. Three authors interested me above all others: Richard Matheson, [J.] Sheridan Le Fanu, and Edgar Allan Poe. Poe, perhaps, interested me most of all—not just as a writer, but also as a man. Apparently there were not many points in common between his life and mine, yet I completely identified with aspects of his personality.

"In making my choice of one of his tales, I proceeded by process of elimination. First of all, I eliminated everything I knew had already been done in cinema. Of all the Poe films, I had seen only two: Jean Epstein's *The Fall of the House of Usher*, an old film made before the War, and a short television adaptation of 'The Pit and the Pendulum' by Alexandre Astruc. I never saw the others, including the Roger Corman cycle[4]. In avoiding other adaptations, I was not so much afraid of compromising my fresh and original vision as I was wary of unconsciously re-enacting in public cinemas certain cinematic tropes already known.

"All in all, I eliminated anything that could be defined as a thriller... 'Murders in the Rue Morgue,' 'The Mystery of Marie Roget,' 'The Purloined Letter'—those I do not like. I mean, I always enjoy reading them. But while the killer in one of these turns out to be a gorilla, a fore-

---

[4] One cannot help but doubt Vadim's proud and convenient assertion of ignorance, considering that he named Richard Matheson as one of three writers who meant most to him in the world, as Matheson had scripted the first four films in Corman's "Poe cycle." Also, of the three segments in *Histoires Extraordinaires*, Vadim's "Metzengerstein" is by far the closest to the look and feel of Corman's Poe pictures.

runner of King Kong, the other characters do not operate in a fantastic climate.

"The Poe I like best is the one who surrenders to an excess of imagination until it transforms everything, transporting everything into a sort of cosmic storm where every point of reference is lost. My ideal would have been to make 'The Adventure of Arthur Gordon Pym,' but this would not have been possible in a film of less than ninety minutes. Or 'A Descent Into the Maelstrom.' Here too, it was a matter of means. To achieve this, we would have needed greater resources than were available to us at this time.

"Then I thought of his macabre series: those stories, I mean, which take place like [Monteverdi's] 'L'Arianna,' in a labyrinth. A vertiginous labyrinth, in the center of which stands a monstrous woman: Ligeia, for example. But even for 'Ligeia,' it would have required enough footage to feed at least one hour of projection... Finally, I re-read 'Metzengerstein.' And that very night—in a single night—I produced a dozen pages of treatment."[5]

LOUIS MALLE

While Vadim was deciding what to do, Raymond Eger kept moving forward. In revisiting Poe's stories, he had found himself particularly intrigued by the *döppelgänger* tale "William Wilson," which had not been previously filmed—at least not as a straightforward adaptation. He commissioned a script from the American expatriate screenwriter Clement Biddle Wood (1925-1994), a Harvard alumnus and former president of their *Lampoon*, who had published a well-received first novel (*Welcome to the Club*, 1966) and was at the time serving as an overseas editor for *The Paris Review*. He came well-recommended by the fact that he had previously written the English dialogue for René Clément's film *Le jour et l'heure/The Day and the Hour* (1963), starring Simone Signoret, Stuart Whitman and Geneviève Page. Eger was also likely looking ahead to the value of having an English-speaking writer aboard who could appreciate the nuances of Poe in the original and also potentially attract English-speaking talent.

---

[5] *Ibid.*, pp. 177-178.

Wood's script was promptly sent to Eger's most glorious discovery, Alain Delon, who accepted the role of William Wilson at once. It was apparently Delon's idea to approach Louis Malle (1932-1995) to direct; the two men were amicably acquainted though they had not worked together before. Of the three directors ultimately hired to make *Histoires Extraordinaires*, Malle was unique in that he was *not* offered the luxury of filming a Poe story of his own choosing—at least not at first.

Malle would later credit his participation in the project to a strange realization he had experienced on the set of *Le voleur/The Thief of Paris* (1967), his 19th century thriller starring Jean-Paul Belmondo. While blocking a scene on a soundstage at the Studios de Saint-Maurice in Val-de-Marne, he and his cameraman Henri Decaë suddenly realized that they were working on the exact same spot where they had made their breakthrough film *Les Amants/The Lovers* in 1958, eight years before.

So very much had happened in their lives since then, yet so very little had changed.

Malle subsequently found himself obsessing over the notion that his success as a film director had taken him nowhere, that he was standing in the same spot but in a deeper trench. "I was beginning to repeat myself," he recalled. "And what did my future hold? Becoming one of the major French directors, making films one after the other. I decided to shake everything up, [to] question everything. I did not want to keep making a film every eighteen months or two years. I did not want my work to become routine... So when Alain Delon called me and said, 'Will you participate in this series of three films?,' at first I refused."[6]

He refused but, not wishing to offend Delon by dismissing the offer out of hand, he agreed to read the script first. Alas, at that stage, Wood's screenplay was not sufficient to change his mind. Malle knew that, whatever film he might make next, it would have to take him outside France, outside what had become his comfort zone. A project with Delon, the biggest male star in France, did not seem to offer this.

He explained: "The script they submitted to me—[which I found] vaguely melodramatic—was not at all to my liking, and I never make a

---

[6] Unless otherwise noted, all Louis Malle quotes are taken from *Malle on Malle*, edited by Philip French (London: Faber and Faber, 1993), pp. 64-68.

movie that I do not care about. It may even happen that I will pass on a film that might otherwise interest me, in principle, if it doesn't correspond to my current state of mind... So, in the case of 'William Wilson,' I could find no reason to accept their offer because what I most wanted to do was to relax with some friends of mine in Switzerland. Switzerland—a place where one *reads*."[7]

Malle's friends in Switzerland kept an extensive personal library, which on an otherwise empty day he happened to explore. It was there that he discovered, as if providentially, an English edition of Poe's complete works. He decided to read 'William Wilson' in the author's own words. "After reading it in the original," he said, 'William Wilson' appeared to me in a very different light. What won me over was the impression of a constant tension at work inside the character. There was a tension always on the point of exploding, yet dragged-out for some time before its final detonation: it was exactly what was needed, among other things, to combat the sense of frustration I was beginning to experience from my sudden inactivity, following such a feverish period. I immediately telephoned Paris and told them that I had reconsidered. Within a week, I had written a new adaptation at top speed."[8]

Therefore, while "William Wilson" had not been a story of Malle's own choosing, it *became* the story of his own choosing.

In the time between Delon's initial call and Malle's reconsideration, Federico Fellini and his new producer Alberto Grimaldi had become attached to the project, which meant that Malle would be able to direct his segment of the film in Italy, should that prove more to his liking. "And then," he summarized, "things moved very quickly. I ended up spending half of 1967 in Italy."

Knowing that he would be rewriting the script from scratch, Malle arranged for Daniel Boulanger (1922-2014) to be brought aboard. Boulanger—himself a novelist, screenwriter, and occasional actor (he was the lead henchman in *Fantômas contre Scotland Yard*!)—had written the dialogue for Malle's *The Thief of Paris*, as a result of having written several earlier vehicles for Jean-Paul Belmondo (*L'homme de Rio/That Man From*

---

[7] *Tre passi nel delirio*, pp. 102-103.
[8] Ibid.

Rio, 1964; *Les tribulations d'un Chinois en Chine/Up To His Ears*, 1965; *Tendre voyou/Tender Scoundrel*, 1966) and Malle had been pleased with their collaboration. Ultimately, by the time Boulanger arrived, he found that Malle, unexpectedly caught up in his passion for the project, had already gone into production.

"My collaboration was very limited," confessed Boulanger. "Malle was already in the process of shooting, I spent three days in Rome, and, as they say, I 'hogged' the dialogue: that is, I modified his lines slightly to make them sound bit more natural and credible. But the characters had already been identified and characterized." [9]

Learning of the situation, Raymond Eger intuited that Boulanger (who was, after all, on the payroll) might be of greater use to Vadim—whom he knew to be falling behind schedule, as he was dividing his attentions between "Metzengerstein" and the pre-production of *Barbarella*—so he sent the writer on to Brittany to help Vadim develop his scenario.

Boulanger: "Vadim gave me a bit of a treat by establishing the situation: he left the task of inventing scenes to me, and then, from those, he would flesh-out his ideas. Then he began filming, improvising freely during the shooting."

BAIT AND SWITCH

As the production began to grow, Eger realized it was developing beyond his capacity to afford it single-handedly, so he went into partnership with Les Films Marceau of Paris, which had begun as a pre-war distribution company and started producing and co-producing films in the early 1950s. Among their most notable releases were Orson Welles' *Othello* (1951), Federico Fellini's *La Strada* (1954) and *Le notti di Cabiria/The Nights of Cabiria* (1957), Ingmar Bergman's *Sommarnattens leende/Smiles of a Summer Night* (1955), and Steno's *Mio figlio Nerone/Nero's Mistress* (1956), featuring Brigitte Bardot—all of which harbored ravens that could now be invited to knock at the chamber door of Eger's Poe project.

Curiously, when the first announcements of *Histoires Extraordinaires* were made, no mention was made of the two directors already at work on

---
[9] Ibid., pp. 188-189.

it. Instead, Les Films Marceau's press releases and trade paper advertisements trumpeted the participation of bigger guns: Ingmar Bergman, Luchino Visconti (whose 1960 film *Rocco e i fratelli/Rocco and His Brothers* had been a hit for the company), Joseph Losey, and Claude Chabrol (whose 1959 film *Les Cousins* was another LFM success). It was said that Chabrol was developing an adaptation of "The System of Doctor Tarr and Professor Fether,"[10] while Joseph Losey's tastes were running more toward the Venice-set tale "The Assignation." Luchino Visconti was mentioned in connection to a conflation of "The Tell-Tale Heart" and "Maelzel's Chess Player." It isn't known how far any of these individual projects got, but surely there was a limit to how long the eventual feature could be.

Inevitably, as new names were added to the banner, others began to fall away. Ingmar Bergman, never mentioned in connection to a specific Poe story, dropped out at some point (if he ever was truly involved) — and then proceeded to direct his only horror film, *Vargtimmin/Hour of the Wolf* (1968). In an interesting coincidence, it is the story of an artist who travels with his wife to a remote island to recover from a nervous collapse. Needing strict rest and quiet, he finds his conscious mind suddenly under siege by the darkest figments of his graphic imagination — a very Poe-like conceit.

At some point prior to Bergman's leavetaking, the project entered a kind of golden phase when Orson Welles joined the roster with a proposed new version of "The Masque of the Red Death." His script (said to be co-authored by his companion, Oja Kodar, though the cover page bears only his name) turned out to be a conflation of "Masque" and "The Cask of Amontillado," a story that had previously found its way into Richard Matheson's darkly comic adaptation of "The Black Cat" for Roger Corman's *Tales of Terror*. To provide Kodar with a role, the character of

---

[10] While it is unknown whether Chabrol generated a script at this time, he did eventually direct a short film of the story, *Le Système du Docteur Goudron et du Professeur Plume*, for French television in 1980. This project also yielded adaptations of "The Fall of the House of Usher" and "Ligeia." According to *The Cambridge Companion to Edgar Allan Poe*, edited by Kevin J. Hayes (Cambridge University Press, 2002): "These productions are fairly faithful to Poe's stories, and they do not resort to the use of stagy Gothic settings and effects. The best of the three is [Chabrol's film], which creates a sumptuously baroque atmosphere of increasing madness. In this French version, the fact that Monsieur Maillard repeatedly demonstrates that he does not know how to pour, much less drink, good wine is a clear hint that he is, in fact, insane."

Fortunato (from "Amontillado") was re-envisioned as a splendidly female rope-dancer named Fortunata. Surprisingly, the original typescript on file at the Filmmuseum in Munich, Germany runs to 57 pages—a length that could have been easily extended in production to feature length. One cannot help wondering if the project's ambitions were not part of its ultimate downfall.

The Welles Scenario

As the only unproduced element of this production known to survive on paper, it is worth paraphrasing what Welles and Kodar created, not least of all because their liberal and inventive approach to the material is so complementary to the approaches taken by the segments finally composing *Histoires Extraordinaires*, wildly diverse as they are.

The script opens with the decadent Prince Prospero (Welles) hosting festivities in his medieval castle for an elite gathering of friends, who seek his shelter from the Red Death, a plague running rampant through local territories. At the stroke of midnight, one of the more mysterious guests reveals himself to be the Red Death incarnate—and at his introduction "a great cloud of scarlet-colored dust hangs motionless over the monstrous heap of dead revelers frozen in the last agonies of the Peste, sprawling grotesquely on the ballroom floor..." There is then, as in the closing moments of Corman's adaptation (scripted by R. Wright Campbell), a quotation of Poe's closing lines, "And Darkness and Decay and the Red Death held illimitable dominion over all"—this time, however, spoken in Welles' unmistakable tones as the camera pans across the crimson carnage to reveal another Welles standing at a podium, acknowledging the applause of an audience assembled for the performance.

Acknowledging the cheers of the crowd, the Narrator makes his way across the cluttered ballroom set as the dead actors begin to stand and joke among themselves about their costumes and gruesome makeups. Prospero is among them and, at the Narrator's approach, he removes his mask and bows—revealing himself to be a real Prince, in fact the owner of the Italian *castello* wherein the performance has been staged. Welles is said to have specifically written this role for the English actor Charles Gray. The script describes the Prince quite colorfully, almost in the manner of Welles' eponymous earlier character in the film *Mr. Arkadin* aka *Confidential Report* (1953).

"A great dandy, he is most elaborately primped and corseted; his hair is dyed and curled, his cheeks are rouged, and under it all he looks like one of the very late Roman Emperors gone badly to seed. And yet, in a way, he manages to give the impression that the ruin and decay is of something rather impressive. He is flourishing (like the Green Bay Tree) a few years after the death of Byron, and somewhat before the rise of Oscar Wilde, but there is something of both in him; a matter of style, however, not of genius. The truth? He has flair, personality; it doesn't go much further than that. The evil is real enough, though. There are thick dossiers on His Highness' escapades in every police department in civilized Europe."

That last part certainly allies the Prince with Arkadin, and one can easily imagine Welles filming the story's opening festivities in the manner of *Mr. Arkadin's* costume ball.

However, we eventually learn that the setting of this adaptation is in the year 1860. As a second entertainment for his guests, the Prince introduces a circus troupe from Trieste, whose star performer is Fortunata, a beautiful rope dancer. The Prince and the showgirl share a history, as yet unknown to the performer: she once humiliated the Prince by rejecting his romantic attentions, something no woman before her had ever dared to do. It is only after her dazzling performance that she finds herself abandoned by her fellow circus workers, leaving her alone to collect her salary from the man who still desires her. Again, she rejects him—and his money, telling him that she is "not a whore." Putting a friendly face on his seething anger, the Prince tempts Fortunata into his wine cellar, where he puts her at ease by opening a conciliatory bottle of amontillado. As he leads the tour, his highly listenable, amusing narrations of the cellar's history gradually segue into hair-raising stories about its past uses as a torture chamber. He tells her the story of the infamous child murderer Gilles de Rais, then catches her off-guard by confessing that he too, like Gilles de Rais, sometimes indulges in the drinking of human blood.

When they take the last step down into his catacombs, the Prince manacles Fortunata and prepares to erect a brick wall, burying her alive.

Ultimately, he realizes that he doesn't wish to kill her, only to see her admit to his mastery over her—an emollient to his humiliation and implied impotence. According to the notes in the script:

"His requisite is darkness. Just as the girl is light itself, sunshine. He must put out that light, black it out, kill the sun. But in his heart, does he really want her to die? All he is sure of is that he wants her to fear death, to fear it in his own person. He feels that to the girl he has been, up to now, only a sort of harmless ghost, a ghost she neither fears nor even quite believes in. He has never been real to her, but now he will make himself real. Through terror, she will learn to believe in him. This is a last, despairing gesture of impotence. Assuredly, he is a sick man yearning to infect the object of his love with his own fatal disease, his own Red Death."

At the psychological moment, as it were, the Prince offers to release Fortunata—on the condition that she first cry out and admit her terror, but she refuses to submit in this way to his perverse tyranny. And so he leaves her there to die, having conquered her for the moment, but ultimately damning himself to madness as he eventually succumbs to her disembodied reproaches, cutting loose "a hoarse and terrible roar, like the roaring of some rabid beast. It is the Prince in hopeless pain, a voice out of hell... but we see that there is no real place for him to go. He will never escape."

Federico Fellini

One great name in European cinema, the most purely fantastic of them all, remained conspicuous in its omission from Eger's list. In 1967, Italian director Federico Fellini (1920-1993) had not directed a film in almost two years, not since the commercial and critical disappointment of his first film in color, *Giulietta degli spiriti/Juliet of the Spirits* (1965). Fellini himself was mired in a terrible mental crisis: it had begun with the death of his Jungian analyst Ernst Bernhard in June 1965, the man to whom he had entrusted his deepest secrets and inner workings over the past four years (and whose warnings he had ignored when he chose to take LSD therapy with another analyst in 1964); this trauma was followed in February 1966 with the sudden death of his closest collaborator, the cinematographer

The Facts of the Case of *Histoires Extraordinaires*

Gianni de Venanzo, at the age of only 45. Both of these deaths occurred after he had begun working on a new screenplay, *Il viaggio di G. Mastorna* ("The Voyage of G. Mastorna"), about the after-life wanderings of a concert cellist who has died in an airline crash, for producer Dino De Laurentiis (1919-2010). Fellini's development of the screenplay was agonized and characterized by fitful departures and returns to the project. Once, shortly after coming back to the project in an effort to reclaim personal valuables that De Laurentiis had seized with other property, Fellini collapsed and was hospitalized with an illness that nearly claimed his life. When he was released, he made an effort to continue with the project but his own near-death experience had persuaded him that to proceed would be to court his own death. Some three months after the sets for the film had begun construction at Dinocittà, Fellini wrote an emotional rambling letter to De Laurentiis explaining his inability to make the film. They came to a costly settlement: Fellini would be released from *Mastorna* (which would remain De Laurentiis' property) on the condition that he would agree to make three other pictures for De Laurentiis instead. Fellini signed the contract, but never made those movies.

At the height of these difficulties, Fellini was approached at home by a man named Alberto Grimaldi (b. 1925), who announced himself as a lawyer. Imagining the worst, Fellini managed to avoid Grimaldi for awhile but was eventually caught while trying to sneak around his uninvited guest to reach his car. As the men talked, Grimaldi explained that, yes, he was a lawyer, but he was more pertinently the successful producer of two recent Sergio Leone Westerns starring Clint Eastwood—who had just starred opposite De Laurentiis' wife Silvana Mangano in an episode of the recent portmanteau film *Le streghe/The Witches* (1967); this particular episode, directed by Vittorio de Sica, had some fantasy sequences that were so Felliniesque in flavor, that Fellini had met with and hired its cameraman Giuseppe Rotunno to come and work with him on *Mastorna*. For Grimaldi to say that he was the producer of two recent Sergio Leone Westerns was something of an understatement: *Per qualche dollar in più/For a Few Dollars More* (1965) and *Il buono, il brutto, il cattivo/The Good, The Bad, and The Ugly* (1966) happened to be—by far—the most commercially successful Italian films of the last several years. Indeed, they had shattered all Italian and French box office records. Now it was Grimaldi's dream, he made known, to produce a film signed by the *maestro*, Fellini. They briefly discussed the possibility of reviving the *Mastorna* project—Grimaldi actually acquired the rights to the project from De Laurentiis at great cost, dissolving Fellini's debt—but Fellini's renewed superstitious feelings prevailed again. Grimaldi was disappointed but not angry; the two men shook hands in agreement that they would someday work together when the stars were more correctly aligned.

It was at this juncture that Fellini was approached by Raymond Eger, who invited him to take part in his Poe *"film à sketches."* Fellini was an obvious choice, from Eger's perspective: he was experienced at making short films, as long ago as *"Un agenzia matrimoniale"* in 1953's *L'amore in città/Love in the City* and as recently as the unforgettable *"Le tentazioni del dottor Antonio"/*"The Temptation of Dr. Antonio" in *Boccaccio '70* (1962). Furthermore, Les Films Marceau had distributed two of his feature films with great success, establishing a happy prior connection.

Fellini's initial response was to challenge Eger: "Now tell me, what sense does it make to film Poe? Apart from the fact that such transplants, such associations are always unnatural and ill-fated, Poe is such a great writer that his language is a perfect unity in which the images and their meanings permeate and illuminate one another. To remove Poe from his written word, especially today, after the experiences of Existentialism, Surrealism and psychoanalysis, would be arbitrary and uninteresting, it would kill any attraction in the two fantastic institutions and constructions. And what about translating him literally? In that case, Mario Bava is the most qualified man, he would be the most rigorous and suitable director for the job."[11]

That Fellini's first recommendation was that Eger redirect his invitation to Mario Bava is enlightening, particularly in terms of how his eventual segment for the Poe film turned out. However, Eger was more interested in appending the Fellini name to his banner than acquiring the "most qualified" man for the job, so he pressed on—upping the ante by informing Fellini that he would be directing this tribute to the great writer in tandem with Ingmar Bergman and Orson Welles. "They assured me that, of the

---

[11] Betti, Liliana. *Fellini: An Intimate Portrait* (Boston, Toronto: Little, Brown and Company, 1979), translated by Joachim Neugroschel. P. 135.

three stories, I would make one, Bergman another, and Welles the last," remembered Fellini. "So I said yes. With me, Welles, and Bergman—three visionary artists whose images have a richness of meaning—there would have been some common quality in this homage to Poe. That's why I signed, not for monetary considerations."[12]

As intrigued as Fellini was to work in tandem with Bergman and Welles, he and Eger hit an impasse when they began discussing logistics; Eger could not produce outside France, and Fellini—who had spent much of the previous year in seriously poor health—was unable to travel. The briefly insurmountable problem was then overcome when Fellini had the brainstorm to introduce M. Eger to Alberto Grimaldi. He was gratefully welcomed into the fold as co-producer, and Fellini would be free to film in Rome.

For undetermined reasons, Fellini was not informed of Roger Vadim's participation at the time of his signing. Perhaps because, when Louis Malle was approached—evidently around the same time—he *had* been so informed, made it clear that he did not care for Vadim nor his work, and initially refused the project. However, both Fellini and Malle were lured in, at least in part, by the possibility of having their work presented in tandem with that of Orson Welles. Alas, in September 1967, Welles officially parted company with the project, going on to direct *Dead Calm*, an adaptation of a suspense novel by American writer Charles Williams. As Fellini later suggested, Welles' departure may have had something to do with his distrust of the producers, who may have baited him as well with attractive, companionable names that vanished from the advance ballyhoo as quickly as one of the rabbits in Welles' magic act.

It is also possible that Welles' submission was ultimately deemed unsuitable—either for its frankly incommodious length (which threatened to make Eger's project a diptych at best), or because the stories he had chosen had been recently filmed by Roger Corman for AIP—"The Cask of Amontillado" in *Tales of Terror* (1962) and "The Masque of the Red Death" as a stand-alone feature in 1964. Both of these had received theatrical releases throughout Europe at still more recent dates. It didn't matter that the stories themselves were in the public domain; AIP might

---

[12] Samuels, Charles Thomas. *Encountering Directors* (New York, NY: Putnam, 1972).

have legitimate cause to file a lawsuit if Les Films Marceau appeared to "remake" one of their productions.

Fellini was not pleased and considered pulling out of the deal—which he insisted would have been his legal right as the project he had signed onto had substantively changed from the letter of his contract. However, by this time, his work on the script was too far along, and he didn't want to add a second unfinished film to his train. According to his personal assistant Liliana Betti, "Whenever [Fellini] had to mention his two colleagues, he always said, with embarrassing nonchalance: Malle and Bergman. If someone pointed out the mistake, he would burst out laughing, pretend to think a moment and then, serious once more, say: Bergman."[13]

Raymond Eger had finally sifted through all the possibilities he had envisioned to the finality of what his Poe project would be. He had his troika.

Though on the surface a motley crew, ill-matched by their own argumentative assent, the three directors finally chosen to helm *Histoires Extraordinaires* shared something significant in common at the time of their collaboration: each of them had come to the end of a road. Louis Malle knew that he could only proceed with his career in a radically new environment. Federico Fellini could only move forward in the context of a wholly new creative support system. Roger Vadim did not know at the time that he was about to make his last film with his wife, Jane Fonda (b. 1937)—but, as his then-brother-in-law Peter Fonda (b. 1940) observes in his autobiography, Vadim was the sort of man who could smoke pot, take mescaline, or drop a tab of acid and make it known at the height of its effect that he felt nothing whatsoever.

To meet their respective futures would involve extreme, even unthinkable change, but... *they were going to get across.*

The first story in *Histoires Extraordinaires* is "Metzengerstein"—so let us begin there.

---

[13] Betti, *ibid.*, p. 152.

METZENGERSTEIN

"A Tale in Imitation of the German"
by Edgar Allan Poe, 1832

Pestis eram vivus — moriens tua mors ero.[14]
— *Martin Luther*

HORROR AND FATALITY have been stalking abroad in all ages. Why then give a date to this story I have to tell?[15] Let it suffice to say, that at the period of which I speak, there existed, in the interior of Hungary, a settled although hidden belief in the doctrines of the Metempsychosis. Of the doctrines themselves—that is, of their falsity, or of their probability— I say nothing. I assert, however, that much of our incredulity (as La Bruyere says of all our unhappiness) *"vient de ne pouvoir être seuls."*[16]

But there are some points in the Hungarian superstition which were fast verging to absurdity. They—the Hungarians—differed very essentially from their Eastern authorities. For example, *"The soul,"* said the former—I give the words of an acute and intelligent Parisian—*"ne demeure qu'un seul fois dans un corps sensible: au reste—un cheval, un chien, un homme meme, n'est que la ressemblance peu tangible de ces animaux."*[17]

---

[14] Translation: "In life, I have been your plague; in death, I shall be your death."

[15] These two lines, presented as a handwritten epigram signed by Poe, appear onscreen following the main titles of *Histoires Extraordinaires*, before "Metzengerstein" begins. The source of the quotation is not identified, so it is assumed to apply to the whole of the film – which indeed covers a variety of time periods – and not the first story in particular.

[16] "… comes from being unaccustomed to solitude."

[17] "The soul lives but once in corporeal form: for the rest, a horse, a dog, even a man, there is nothing like a tangible resemblance to such animals."

The families of Berlifitzing and Metzengerstein had been at variance for centuries. Never before were two houses so illustrious, mutually embittered by hostility so deadly. The origin of this enmity seems to be found in the words of an ancient prophecy—"A lofty name shall have a fearful fall when, as the rider over his horse, the mortality of Metzengerstein shall triumph over the immortality of Berlifitzing."

To be sure, the words themselves had little or no meaning. But more trivial causes have given rise—and that no long while ago—to consequences equally eventful. Besides, the estates, which were contiguous, had long exercised a rival influence in the affairs of a busy government. Moreover, near neighbors are seldom friends; and the inhabitants of the Castle Berlifitzing might look, from their lofty buttresses, into the very windows of the Palace Metzengerstein. Least of all had the more than feudal magnificence, thus discovered, a tendency to allay the irritable feelings of the less ancient and less wealthy Berlifitzings. What wonder, then, that the words, however silly, of that prediction, should have succeeded in setting and keeping at variance two families already predisposed to quarrel by every instigation of hereditary jealousy? The prophecy seemed to imply—if it implied anything—a final triumph on the part of the already more powerful house; and was of course remembered with the more bitter animosity by the weaker and less influential.

Wilhelm, Count Berlifitzing, although loftily descended, was, at the epoch of this narrative, an infirm and doting old man, remarkable for nothing but an inordinate and inveterate personal antipathy to the family of his rival, and so passionate a love of horses, and of hunting, that neither bodily infirmity, great age, nor mental incapacity, prevented his daily participation in the dangers of the chase.

Frederick, Baron Metzengerstein, was, on the other hand, not yet of age. His father, the Minister G—, died young. His mother, the Lady Mary, followed him quickly. Frederick was, at that time, in his eighteenth year. In a city, eighteen years are no long period; but in a wilderness—in so magnificent a wilderness as that old principality, the pendulum vibrates with a deeper meaning.

From some peculiar circumstances attending the administration of his father, the young Baron, at the decease of the former, entered immediately upon his vast possessions. Such estates were seldom held before by a nobleman of Hungary. His castles were without number. The chief in point of splendor and extent was the "Palace Metzengerstein." The boundary line of his dominions was never clearly defined; but his principal park embraced a circuit of fifty miles.

Upon the succession of a proprietor so young, with a character so well known, to a fortune so unparalleled, little speculation was afloat in regard to his probable course of conduct. And, indeed, for the space of three days, the behavior of the heir out-heroded Herod, and fairly surpassed the expectations of his most enthusiastic admirers. Shameful debaucheries — flagrant treacheries — unheard-of atrocities — gave his trembling vassals quickly to understand that no servile submission on their part — no punctilios of conscience on his own — were thenceforward to prove any security against the remorseless fangs of a petty Caligula.[18] On the night of the fourth day, the stables of the Castle Berlifitzing were discovered to be on fire; and the unanimous opinion of the neighborhood added the crime of the incendiary to the already hideous list of the Baron's misdemeanors and enormities.

But during the tumult occasioned by this occurrence, the young nobleman himself sat apparently buried in meditation, in a vast and desolate upper apartment of the family palace of Metzengerstein. The rich although faded tapestry hangings which swung gloomily upon the walls, represented the shadowy and majestic forms of a thousand illustrious ancestors. *Here*, rich-ermined priests, and pontifical dignitaries, familiarly seated with the autocrat and the sovereign, put a veto on the wishes of a temporal king, or restrained with the fiat of papal supremacy the rebellious scepter of the Arch-enemy. *There*, the dark, tall statures of the Princes Metzengerstein — their muscular war-coursers plunging over the carcasses of fallen foes — startled the steadiest nerves with their vigorous expression; and *here*, again, the voluptuous and swan-like figures of the dames of days

---

[18] One of the story's few sentences to make its way, with minor changes, into the narration of Roger Vadim's adaptation. It is worth noting too the remarkable similarity between Frederick, Baron Metzengerstein, and what is told of the early life of the irredeemable Duc de Blangis in the Marquis de Sade's *The 120 Days of Sodom*, which was written in 1785 but not published until 1904 – making it most unlikely that Poe ever had access to it.

gone by, floated away in the mazes of an unreal dance to the strains of imaginary melody.

But as the Baron listened, or affected to listen, to the gradually increasing uproar in the stables of Berlifitzing—or perhaps pondered upon some more novel, some more decided act of audacity—his eyes were turned unwittingly to the figure of an enormous, and unnaturally colored horse, represented in the tapestry as belonging to a Saracen ancestor of the family of his rival. The horse itself, in the foreground of the design, stood motionless and statue-like—while, farther back, its discomfited rider perished by the dagger of a Metzengerstein.

On Frederick's lip arose a fiendish expression, as he became aware of the direction which his glance had, without his consciousness, assumed. Yet he did not remove it. On the contrary, he could by no means account for the overwhelming anxiety which appeared falling like a pall upon his senses. It was with difficulty that he reconciled his dreamy and incoherent feelings with the certainty of being awake. The longer he gazed, the more absorbing became the spell—the more impossible did it appear that he could ever withdraw his glance from the fascination of that tapestry. But the tumult without becoming suddenly more violent, with a compulsory exertion he diverted his attention to the glare of ruddy light thrown full by the flaming stables upon the windows of the apartment.

The action, however, was but momentary; his gaze returned mechanically to the wall. To his extreme horror and astonishment, the head of the gigantic steed had, in the meantime, altered its position. The neck of the animal, before arched, as if in compassion, over the prostrate body of its lord, was now extended, at full length, in the direction of the Baron. The eyes, before invisible, now wore an energetic and human expression, while they gleamed with a fiery and unusual red; and the distended lips of the apparently enraged horse left in full view his sepulchral and disgusting teeth.

Stupified with terror, the young nobleman tottered to the door. As he threw it open, a flash of red light, streaming far into the chamber, flung his shadow with a clear outline against the quivering tapestry; and he shuddered to perceive that shadow—as he staggered awhile upon the threshold—assuming the exact position, and precisely filling up the contour, of the relentless and triumphant murderer of the Saracen Berlifitzing.

To lighten the depression of his spirits, the Baron hurried into the open air. At the principal gate of the palace he encountered three equerries. With much difficulty, and at the imminent peril of their lives, they were restraining the convulsive plunges of a gigantic and fiery-colored horse.

"Whose horse? Where did you get him?" demanded the youth, in a querulous and husky tone, as he became instantly aware that the mysterious steed in the tapestried chamber was the very counterpart of the furious animal before his eyes.

"He is your own property, sire," replied one of the equerries, "at least he is claimed by no other owner. We caught him flying, all smoking and foaming with rage, from the burning stables of the Castle Berlifitzing. Supposing him to have belonged to the old Count's stud of foreign horses, we led him back as an estray. But the grooms there disclaim any title to the creature; which is strange, since he bears evident marks of having made a narrow escape from the flames."

"The letters W. V. B. are also branded very distinctly on his forehead," interrupted a second equerry, "I supposed them, of course, to be the initials of Wilhelm Von Berlifitzing—but all at the castle are positive in denying any knowledge of the horse."

"Extremely singular!" said the young Baron, with a musing air, and apparently unconscious of the meaning of his words. "He is, as you say, a remarkable horse—a prodigious horse! although, as you very justly observe, of a suspicious and untractable character; let him be mine, however," he added, after a pause, "perhaps a rider like Frederick of Metzengerstein, may tame even the devil from the stables of Berlifitzing."

"You are mistaken, my lord; the horse, as I think we mentioned, is *not* from the stables of the Count. If such had been the case, we know our duty better than to bring him into the presence of a noble of your family."

"True!" observed the Baron, drily; and at that instant a page of the bedchamber came from the palace with a heightened color, and a precipitate step. He whispered into his master's ear an account of the sudden disappearance of a small portion of the tapestry, in an apartment which he designated; entering, at the same time, into particulars of a minute and circumstantial character; but from the low tone of voice in which these latter were communicated, nothing escaped to gratify the excited curiosity of the equerries.

The young Frederick, during the conference, seemed agitated by a variety of emotions. He soon, however, recovered his composure, and an expression of determined malignancy settled upon his countenance, as he gave peremptory orders that the apartment in question should be immediately locked up, and the key placed in his own possession.

"Have you heard of the unhappy death of the old hunter Berlifitzing?" said one of his vassals to the Baron, as, after the departure of the page, the huge steed which that nobleman had adopted as his own, plunged and curveted, with redoubled fury, down the long avenue which extended from the palace to the stables of Metzengerstein.

"No!" said the Baron, turning abruptly toward the speaker, "dead! say you?"

"It is indeed true, my lord; and, to the noble of your name, will be, I imagine, no unwelcome intelligence."

A rapid smile shot over the countenance of the listener. "How died he?"

"In his rash exertions to rescue a favorite portion of his hunting stud, he has himself perished miserably in the flames."

"I—n—d—e—e—d—!" ejaculated the Baron, as if slowly and deliberately impressed with the truth of some exciting idea.

"Indeed," repeated the vassal.

"Shocking!" said the youth, calmly, and turned quietly into the palace.

From this date a marked alteration took place in the outward demeanor of the dissolute young Baron Frederick Von Metzengerstein. Indeed, his behavior disappointed every expectation, and proved little in accordance with the views of many a maneuvering mamma; while his habits and manner, still less than formerly, offered anything congenial with those of the neighboring aristocracy. He was never to be seen beyond the limits of his own domain, and, in this wide and social world, was utterly companionless—unless, indeed, that unnatural, impetuous, and fiery-colored horse, which he henceforward continually bestrode, had any mysterious right to the title of his friend.

Numerous invitations on the part of the neighborhood for a long time, however, periodically came in. "Will the Baron honor our festivals with his presence?" "Will the Baron join us in a hunting of the boar?"—"Metzengerstein does not hunt"; "Metzengerstein will not attend," were the haughty and laconic answers.

These repeated insults were not to be endured by an imperious nobility. Such invitations became less cordial—less frequent—in time they ceased altogether. The widow of the unfortunate Count Berlifitzing was even heard to express a hope "that the Baron might be at home when he did not wish to be at home, since he disdained the company of his equals; and ride when he did not wish to ride, since he preferred the society of a horse." This to be sure was a very silly explosion of hereditary pique; and merely proved how singularly unmeaning our sayings are apt to become, when we desire to be unusually energetic.

The charitable, nevertheless, attributed the alteration in the conduct of the young nobleman to the natural sorrow of a son for the untimely loss of his parents;—forgetting, however, his atrocious and reckless behavior during the short period immediately succeeding that bereavement. Some there were, indeed, who suggested a too haughty idea of self-consequence and dignity. Others again (among them may be mentioned the family physician) did not hesitate in speaking of morbid melancholy, and hereditary ill-health; while dark hints, of a more equivocal nature, were current among the multitude.

Indeed, the Baron's perverse attachment to his lately-acquired charger—an attachment which seemed to attain new strength from every fresh example of the animal's ferocious and demon-like propensities—at length became, in the eyes of all reasonable men, a hideous and unnatural fervor. In the glare of noon—at the dead hour of night—in sickness or in health—in calm or in tempest—the young Metzengerstein seemed riveted to the saddle of that colossal horse, whose intractable audacities so well accorded with his own spirit.

There were circumstances, moreover, which coupled with late events, gave an unearthly and portentous character to the mania of the rider, and to the capabilities of the steed. The space passed over in a single leap had been accurately measured, and was found to exceed by an astounding difference, the wildest expectations of the most imaginative. The Baron, besides, had no particular *name* for the animal, although all the rest in his collection were distinguished by characteristic appellations. His stable, too, was appointed at a distance from the rest; and with regard to grooming and other necessary offices, none but the owner in person had ventured to officiate, or even to enter the enclosure of that particular stall. It was also to be observed, that although the three grooms, who had caught the steed as he fled from the conflagration at Berlifitzing, had succeeded in arresting his course, by means of a chain-bridle and noose—yet no one of the three could with any certainty affirm that he had, during that dangerous struggle, or at any period thereafter, actually placed his hand upon the body of the beast. Instances of peculiar intelligence in the demeanor of a noble and high-spirited horse are not to be supposed capable of exciting unreasonable attention, but there were certain circumstances which intruded themselves per force upon the most skeptical and phlegmatic; and it is said there were times when the animal caused the gaping crowd who stood around to recoil in horror from the deep and impressive meaning of his terrible stamp—times when the young Metzengerstein turned pale and shrunk away from the rapid and searching expression of his earnest and human-looking eye.

Among all the retinue of the Baron, however, none were found to doubt the ardor of that extraordinary affection which existed on the part of the young nobleman for the fiery qualities of his horse; at least, none but an insignificant and misshapen little page, whose deformities were in every body's way, and whose opinions were of the least possible importance. He (if his ideas are worth mentioning at all) had the effrontery to assert that his master never vaulted into the saddle without an unaccountable and almost imperceptible shudder; and that, upon his return from every long-continued and habitual ride, an expression of triumphant malignity distorted every muscle in his countenance.

One tempestuous night, Metzengerstein, awaking from a heavy slumber, descended like a maniac from his chamber, and, mounting in hot haste, bounded away into the mazes of the forest. An occurrence so common attracted no particular attention, but his return was looked for with intense anxiety on the part of his domestics, when, after some hours' absence, the stupendous and magnificent battlements of the Palace

Metzengerstein, were discovered crackling and rocking to their very foundation, under the influence of a dense and livid mass of ungovernable fire.

As the flames, when first seen, had already made so terrible a progress that all efforts to save any portion of the building were evidently futile, the astonished neighborhood stood idly around in silent, if not apathetic wonder. But a new and fearful object soon riveted the attention of the multitude, and proved how much more intense is the excitement wrought in the feelings of a crowd by the contemplation of human agony, than that brought about by the most appalling spectacles of inanimate matter.

Up the long avenue of aged oaks which led from the forest to the main entrance of the Palace Metzengerstein, a steed, bearing an unbonneted and disordered rider, was seen leaping with an impetuosity which outstripped the very Demon of the Tempest.

The career of the horseman was indisputably, on his own part, uncontrollable. The agony of his countenance, the convulsive struggle of his frame, gave evidence of superhuman exertion: but no sound, save a solitary shriek, escaped from his lacerated lips, which were bitten through and through in the intensity of terror. One instant, and the clattering of hoofs resounded sharply and shrilly above the roaring of the flames and the shrieking of the winds—another, and, clearing at a single plunge the gateway and the moat, the steed bounded far up the tottering staircases of the palace, and, with its rider, disappeared amid the whirlwind of chaotic fire.

The fury of the tempest immediately died away, and a dead calm sullenly succeeded. A white flame still enveloped the building like a shroud, and, streaming far away into the quiet atmosphere, shot forth a glare of preternatural light; while a cloud of smoke settled heavily over the battlements in the distinct colossal figure of—*a horse.*

"METZENGERSTEIN" WAS POE'S FIRST published short story. It made its debut in the pages of Philadelphia's *Sunday Courier* on January 14, 1832. The subtitle "A Tale in Imitation of the German"—a reference to Germany's standing as the 19th century mainspring of what is now known as Gothic fiction—indicates that Poe undertook the story in the manner of a pastiche, thus imposing upon it the sense of ironic distance or detachment that now tends to be viewed as "Brechtian." It may well have been added to shield its young author from direct or overly harsh criticism. It is the kind of literary device that might come naturally to a writer who was also a professional critic.

Stephen Peithman, author of *The Annotated Tales of Edgar Allan Poe* (1981), has valuably identified some antecedents of this story: Horace Walpole's 1764 novel *The Castle of Otranto*, in which a picture comes to supernatural life, whose 1811 introduction by Walter Scott also apparently contributed some ideas; Benjamin Disraeli's 1826 novel *Vivian Grey* (which Poe is known to have reviewed), in which a character becomes absorbed in a portrait of an ancestor astride a ferocious looking horse; and Richard Henry Dana's 1827 poem "The Buccaneer," in which a woman's horse returns three times to avenge her violent death.

Peithman goes on to observe that "Metzengerstein" is unique among Poe's tales in that it offers only a single explanation for its mystery—an explanation that is, furthermore, supernatural; exactly the kind of explanation that the author's later stories were eager to challenge or at least balance with more rational, logical reasoning. The explanation of this tale of "metempsychosis" (or transmigration of souls) that Peithman recognized is that the soul of the aged Baron William von Berlifitzing migrates at the moment of his death in the inferno into the body of a horse—a horse branded on its brow with his own initials, though it is not recognized as one of his own by his stablemen, presumably because the animal is so outwardly changed in character by its possession.

However, there are at least two other explanations that occur to me. The first is that the centuries-long enmity between the two houses, an inheritance that has contaminated young Frederick with a desire to commit constant evil, dies within him when the last surviving heir of his rival house expires. The second explanation—which I feel is strongly suggested by the sentence "From this date a marked alteration took place in the outward demeanor of the dissolute young Baron Frederick Von Metzengerstein"—is that Frederick "becomes" William at the moment of his death, rather than the horse. This would allow for the displacement of Frederick's angry spirit into the horse, which would explain its cowering effect on his equirees, the human look that Frederick sees in its eyes, and even the W. V. B. branding on its brow—because a brand does not signify the owner, but rather the property of an owner. The locus of this transference of souls would appear to be the tapestry. The simpler reading, that William is reborn as the horse, does not account for the horse's indomitable fury, but if we read this as Frederick's bucking anger at having been so mastered, it makes sense—as does the means by which the horse and rider meet their common end.

Though "Metzengerstein" was never adapted to film prior to *Histoires Extraordinaires*, and remains one of his more obscure stories, there is much about it that seems familiar, due in part to Poe's reworkings of its concepts in later works, as well as other adaptations of his creations to cinema. Its depiction of a dark animal suddenly appearing as an avenger of wrong, or harbinger of doom, is echoed in the story "The Black Cat" (1843) and in the poem "The Raven" (1845), and Roger Corman's film *The Tomb of Ligeia* ends with a fiery conflagration in which the tragic hero, Verden Fell (Vincent Price), nearly survives but is dragged back into the flames by a struggle with a black cat possessed by the spirit of his first wife.

However, prior to *Histoires Extraordinaires*, there was at least one other adaptation of "Metzengerstein" that demands recognition. In 1963, author André Pieyre de Mandiargues (1909-1991) scored an unexpected commercial success with his novel *La Motorcyclette* , first published in Paris by Éditions Gallimard. The novel begins with an epigram from Poe's "Metzen-gerstein": "One tempestuous night, Metzengerstein, awakening from a heavy slumber, descended like a maniac from his chamber, and mounting in hot haste, bounded away into the mazes of the forest." This makes clear the otherwise obscure relationship between the two works, that *La Motorcyclette* is a modernistic retelling of "Metzengerstein."

The novel contains very little dialogue, instead attending to an interior third person delineating the innermost thoughts of Rebecca Nul, a young married woman who one morning leaves her sleeping husband, zips her naked body inside a leather outfit that includes a facial covering and goggles, and mounts a powerful Harley-Davidson motorcycle (a liberating gift from her lover Daniel Lionart), whose throbbing energy she savors between her thighs as she rides from Geneva to Karlsruhe with the intention of giving herself to Daniel, body and soul. The journey—which recounts the stories of her childhood with her father, her marriage, her affair, and her sexual awakening under Daniel's control—climaxes in her senseless and accidental death aboard the machine.

The novel was subsequently translated into English by Richard Howard as *The Motorcycle* and first published by Grove Press in 1965. *The Girl on the Motorcycle*, a competing English translation by Alexander Trocchi, was published by Calder and Boyars in 1966. It was filmed as *The Girl on the Motorcycle* in 1968 by director and cinematographer Jack Cardiff, with Marianne Faithfull and Alain Delon in the lead roles—it was Delon's first assignment after *Histoires Extraordinaires*, and his first film as a co-producer. The film was subsequently distributed in America under the more exploitative title *Naked Under Leather*.

It could be said that Mandiargues' novel—and thus "Metzengerstein" itself—played a significant role in releasing the Harley Davidson motorcycle into the 1960s *zeitgeist* (to use a good old German word), where it would play a significant role in the careers of two other *Histoires Extraordinaires* participants: Peter Fonda as the star of Roger Corman's *The Wild Angels* (1966) and *Easy Rider* (1969), both of which end on a nihilistic note; and also Brigitte Bardot, who scored a hit single with Serge Gainsbourg's song "Harley Davidson" in 1967.

The song's lyrics serve as a plausible metaphor for Frederick, who "never vaulted into the saddle without an unaccountable and almost imperceptible shudder":

> *I don't need anyone*
> *When I'm on my Harley Davidson!*
> *I don't see anyone*
> *When I'm on my Harley Davidson!*
> *I push the starter button*
> *And leave the world behind.*
> *Perhaps I'll go to Paradise*

On a hellbound express.
I don't need anyone
When I'm on my Harley Davidson!
I don't see anyone
When I'm on my Harley Davidson!
And if I die tomorrow,
This was meant to be my fate.
I value my life infinitely less
Than this thundering engine.

I don't need anyone
When I'm on my Harley Davidson!
I don't see anyone
When I'm on my Harley Davidson!
When I feel the urge to travel,
The vibrations of my machine
Cause desire to mount
In the hollows of my kidneys.

I don't need anyone
When I'm on my Harley Davidson!
I don't acknowledge anyone, never more
When I'm on my Harley Davidson!
As I go over a hundred
I feel flames spread through my blood
If I die, why should I care
If the wind is in my hair?
If I die, why should I care
If the wind is in my hair?[19]

    I do not know with certainty that Mandiargues' novel was the inspiration for Gainsbourg's song, but the lyrics of another song from Gainsbourg's album *Initials B.B.* offers a compelling reason to assume as much. In "Ford Mustang"—intended as a duet with Bardot but ultimately sung with

---

[19] Translated from the original French by the author.

SPIRITS OF THE DEAD

African-American vocalist Madeline Bell at London's Chappell Studios in May 1968—Gainsbourg offers an impressionistic list of moments and tangibles associated with the car of his fantasies:

> *A flash*
> *A Browning and a pick-up*
> *A volume of Edgar Poe*
> *A cigarette lighter, brand Zippo.*
> *We kiss with our tongues*
> *In a Ford Mustang*
> *And…bang!*[20]

---

[20] Ibid.

"METZENGERSTEIN"
by Roger Vadim

SCRIPT by Roger Vadim and Pascal Cousin, with dialogue by Daniel Boulanger.
DIRECTOR OF PHOTOGRAPHY: Claude Renoir (Eastmancolor/Technicolor Roma).
CAMERA OPERATORS: Vladimir Ivanov, Philippe Brun, Alain Douarinou, Bernard Noisette.
MUSIC: Jean Prodromides. Editor: Hélène Plemmianikov, assisted by Catherine Gabrielides and Claire Griniewsky.
ART DIRECTOR: Jean André.
COSTUMES: Jacques Fonteray. Hairdresser to Jane Fonda: Carità.
SET DECORATOR: Jean Forestier.
ASSISTANTS TO THE DIRECTOR: Michel Clement, Serge Vallin, Jean Michel Lacor.
PRODUCTION SECRETARIES: Ludmila Goulian, André Coultet.
CONTINUITY: Suzanne Durrenberger.
CAST: Jane Fonda (Countess Frédérique), Peter Fonda (Baron Wilhelm), Serge Marquand (Hugues), Philippe Lemaire (Philippe), Carla Marlier (Claude), Georges Douking (tapestry repairer), Maurice Ronet (narrator, French version), Clement Biddle Wood (narrator, English version)[21], Andreas Voutsinas, David Bresson, Marlene Alexander, Marie-Ange Agnès. Cut from film: James Robertson Justice (Countess' advisor), Françoise Prévost (friend of the Countess).

---
[21] Some sources wrongly attribute the English narration to Canadian actor Donald Sutherland.

FILMED in Sibiril and Roscoff, Brittany in March 1967, November-December 1967, and February 1968.
RUNNING TIME: 37:55.

ROGER VADIM'S "METZENGERSTEIN" is the segment of *Histoires Extra-ordinaires* most commonly derided by viewers and critics. Vincent Canby, reviewing *Spirits of the Dead* for *The New York Times*, described Vadim's segment as "overdecorated and shrill as a drag ball."[22] Meanwhile, *Time*'s anonymous reviewer snarked, "It's all terribly kinky, with Peter [Fonda] in his leather pants, Jane in her *Story of O* décolletage, and the stallion with his quivering nostrils and muscular flanks—a pornographic *My Friend Flicka*."[23]

It's a position I can well understand, in light of the more accomplished company it keeps, but despite a tendency to say through its narrator more than it is able to show through its actors ("Somber forebodings possessed her, terror fell like a pall upon her senses"), I cannot agree that "Metzengerstein" is without value.

It is important to remember that Vadim was the only director of this particular grouping with previous experience of directing in the horror genre. It was a genre he deeply loved and in which he had excelled. His *Blood and Roses* is an exquisite and remarkable adaptation of J. Sheridan le Fanu's 19th century lesbian vampire novella "Carmilla," starring Mel Ferrer, Elsa Martinelli and, as Carmilla, Vadim's second wife Annette Stroyberg. In it, he had taken a similarly audacious stance in relation to le Fanu as Fellini would take to Poe in *Histoires Extraordinaires*; he had adapted the period novella as a contemporary story about a woman psychologically burdened and unhinged by the legends attending her family history. Such was Vadim's celebrity in the wake of the film's success that the publisher Roger Laffront hired him to select and edit a compendium of classic stories, *Histoires de Vampires*, that ran close to 600 pages.[24] In Vadim's later film, the somewhat autobiographical *La jeune fille*

---

[22] Canby, Vincent. "3 Unrelated Stories by Poe:' *Spirits of the Dead*' at Rivoli and Pacific East," *New York Times*, September 4, 1969.

[23] Uncredited. "New Movies Two Dead Spirits Out of Three," *Time*, September 12, 1969, p. 62.

[24] In 1965, the British publisher Pan Books released an English paperback edition of this volume,

assassinée/Charlotte (1974), the story's protagonist—novelist Georges Viguier, portrayed by Vadim himself—declares that his love affair with the title character had been founded upon their mutual love of *"films de vampires."*

"Metzengerstein" is not a vampire film, yet it shares with that subgenre some of its traditional trappings: decadent nobles and their cruel oppression and exploitation of the poor, ruined castle settings, human into animal metamorphosis, and the notion of metempsychosis: the idea that one might die out of one existence to awaken in another on the same plane of reality. In order to make use of his most impressive resource, his wife Jane Fonda, he adapted the central character of Frederick, Baron of Metzengerstein, to Frédérique, Countess of Metzengerstein, and in turn introduced to the screen a kind of female character seldom if ever seen in films before: a female Sadist in the true historical and literary sense.[25] In so doing, his epicurean attention to expressions of sophisticated and sexualized cruelty brought something novel to horror cinema that was promptly carried over into the Sadean excesses of the many female vampire films that appeared in its wake.

Vadim's calling card as a film director was his way with women. His career in films effectively began in 1950, when his wandering and acquisitive eye fell upon 15 year-old Brigitte Bardot on the cover of March 8th edition of *Elle*. He promptly brought the photo to the attention of his mentor, the film director Marc Allégret, whom he had been assisting for a few years. His intervention resulted in Bardot being cast in *Les lauriers sont coupés*—a film that was never made, though Vadim humself managed to "close the deal." He made sure he was present at her audition, subsequently entitled *The Vampire*.

[25] Most extravagantly cruel women in earlier cinema are motivated by cold-blooded, practical concerns such as revenge (*Thirteen Women*, 1933), greed (*Freaks*, 1932), or mental illness (*Leave Her to Heaven*, 1946). Truly Sadean female characters, whose evil is motivately strictly out of voluptuous pleasure, are more scarce but would include Marlene Dietrich in several of her performances for Josef von Sternberg (particularly *Der blaue Engel/The Blue Angel*, 1930 and *The Devil is a Woman*, 1935), Myrna Loy's Fah Lo See in *The Mask of Fu Manchu* (1932), Silvana Pampanini's Marguerite de Bourguignon in Abel Gance's *La tour de Nesle* (1955), and two particularly notable Disney characters, the evil Queen of *Snow White and the Seven Dwarfs* (1937) and Cruella de Ville of *One Hundred and One Dalmatians* (1961) – both of whom preside over death as a boon to their personal vanity. Such female characters also appeared with frequency in Italian sword-and-sandal fantasies, played by the likes of Gianna Maria Canale and Fay Spain.

became involved with her, continued to promote her for films, and eventually married her in December 1952, after her 18th birthday. The couple had wanted to marry sooner, but Brigitte's parents were against the union and withheld their permission, which led the distraught Bardot to the first of many admitted suicide attempts over a lifetime.

Once married, Vadim then embarked on a history of making erotic films with the women in his life, beginning with Bardot, to whom he was married from 1952 till 1957 (his script for *Plucking the Daisy* led to his writing and directing...*And God Created Woman*); then the Danish actress and model Annette Stroyberg, his wife from 1958 to 1961 (*Les liaisons dangereuses, Blood and Roses*); followed by Catherine Deneuve, whom he did not marry but who bore him a son, Christian, in 1963 (she appeared in his 1963 film *Le vice et la vertu/Vice and Virtue*). At the point in time that interests us, Vadim had already made two films with the American actress Jane Fonda (*La ronde/Circle of Love*, 1964; and *La curée/The Game is Over*, 1965), whom he married on August 14, 1965.

Theirs had been a long process of seduction, beginning with a first encounter in 1957, when Fonda was newly graduated from Vassar University and exploring her liberty in Paris. She recalled: "I went to Maxim's one night with Christian Marquand, the actor—Vadim's best friend...Vadim came into the restaurant with Annette Stroyberg, who was 20 and very pregnant. They weren't married yet, as he was still married to Brigitte...I was really a typical young American girl, and they all terrified me. I had this very proper façade that I used to cover up my shyness, but underneath I was intimidated and frightened! I'd heard a lot about this wild, sinister, cynical, debauched, crazy man, and when I saw this creature arrive, with his slanted Russian eyes, I thought, 'Oh, God!' I know now that I was attracted to him, although at the time I thought I hated him."[26]

Fonda became a film actress in 1960 with *Tall Story*. At some point after this, possibly in 1961 when Vadim had American business with Paramount

---

[26] Quoted in Lawrenson, Helen. "I Make Women Bud and Bloom: An Afternoon with Jane Fonda's Lousy First Husband" in the book *Latins Are Still Lousy Lovers* (Hawthorn Books, 1968). In her interview, Fonda mistakenly remembered the year of their meeting as 1960, but Stroyberg gave birth only once with Vadim, a daughter named Nadine, in 1957.

concerning the release of *Blood and Roses*, he came to Hollywood and arranged to meet her again. She remembered: "He telephoned me, and we met in the coffee shop of the Beverly Hills Hotel. We had nothing to say to each other. He wanted me to play a part in *La Ronde*, but I had my agent send a wire saying that under no circumstances would I make a movie with Roger Vadim." Instead, almost as if to flaunt her indifference to him, she decided to make her next film in Paris, acting opposite Alain Delon in René Clément's film *Joy House* (1963).

On the last night of 1964, Fonda happened to meet Vadim again—at a New Year's Eve costume ball in the Bois de Boulogne in Paris. Fonda was dressed as Charlie Chaplin, Vadim as a Red Army officer. He chased her all night until he scored a New Year's kiss at 5:00am. Fonda decided: "When a woman is that aggressive about a man, there's something behind it. He knew this, too. I found out he was all the way down the line, totally the opposite of what I'd thought he was. We started seeing each other."

The couple was soon cohabitating at Fonda's 19th century farmhouse, in the French countryside. "We had no furniture, no heat, no electricity," she recalled. "We slept in sleeping bags on the floor and ate on a board propped on sawhorses." As *Chicago Tribune* journalist Helen Lawrenson revealed in her report: "She was her own architect, and she taught workmen how to build a stone wall without cement. She found a medieval town 50 kilometers from there that was going modern and putting in sidewalks, so she bought their cobblestones, several tons of them, and had them put in her courtyard, with grass planted between them. She had birch and oak trees planted. She put fireplaces in every room; and she designed the bathroom, separated from her bedroom by a wall of glass 'because Vadim likes to lie in bed and watch me in the bathroom.'"

Vadim admitted to occupying the traditional female role in their relationship; in turn, Fonda turned their farmhouse into a home, cooked his meals, waited on him hand and foot, pampered him with sports cars and paid his frequent gambling debts, which were rumored to have laid waste to his own personal fortune. Furthermore, according to Patricia Bosworth's bio-graphy *Jane Fonda: The Private Life of a Public Woman*, when the couple married, Vadim made it clear to his new wife that he would never be sexually exclusive to her, yet this would not mean he was "unfaithful" to her. He loved her, he insisted, but he would continue to have other women. When she finally objected, Vadim advised her to try living as he did, to take lovers of her own—and soon enough, they were sharing lovers, having threesomes and later foursomes. Asked by her biographer about the extent of her gay and bisexual experiences, Fonda said "'Look, can't we leave something to the imagination? Frankly, I've probably done everything."

It is necessary to know this much of Vadim, and of Fonda and their personal relationship, to appreciate the extent to which "Metzengerstein" is expressive not only of Poe but their own lifestyle and relationship.

Filming began in March 1967 in Sibiril, in the Finestère region of Brittany, northwestern France, at the Chateau de Kérouzéré, a Breton castle whose construction began in 1425. All the castle interiors were shot there, as were the exteriors showing Wilhelm's farmhouses and stables, all standing parts of this main property, which was declared historic in 1883. The film's construction crew built a stable on the chateau grounds at a safe distance from other structures, with a view toward it being burned to the ground at the end of shooting.[27] When Vadim received word from Dino De Laurentiis that the first sets for *Barbarella* were ready for filming, "Metzengerstein" went on immediate hiatus. Shooting did not resume until late November—leaving Vadim and Fonda exactly one day to recuperate at their farmhouse before they resumed filming in the coastal village of Roscoff, in northeastern Brittany. This period of filming focused on the scenes at and around the castle of Baron Wilhelm, such as the scene in the dovecote, which were filmed on the grounds of the Château de Kergournadéac'h, not far from the hotel where the cast and crew were sequestered. The beach scenes were also filmed along its coastline under gray skies.

The filming concluded in February 1968 with some minor pick-up shots needed by the film's editor Hélène Plemiannikov (b. 1936), who happened to be Vadim's sister. (The film really was what *Time*'s reviewer called "a family affair.") Plemiannikov had previous experience with Poe, having edited Robert Lachenay's short film *Le scarabée d'or* ("The Gold Bug,"

---

[27] Bertrand Tavernier used the same location for his 1975 film *Que la fête commence…/Let Joy Reign Supreme.*

1964). Her later accomplishments would include Alain Jessua's *Traitement de choc/Shock Treatment* (1973), also with Alain Delon, as well as the three final films of Luís Buñuel: *Le charme discret de la bourgeoisie/The Discreet Charm of the Bourgeoisie* (1974), *Le fantôme de la liberté/The Phantom of Liberty* (1974), and *Cet obscur objet du désir/That Obscure Object of Desire* (1977).

Daniel Boulanger worked closely with Plemiannikov while scripting the film's narration. He said, "As for the narration, which accompanies and illustrates all of 'Metzengerstein'—and which is derived almost entirely from Poe's original text—I wrote it directly to the completed scenes, once they had been edited. I had recorded on the tape those excerpts I found appropriate: then, in the editing room, together with Hélène Plemiannikov (Vadim's sister), I tried to match them to some image or other, enlarging or rearranging them as needed. I generally reduced the conversation between the characters to the minimum. What a wonderful movie you are talking about! A few words there, half a word here!"[28]

Roger Vadim had the following insights into the story he selected: "'Metzengerstein' is one of Poe's earliest stories. Its theme, however, was one of those dearest to Poe, as he would repeat it many times. The protagonist sets in motion the device that will bring about his own destruction. At first he does not see this but, as soon as the danger acquires a visible form, instead of retreating, he becomes fascinated. Indeed, the closer he comes to death, the more its charm increases. 'Metzengerstein' is the story of a victim fascinated by his killer, who forces him to die the same death to which he himself has been condemned by the other man. It is a perfect story: two symmetrical antagonists face each other and both die because of the other, and in the same way the other died. In their case, instead of separation, death constitutes their supreme union. Baudelaire said that Poe ignored love stories but, for me, 'Metzengerstein' is one of the most erotic stories I have ever read. In my adaptation, I have therefore proposed, above all, to highlight Poe's violent, though subliminal, eroticism."[29]

As the opening title cards of *Histoires Extraordinaires* dissolve to an

---

[28] *Tre passi nel delirio*, p. 189.
[29] Ibid., pp. 178-179.

image of billowing smoke, the following epigram is superimposed onscreen in scratchy, golden handwriting: "Horror and fatality have been stalking abroad in all ages. Why then give a date to the story I have to tell? — Edgar Allan Poe."

Though it precedes the title cards for Vadim's episode by a good distance, this epigram consists of the opening words from Poe's "Metzengerstein" and were possibly meant to apply only to it — yet they also relate to *Histoires Extraordinaires* as a whole, as all three stories occupy three very different eras, all of which are at least mildly bent by surreal, unreal or unusual content.

The first thing we see is a high angle view of handsome young man lying dead on the ground, an ugly gash across his temple complementing a nearby splash of bright red blood. He appears to have fallen from a great height onto a circular and concentric arrangement of stones separated by patches of grass.[30] The high angling of the opening shot is then explained with a cutaway to a close-up of Frédérique, Countess of Metzengerstein (Jane Fonda), framed by a turret window in her castle, where she looks down upon the body with an ambiguous expression.

---

[30] This shot was likely one of the pick-up shots collected in post-production and may have been filmed on the French farm property where Vadim lived with Fonda, who (as previously mentioned) had installed such a stone garden, placing the stones herself.

"Metzengerstein" by Roger Vadim

According to the script of Vadim's segment, these color shots are remnants of an opening nightmare sequence that was intended to be shot in "grainy black-and-white":

Frédérique, a young and beautiful woman, looks at a young man whose face is pressed against a wall of granite. Her mouth wrinkles in an expression of disgust, of odiousness. Close beside her is another young woman, Claude, her head resting on her shoulder as if in the depths of despair.

Frédérique (in a low voice): What about him?

Frédérique turns to her companion, who doesn't answer. She lifts her head, holding it up. The other woman opens her eyes.

Claude (in a deep voice): Alright.

Frédérique's hand trifles with a dagger.

The boy's face has a foolish aspect, a piece of straw is sticking up out of his hair. He looks like a caged bird. Frédérique stabs him four times.

The boy, visible from the waist up, buckles slightly. Two hands clutch his shoulders.

A window opens.

Below, the pavement of the courtyard.

The boy is thrown out.

His fall.

Frédérique looks down from the window, then she scrambles up onto the sill; a moment later, she also falls.

Her cry.

Frédérique awakens.[31]

The script's separation of monochromatic dream from colorful reality would have been consistent with the approach taken by Vadim and his director of photography Claude Renoir[32] — during the filming of *Blood and Roses*, which includes a surreal black-and-white dream sequence, influenced by Jean Cocteau's *La sang d'un poète/The Blood of a Poet* (1932), in which the only color permitted is blood-red.

If the opening images were meant as fragments of a bad dream, we never see Frédérique awaken. Instead, the film cuts to her, fully awake, impatiently pacing a disordered but sumptuously appointed bedroom, which she apparently shares with a young ocelot. Like a spoiled child, she loudly summons her ever-ready majordomo Hugues (Serge Marquand) and orders him to rouse her guests, regardless of the early hour, and to ready some fresh horses.

In *Histoires Extraordinaires*, this entire scene is played in French with live sound recording; in *Tales of Mystery and Imagination* and *Spirits of the Dead*, Jane Fonda dubs her own performance in English.

"I want to ride, to forget this dream I had!"

"Are you sure it was a dream? Sometimes you forget what is true and I am the only one that can tell you what is real," the servant reasons with her, in French. In the English versions, his words overstep his station (". . . and I am the only one who can remind you you are *lying*"); either way, his words provoke an outraged glance from the Countess. Neither the English track nor the English subtitles reflect the severity of her words in French as she strikes him, calls him a *con* "cunt," and orders him to go and do what she said.

A male narrator proceeds to inform us that, at 22 years of age,

---

[31] *Tre passi nel delirio*, p. 200. Translated by the author. This rare Italian-language hardcover, the 37th in a series of screenplay editions by its publisher, contains the original shooting scripts of each segment, along with the original Poe stories, behind-the-scenes articles and interviews, and 96 illustrations.

[32] Renoir (1913-1993) was the nephew of film director Jean Renoir and the grandson of famed Impressionist painter Pierre-Auguste Renoir.

"Metzengerstein" by Roger Vadim

Frédérique, the Countess of Metzengerstein, "inherited a vast family fortune. Seldom had a noble of her country possessed an estate of such magnificence. She ruled capriciously, day was night or night day, according to her fancies"—a comment that might have better been placed before her scene with Hugues, which demonstrates it. Frightened by her dream, Frédérique decides to abruptly relocate her guests to another castle she owns, one where she spent much of her childhood. En route, she rides alongside one of her guests, a Marquis, a stout bearded man resplendently dressed in red, and demands from him something to quench her thirst. (This and one more brief shot in the next scene by the scaffold are the only appearances in the film by the prominently billed English actor James Robertson Justice, whose part was otherwise eliminated in the editing.) He presents her with a wineskin apparently filled with blood, which she spits out with another insult. The Marquis rides away, laughing. When Hugues appears in response to her apparent need, Frédérique begins laughing too. "What, we have no right to amuse ourselves anymore?" she says, mastering the moment of her brief disadvantage as her laughter echoes over a seascape where we see her entire retinue of harlequins and fairy tale regents riding in a procession. Over this image, the story's title and brief credits are superimposed, to sighing, nerve-scraping music. These exterior dialogue scenes were shot MOS (without sound) but in both French and English, allowing for precise post-synchronized sound.

The castle of Frédérique's childhood is introduced with a helicopter shot. Riding to a halt in front of a nearby scaffold where a local man has been hung, the Countess proclaims—within earshot of his grieving family—"I love this place. It's beautiful!" In *Histoires*, Hugues reminds her that she owns ten finer castles than the one where she is dragging her entourage; in *Tales/Spirits*, it is an unseen female companion who makes the observation.[33] Both comments invite her displeasure: "Better than the home of my childhood? Fool!"

There is no scene of arrival, no scene to formalize a separation between the castle of the opening scene and the new one; they seem, and probably are, indistinguishable. In the bending corridor of a castle turret, one of the aristocratic guests, Philippe (Philippe Lemaire) dashes into view as if chasing someone. He notices a teenage boy caressing Frédérique's pet ocelot as she looks on. Philippe demands to know if the boy is bothering the Countess and offers to throw him out the nearest window should it please her. Frédérique hesitates—a hesitation in which we are supposed to read the recollection of her nightmare, though this is a different boy. Instead, the scene cuts outdoors, where Frédérique entertains her decadent coterie by using the boy, standing on a barrel with a noose around his neck, as a live target for her archery practice. Cue narrator, quoting more or less from the original story: "Shameful debaucheries, flagrant treacheries, unheard-of cruelties—soon taught her vassals that nothing would guarantee them security against the remorseless [indistinguishable] of this Lady Caligula." Every arrow misses the boy until an attendant kicks the supporting barrel out from under the boy's feet, literally hanging him, until Frédérique's expert aim secures his release. Seductively, she beckons the boy closer, demanding his "necklace" as a souvenir before brusquely kicking him away.

The young ocelot is shown at oblivious, pampered rest atop furs of its own related species as we cut to a bedroom episode. Here, Philippe is shown attempting to seduce an attractive young woman—the first appearance in the film by Claude (Carla Marlier), a character introduced in the script as a participant in the opening discarded nightmare sequence.

---

[33] This may be a lingering trace of a character excised from the final cut, listed as "Friend of the Countess" and played by French actress Françoise Prévost (1929-1997), whose name still appears onscreen during the end titles scroll.

"Metzengerstein" by Roger Vadim

So intent is Vadim on telling his story elliptically, the character's name is never invoked, neither in French nor in English, making it a surprisingly anonymous role for an actress as accomplished in French cinema as Marlier, whose screen debut was as Albertine, the comically gentle and blank wife of Philippe Noiret's character in Louis Malle's *Zazie dans le Métro* (*Zazie*, 1960). She had also played Constance in Carlo Ludovico Bragaglia's *I quattro Mosquettrieri* (*The Three Musketeers*, 1963), and Nicole in Alain Resnais' *Je t'aime, je t'aime* (1968). Telling Claude that he has a surprise for her, Philippe pulls back the bedcovers to reveal Frédérique lying there in wait. Working together toward her seduction, Philippe and Frédérique pull her onto the bed between them, but she resists — running away and initiating a chase that she sees as survival, but which they see as foreplay. The pursuers split up to catch Claude between them in the curving corridors of the castle turret. She responds warmly to Philippe's advances but, as Frédérique joins them, mashing her between them, the scene cuts abruptly from this private struggle to the orgiastic revels of (we imagine) later that evening, leaving the pay-off of the encounter to our imagination.

The orgy scene that follows is strangely diffident, its costumed revelers evoking pale memories of Corman's bolder, more full-blooded *The Masque of the Red Death* (1964). Frédérique, brandishing a dagger, kisses an unnamed but always prominently-placed man as he fondles another woman, then uses the blade to taunt a nervous, distracted woman we only belatedly recognize as Claude, now wearing a radically different hair style. (This Mephistophelean-looking fellow is played by Andreas Voutsinas, a Greek-born Actor's Studio member who was responsible for "discovering" Jane Fonda and casting her in her first Broadway play, *Fun Couple*, in 1960. He continued to serve as her acting coach through the 1960s, until founding his own acting workshop, Le Théâtre des Cinquante, in Paris.) Claude then rushes away from her hostess, out of the room, at earliest opportunity.

We next see Frédérique and Claude horseback-riding together along the edge of the coast, then sharing a bath—attended by two children and a parrot—in which they playfully reach out to tweak each other's nipples, perhaps in emulation of the anonymous 16th century painting *Gabrielle d'Estrées et une de ses sœurs* ("Gabrielle d'Estrées and One of Her Sisters"). All of this is so passively directed, as if to posit the viewer in such amoral regard of the action, that it may well escape the viewer's notice that the woman who earlier fled the *ménage à trois* and orgy and the woman now so happily riding beside Frédérique and sharing her bath are one and the same.

On another riding excursion, Frédérique and her guests venture out to the edge of her property, where it adjoins the castle grounds of her cousin, Baron Wilhelm of Berliftizing (Peter Fonda).[34] As they mock him from afar, the narrator tells us that the cousins had never spoken, owing to an enmity between their families so ancient that it cannot be dated. The young Baron is a misanthrope but not unloving; his fellow creatures are his animals. He is shown speaking, directly and warmly, to his favorite horse as Frédérique and entourage mock his eccentric ways.

Peter Fonda had just finished making *The Trip* for Roger Corman when he flew to Paris for his costume fittings with Jacques Fonteray in February 1967; it was there, at this time, that he and Jane attended the French premiere of his previous film for Corman, *The Wild Angels*. He arrived in Roscoff in October but was not needed until sometime in November. He recalled spending about four hours of each day "working on the story of *Easy Rider* while watching the tides... But I became bored with this

---

[34] The English narrator's voice pronounces Berlifitzing as "Belifitchin." When Jane Fonda has to say it, it comes out "Bellafitzing."

bucolic life, and began heading to the set, where the food was terrific, and free. I had many great lunches with the famous British character actor James Robertson Justice. The production headquarters were in a very old castle, as were the dressing rooms, wardrobe, makeup, and even several sets. It was a true castle, spooky and kind of fun, with a moat, now dry, a drawbridge, and a very large courtyard. Sometimes I would get in costume, ready to shoot, but the shot would be put off, or the scene being shot would be apparently endless. I had already earned more in my *per diem* than I was paid for the gig."[35]

That night, as Frédérique's guests indulge in orgiastic delights, their hostess is shown seated amidst them looking distracted as couples and triples dally and carve meat from the half-skinned carcass of a wild boar. The implication of her distraction, supported by the words of the narrator, is that Frédérique was attracted to her strange cousin—but there is really nothing evident in her distraction to differentiate it from the alienation she was clearly feeling in the previous orgy scene.

We next see Frédérique in another of her outrageous costumes (this one with thigh-high boots and an impractical plumed hat) walking beside her horse through a leaf-strewn wood on Wilhelm's property. Suddenly her ankle is caught in a trap—and the only person near enough to respond to her demands for help is the Baron himself. He sprints to her side over immense moss-covered stones, set inside the chuckling water of a stream. Projecting an intimate knowledge of the woods, Peter Fonda looks very much as though he's jumped straight out of one of the Big Sur fantasy sequences in *The Trip*. He bends down and frees her, to which she responds insolently—but in the following days, we're told, "she had but one desire—to see Wilhelm again."

We count the days in further costume changes until the Countess and the Baron finally meet again within the embrace of a convex castle ruin, where he sits in the window of a dovecote, feeding an owl. As Wilhelm descends to approach Frédérique, their horses (Prince and Sultan) run off together—perhaps to do what they are too inhibited to do. Seeing him warmly cloaked, she petulantly mentions that she's cold and that a Metzengerstein would have the courtesy to offer his cape—at which point

---

[35] Fonda, Peter. *Don't Tell Dad: A Memoir* (New York, NY: Hyperion), p. 245.

SPIRITS OF THE DEAD

Wilhelm wordlessly enfolds her in it, without removing it. Nervously joking that he seems to speak only to animals, she invites him to her evening revels, sweetening the offer by noting that his love of animals would be appeased as "most of my guests are boars, buzzards and bears." He declines, saying that he won't be part of her "collection."

"Who do you think you are?"

"A happy man."

The scene was shot in French and in English, but it's the latter version that resonates; it's the kind of simple but "heavy" retort (in the hippie sense)

"Metzengerstein" by Roger Vadim

that Peter Fonda could sell like no one else back in 1968. (Indeed, the preamble of his auto-biography *Don't Tell Dad* reveals that "A Happy Man" was his original title for the book, though he doesn't concede where it came from.) Young moviegoers of the 1960s saw him as a rock star among actors of their generation; he had evolved beyond tepid early roles like *Tammy and the Doctor* by way of his performance as a mental patient in Robert Rossen's *Lilith*, which presented him in a more introspective, quietly intensive light. He began to play mavericks, searchers, young men who lost their way in order to find it. Wilhelm of Berlifitzing is unusual among his characters in that he seems a natural heir to wisdom, a kind of placid wiccan in relation to Frédérique's flaring witchery. In a strange way, "Metzengerstein" throws Peter's screen persona against Jane's with interesting results, in that Jane was by far the bigger star at this time, though her career choices up to this time now look far more offbeat, floundering and confused. In later years, she would admit that she looks "artificial" in films like *Barbarella*, and so she does here—until the moment she speaks with Wilhelm, her relationship to this cousin made believable by her even closer relationship to Peter. When he tells Frédérique in those few words exactly who she is, the reverse shot to her response conveys the feel of a Zen slap. Wilhelm represents Frédérique's awakening—to life, to feeling, to love—and we can see that it terrifies her, just as the casting of Jane Fonda opposite her brother gives their dynamic a substance of perversion that would be irresistible to Frédérique.

However, no one can speak that way to the Countess Frédérique of Metzengerstein and walk away unscathed. As her horse returns, before she can mount it, Vadim cuts to another close-up of her face as she hears a voice whisper her name with some urgency. She looks around and no one is there. No explanation is given as she mounts the horse and rides away, but we may presume from the actions immediately following that it represents a temptation of the Devil.

Baron Wilhelm's stables are now ablaze, his farmhands passing pails of water to combat the flames. In the mounting chaos—the horses inside bolting free or struggling against their constraints, the inferno gathering force and rising higher, consuming more and more of the outer structure, as Wilhelm runs inside to help the animals—a camera pan reveals a covertly placed Hugues, observing the fruits of his arson with pleasure. All things told, it's one of the most impressive fire sequences in cinema, Renoir's camera attending to the patterns of the fire, the minute interlacings of the smoke, the collapsing of the thatched roof, the reduction of a beautiful structure to wreckage, with the strings of Jean Prodromides' orchestra detuned, wound down and flaccidly strummed; it is—as it needs to be—a counterpart to the tapestry, the stable's deconstruction a prologue to the damage still to come. A setting sun is seen behind its roiling smoke, peering through it like a bold and pitiless eye.

Frédérique happens to be walking past an ancient family heirloom tapestry depicting the conflict between her and Wilhelm's families when she is suddenly shaken out of her self-satisfaction by its image of a large, angry-eyed black stallion, which appears to be gazing in her direction with eyes the color of fire. The image in art is then mirrored in reality as the scene cuts to a slow-motion, low-angled shot of a black stallion bolting through a smoky archway that we presume, from the smoke, to be on the Berlifitzing grounds. It's a huge, powerful animal, never before seen as part of Wilhelm's stables, and a number of workers are required to subdue and calm it. When the camera rises from the scene to show Frédérique on a high balcony inquiring what's going on, we realize that the horse has actually arrived on *her* grounds—but in the confusion and smoke, we have

"Metzengerstein" by Roger Vadim

made an unmistakable connection between the horse and Wilhelm. Hugues informs Frédérique that no one knows this horse, it did not belong to Wilhelm, and no one can calm it—but Frédérique instantly accepts the challenge. Acting now more like Wilhelm than herself, she just as quickly calms the animal, which responds gently to her touch. When one of her staff informs her that Baron Wilhelm died in the fire trying to save his favorite horse, she is shocked and goes back inside... where she discovers the horse formerly woven into the tapestry now completely burnt out.

Had the tapestry been introduced into the story earlier, this could have been a powerful moment; as it is, the tapestry feels introduced only for the purpose of providing this parallel and this later discovery. We have not seen enough of it intact to feel the inexplicable violation of its mystical loss. In a moment acted in French and badly synchronized in English, Frédérique orders Hugues to find "the best weaver there is" and have the piece restored. "You will, because I wish it!"

Time passes and we see Frédérique succumbing to frustration in the wake of Wilhelm's death, her revenge thwarted by her love, and we see her recruited to participate in her usual orgiastic activities without interest or enthusiasm. We also see a clumsily photographed encounter between her and a man she was shown kissing earlier, during which he says something we do not hear, but which seems to repel her. She is becoming as Wilhelm was, more attuned to animals. She retreats to her stables, where the black stallion has been sequestered unhappily and restlessly; her arrival seems to soothe it. She saddles the horse and rides it to the edge of the sea, everything seemingly restored to harmoniousness in their communion. The narrator explains that the Countess soon realized she was only happy when riding the horse and that she sent her fellow decadent revelers away, thereafter living the life of a recluse, attuned only to her horse, as her cousin used to be. Indoors, she watches with fascination as an elderly artisan (Georges Douking) patiently attempts to recreate what was destroyed in the tapestry.

"Fascinated," says the Narrator, "she watched the agile hands of the old man bringing back to life the great black steed, his fingers so deftly knotting the threads seemed to be weaving with a fatal logic her own destiny."

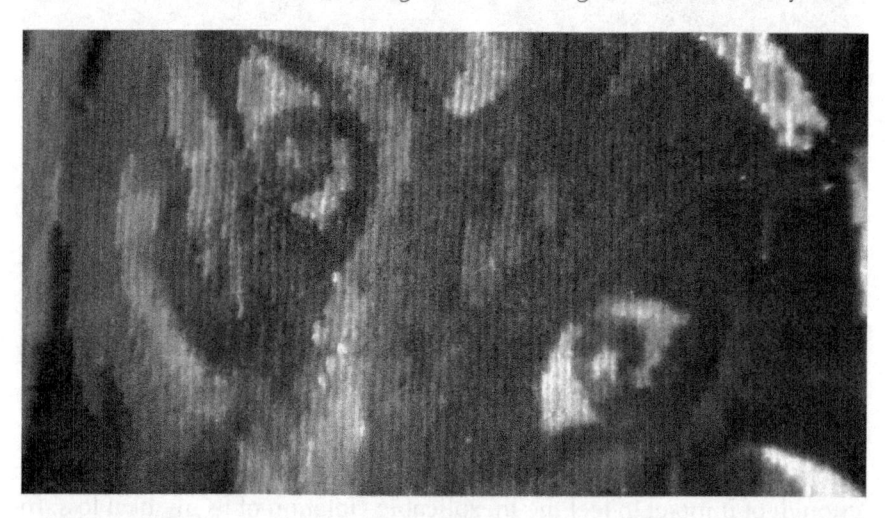

With the exception of a brief moment in which the weaver beseeches his hands not to fail him—and another in which we see him explain his success by telling a little girl that the horse's eyes needed to be red as fire—the remainder of the episode unfolds in wordless fulfillment of the Narrator's eloquence. We see Frédérique and the black steed riding, playing, communing, nuzzling—we even see her lustily strumming a lute for its entertainment. This catalogue of shared experience builds to a storm that starts a fire, and Frédérique's attunement to the stallion's nervousness raises her

"Metzengerstein" by Roger Vadim

out of a warm bed to race to its side. This leads to an impromptu early morning ride in which the horse carries her into the country, to the very source of the flames, where—as the music acquires a kind of galloping, pounding heartbeat evoking a stallion's heated breath, evidently combining rhythmic mashings of the bass keys of a pipe organ with tortured, electronic high end accompaniment—they are both engulfed in a shared destiny of hellfire. As Frédérique and her deliverer fall behind a wall of flames, nothing is left but a red sky and the cold, remorseless eye of the sun.

SPIRITS OF THE DEAD

THE SCORE FOR "METZENGERSTEIN" was the work of Jean Prodomidès (1927-2016), who had previously composed the highly affecting music for Vadim's *Blood and Roses* in 1960. His earliest film music was written for shorts, but these were of uncommonly high artistic caliber, including René Lucot's A *l'aube d'un monde* (1955, written and narrated by Jean Cocteau) and Paul Paviot's *Un jardin public/In the Park* (1955, a showcase for the celebrated mime Marcel Marceau). The first widely seen feature that he scored was Gilles Grangier's *Archimède, le clochard/The Magnificent Tramp* (1959) starring Jean Gabin, and its success led to two more films with Gabin: *Maigret et l'affaire Saint-Fiacre/Maigret and the St. Fiacre Case* (1959) and *Le baron de l'écluse/The Baron of the Locks* (1960), both directed by Jean Delannoy.

Prodomidès' propensity for musical enchantment made itself known in Albert Lamorisse's *Le voyage en ballon* (1960), a film reputedly filmed in the process of "Helivision," in which a young boy stows away on a hot-air balloon voyage with his grandfather. Most of the film was shot from aloft, but it was Prodomidés' musical colorations that gave the film its beguiling sense of timelessness and weightlessness.

His score for *Blood and Roses* is quite limited, consisting of only a few cues amounting to slightly more than twelve minutes, but its main theme (played on the Irish harp by Elena Polonska, and in a separate cue by a full orchestra) is one of the horror genre's most haunting—tender, tactile, regretful, tortured, its gently plucked bittersweetness seeming to mourn the impermanence of the film as it runs through a projector.

The music in "Metzengerstein" is among the genre's most underrated, but it is similarly limited in length. There has never been a proper soundtrack release of the music for the probable reason that it wouldn't lend itself to stand-alone listening; it was meant to sigh and scrape and pant against the film's images.

The first music we hear—before the imagery begins, and then continuing with Frédérique's dream of the defenestrated young man—is less bittersweet than semi-sour, and far less inclined to beauty than unease.

"Metzengerstein" by Roger Vadim

The sustained notes of a sickly, mewling string section are dragged out below the atonal plunking of a cimbalom. It's pensive, unmistakably *psychological* music, much in the same character as Les Baxter's impressionistic score for Roger Corman's *Pit and the Pendulum*.

The orgiastic scenes are accompanied by a melodic, courtly theme played on lute and flute with strummed accompaniment on guitar and harp.

During the scenes of Frédérique riding the stallion, a highly experimental horse theme is introduced, founded on an electronic recreation of a racing horse's labored breathing, and also what could be called a forest theme, more orchestral and sorcerous, all strings and organ.

Prodomidès bade his farewell to writing music for films with Andrzej Wajda's *Danton* (1983), after which he wrote music for the ballet and the last three of his five operas. He was named President of the *Académie des beaux-arts* in 2005.

Before the filming of "Metzengerstein" commenced, Roger Vadim issued the following statement of his intentions with this segment: "The story I chose to adapt is rather short. The action is suggested rather than described, thereby providing the filmmaker with some leeway in the cinematographic interpretation of this work by Edgar Allan Poe. I intend to use this tale simply as a starting point and to overcome its limitations by involving some of the author's obsessions in my scenario. If I take great liberties with the original text, I do so in the hope of delving as deeply as possible into Poe's universe. In other words: I chose not to follow the text to the letter in order to come into greater communion with his spirit. I don't want to state too precisely the time and location where this story takes place. Not even the costumes will belong to a period that is too easily recognizable, yet they should look relatively ancient and romantic. An almost subliminal narration will hold the story together, punctuated by some barbed dialogue. The narration will be written after the editing and will thus be able to attend perfectly to the articulation of the images."[36]

Of the three stories that compose *Histoires Extraordinaires*, only Fellini's "Toby Dammit" admits to being "liberally adapted," yet "Metzengerstein"

---

[36] *Tre passi nel delirio*, p. 199.

also takes a great many liberties with its source story. We can tell from this statement why Vadim made some of the creative choices he did.

The most obvious change, necessitated by the need to create a vehicle for Jane Fonda, was changing the gender of Frederick, Baron Metzengerstein, who became the Countess Frédérique of Metzengerstein, while William, the aged heir of the Berlifitzing family—who was not related, just too geographically close for comfort—became her handsome young cousin Wilhelm to provide a plausible role for Jane's brother Peter Fonda. In not following this aspect of the story to the letter, Vadim was able to invite into his segment other resonances of Poe—namely, the fact that Poe had married his own first cousin, Virginia Eliza Clemm, in 1835 when he was 26 and she only 13. Mrs. Poe would die in 1847 at the age of only 24, and Poe's alcoholic grieving contributed as greatly to his own death two years later at age 40 as it informed and enriched what remained to be written of his morbid prose and poetry. As mentioned earlier, the casting of Peter Fonda as the leading man opposite his own sister was a provocative move, and one of which producer Raymond Eger must have strongly approved, as having the actor aboard would make the film doubly attractive to American International Pictures. Also, although such a result could not have been consciously placed, the juxtaposing of Jane Fonda with Peter Fonda gives the segment an interesting resonance with its follow-up, Louis Malle's "William Wilson," in which the decadent lifestyle of a spoiled narcissist is serially mocked and challenged by someone who is, essentially, their own mirror image—yet a counterweight of integrity and contentment. In his original stories, Poe describes both the Baron von Metzengerstein and William Wilson as having "out-Heroded Herod," a phrase he culled from Shakespeare's *Hamlet*, which makes it a certainty that these two characters sprang from the same locus of his imagination. It is a remarkable, rarely acknowledged fact about the film that all three of its segments—though made independently of each other—venture some kind of comment on the other stories, which I will show in due course.

Vadim—whose earlier films made a habit of either adapting classic works to modern times, or shutting out the modern world by secluding contemporary characters in ancient castles—spoke of wishing the time and place of the story to remain obscure. In this case, he achieved this by contrasting authentic castle locations with the Countess' credulity-straining costumes, designed by Jacques Fonteray (1918-2013). They make no sense whatsoever as historical apparel, instead delicately transposing the story's timeframe to that of a fable or fairy tale.

"I did not have to refer to the settings as belonging to any age in particular," Fonteray said. "In every way, they suggested the Middle Ages-early Renaissance, yet interpreted freely. More than the decorativism of the Italian Renaissance—as you find in Piero della Francesca, or Carpaccio—I preferred the inspiration of my two most favorite painters, Lucas Cranach and Albrecht Dürer. Aside from my own personal preferences (an enlargement of Cranach's 'Eve' is always displayed in my study), it seemed to me that the vaguely morbid and demonic eroticism of these painters corresponded to the ambiance desired by Vadim."[37]

The greatest surprise I experienced, while revisiting this film in order to write this book, was seeing it on a large screen for the first time since 1970. While I enjoyed "William Wilson" and "Toby Dammit" as much as I ever have, seeing "Metzengerstein" again in this way was a revelation. It is a sensual feast and not a film that translates well to more compact viewing. To be properly appreciated, "Metzengerstein" must be seen large, in a context that allows the viewer to feel one is actually inhabiting its castles, its ruins, its moss-covered forests, and its turbulent coastlines. Seen this way, it explodes into life, into nature and human perversity, and its elliptic narrative asserts itself all the more as poetry. In all the years I've known this film, I have paid close attention to the work that Jane Fonda does in it, but it was only upon seeing the film properly projected once again that I realized what a spectacle she is—as a movie star as an actress, and yes, as a woman. I don't intend it as a sexist remark to say that she is ravishing here; I say it because her physical beauty is such a production value and such an essential ingredient of the story. In a movie teeming with beautiful women, Fonda eclipses them all with a face that unabashedly demands to be adored—a dimension of her presence, indeed her performance, that I have never felt when watching the film at home. I may prefer the performances given in the film by Alain Delon, Brigitte Bardot and Terence Stamp, whose work translates impeccably when shrunk down to

---

[37] *Tre passi nel delirio*, pp. 185.

more intimate proportions, but Fonda's work only comes into fullest view when she towers over the viewer, when her face becomes a terrain to be explored, examined, and fetishized. On a large screen, when she's modeling her costumes, when she's riding on horseback, bouncing in the saddle, the collision of her fantasy figure with breathtaking panoramas of nature is striking and unforgettable. Likewise, when the black stallion makes its first appearance, it too looks gargantuan, conveying an impression of almost supernatural power that outshines the extras who rush the screen to calm it. Only Fonda has charisma equal to it, and when it calms as her hand caresses its muzzle, there is a powerful sense of meeting—perhaps reunion—that can be seen but not so deeply felt on smaller screens.

The look of the film—produced through its juxtaposition of wardrobe and settings very much tie the story into the milieu of French adult comics (very much on Vadim's mind as he prepared *Barbarella*), evoking in particular the work of Guido Crepax but also that of Poe's great illustrators of the 19th and 20th centuries, Aubrey Beardsley and Harry Clarke. Say what you will about "Metzengerstein," but nowhere else in Poe cinema do you see the Poe visualized by Beardsley, Clarke and Crepax so well represented. And for all of this, the episode's increasingly bizarre costume changes ultimately provide counterbalance to the fashion show grotesqueries of Fellini's "Toby Dammit"—which ends, as "Metzengerstein" does—with its decadent protagonist bound for blazes aboard a nightmare of horse-power.

Horsepower, indeed. Speaking of which, it is not too far a stretch to suggest that "Metzengerstein" might be read as Jane Fonda's analog of her brother's imminent success in his next film *Easy Rider* (1969), with the black stallion her counterpart to Wyatt's chopper on their respective rides to fiery deaths. *Easy Rider*, after all, was actively incubating in Peter Fonda's mind at the time of filming. It had been the summer of 1967, while promoting Roger Corman's *The Trip* in Toronto, that the eureka came:

"I was up in Toronto, out of grass, depressed, sitting in this hotel room. All of a sudden, *Easy Rider* came to me...I drank a few Heinekens and popped a sleeping pill, because there was a big, noisy convention of exhibitors and I wanted to fall out quick. I was a little bit loaded and I looked at a picture that had been left on a table for me to sign for somebody's cousin. It was a photograph from *The Wild Angels* of me and actor Bruce Dern on a chop... and suddenly I thought, that's it, that's the modern Western: two cats just riding across the country, two loners, not a motorcycle gang, no Hell's Angels, nothing like that, just those two guys."[38]

Author Terry Southern, one of the chief writers of the *Barbarella* script, had migrated with the Vadim crowd after that film's completion to Roscoff, in Brittany, for the second half of the filming of "Metzengerstein." When Peter arrived in advance of filming his part, he told Southern what he had in mind for this nascent project, inviting him aboard as screenwriter. If Peter told that story once, he surely told it twice, even many times, so it's possible that something of it was woven, subconsciously or by osmosis, into the tapestry of "Metzengerstein"—yielding a contemporary adaptation akin to Mandiargues' own adaptation, *The Motorcycle*.

Where Vadim ultimately failed to keep all the promises of his prospectus was in his intention to somehow mirror the way in which the action in Poe's juvenilia was "suggested rather than described." The primary fault of "Metzengerstein" is its over-reliance on narration to convey the inner life of Frédérique and the actions within the story, which prevents Jane Fonda from giving much of a performance and causes what might have been compelling psychological cinema to become a lavishly illustrated procession of illustrations from a book for, shall we say, twisted children.

Claude Renoir's cinematography, while often marvelous, includes some peculiarities that defy the story's intended historical setting, however fanciful—for example, the helicopter shot establishing Frédérique's castle, and some frankly inept moments of camera operation when the framing visibly wavers or fails to follow the movements of an actor (see 9:24 or 24:28 on the Arrow Academy disc). It would have served the story tremendously had only one of the many orgy scenes taken care to include a shot of the horse mural in the background; in a couple of the widest shots, its edge can be seen there, but this is before a proper establishing shot occurs to anchor the mural's importance in the narrative. To retain such technical missteps only serves to remind us that we are watching a film.

While there is a sense that it is trying to be innovative, something different, "Metzengerstein" is ultimately the truest of the film's three stories to the

---

[38] *Playboy Interview: Peter Fonda* (Chicago: Playboy Press, 1971), pp. 9-10.

imagery and format forged by Roger Corman's earlier Poe adaptations for American International—despite Vadim's insistence that he had never seen those films. It opens by the sea, it takes place in rotting castles where its characters look back on an undisclosed but accursed past, its costumed orgies recall the revels in *The Masque of the Red Death,* and it culminates with its protagonist and their train of sins consumed by purifying fire. Indeed, the scene of the burning barn far outclasses the stock footage of the same Chicago warehouse fire that Roger Corman utilized in several of his earlier Poe films. Of course, Wilhelm's reincarnation as the black stallion—his metempsychosis not so ambiguous here as I feel the matter is in the original story—also echoes Ligeia's reincarnation in the black cat of Corman's *The Tomb of Ligeia.*

Despite certain caveats, if "Metzengerstein" is any kind of victory, it is its director's victory. As such, despite the uses of the Fondas' voices on the English-dubbed track, "Metzengerstein" is most effective in French, where the narration feels less intrusive and the dialogue generally sounds more impassioned and ethereal. The hard edges of the Fondas' American accents do not belong to this place, too plain and practical for such high-flown gothic romanticism. But the French version should only be trusted if the title *Histoires Extraordinaires* appears on the film, as it is only this version that retains the French visual track.

Though neither of them realized it at the time, "Metzengerstein" would prove to be Roger Vadim and Jane Fonda's swan song as a filmmaking couple. To viewers who had been following the cinematic consequences of their relationship onscreen, this may have come as no surprise. The unquestionable eroticism that Vadim had found in Jane Fonda at the height of *The Game Is Over* had turned literally anti-gravity and cartoonish with *Barbarella,* while "Metzengerstein" feels even more deflated, an alienated study in sexual ennui. Whenever the situations of its story verge on venturing into frank erotic terrain, it cuts to the next scene as if its own *metteur en scène* couldn't be bothered to look.

On the level of her craft, the objectified center of Vadim's universe was seeing the world of cinema around her evolving beyond his pretty games; she craved more opportunity to participate in it. In order to give Vadim his

Barbarella, Fonda had to turn down the female lead in Arthur Penn's *Bonnie and Clyde*—as she had previously turned down the role of Laura in David Lean's *Dr. Zhivago* (which had gone to Julie Christie) to make *The Game Is Over*, a film that was—however unfairly—forgotten almost as soon as it was made. The couple's decision to have a child had prevented her from accepting the lead role she had been offered in Roman Polanski's *Rosemary's Baby*. When Fonda saw *Barbarella*, she was unable to relate to herself amid the high artifice of Vadim's construction; she saw herself as a female cartoon, a vacuous doll assaulted by orgasm after orgasm. She read reviews like the one written by Molly Haskell, which compared Vadim to a Svengali.

After the birth of their daughter Vanessa, Fonda marked the occasion with a new hairstyle. According to Bosworth, "She had decided to cut off her long, thick blonde hair; it had been part of her identity all the years with Vadim. When she came home with her short, cropped bob, dyed honey blonde, her husband realized it was a symbolic gesture. 'I had the vision of Jane leading her own life on one side, and of myself leading a separate life on the other,' Vadim said. 'I knew that the disintegration of our love had started.'"[39]

Fonda's action might well have been unconscious, but she did exactly as her character in *The Game Is Over* had done to commemorate her divorce. Vadim may have realized that she had chosen to make the change in her heart known in cinematographic terms he would understand. As Vadim made himself remote with drink, waiting for his next film offer to materialize, Jane accepted a role in Sydney Pollack's film of Horace McCoy's *They Shoot Horses, Don't They?* (1969), which won her an Academy Award nomination—and, with it, a certain clarity.

As Bosworth writes:

Suddenly, she was tired of playing the passive wife and mistress, and wanted her life to have more significance.
During an interview with a German reporter about They Shoot Horses, *Jane's attention seemed to wander and the reporter pounced.*

---

[39] Bosworth, Patricia. *Jane Fonda: The Private Life of a Public Woman* (New York, NY: Houghton Mifflin Harcourt), p. 273.

> '*What are you thinking of right this minute?*' he demanded.
> '*I'm thinking of getting a divorce,*' she answered. [40]

She thought about it for some time. When the couple finally agreed to divorce in 1973, Jane was already pregnant by her next husband Tom Hayden, as was Vadim's next wife Catherine Schneider by him.

In retrospect, Fonda credited Vadim, her first husband, with challenging her, extending her, liberating her in innumerable ways, but she had now grown to a point where she no longer needed his help or guidance; she had surpassed him. She was literally one film away from receiving her first Academy Award as Best Actress. Vadim then succumbed to a creative crisis — making only one studio work-for-hire assignment, *Pretty Maids All In A Row* (1971) for MGM, based on a script by Gene Roddenberry. In 1972, he returned to France and French cinema, making five small films before his return to America in the 1980s.

Nathalie Vadim, his daughter with Annette Stroyberg, told Jane Fonda's biographer Patricia Bosworth that Jane had been the true love of her father's life and his work supports this observation. A few years after their divorce, Vadim made one of his most extraordinary films in France, in the immediate wake of their divorce: *La jeune fille assassinée/Charlotte* (1974), shot in 16mm, scored with Mike Oldfield's "Tubular Bells", and starring himself as a successful novelist who learns that a sexually licentious girl who was his lover for several years has been found murdered, prompting him to sift through the ashes of their relationship. The name of the girl, played by Sirpa Lane (later the ravished Beauty in Walerian Borowczyk's *La Bête/The Beast*, 1975), is Charlotte — and it is difficult to not interpret the film as Vadim's post-mortem of his marriage to Fonda, with whom he first connected romantically at a masked ball where she wore a Charlie Chaplin costume. (The French refer to Chaplin with the endearment "Charlot.") In the film, Vadim's character goes around collecting stories from Charlotte's grief-stricken friends and former lovers, which include memories of sexual exploration, multiplicity, even some incestuous teasing of her brother, which recalls Vadim's casting of Peter Fonda as Jane's cousin in "Metzengerstein."

---

[40] Ibid., p. 279.

"Metzengerstein" by Roger Vadim

In 1963, when she was denying her consuming attraction to Vadim and making *Joy House* to flaunt her independence of him, her director René Clément described Fonda by saying, "Like a young wild thing, she's galloping too fast, bursting into flame too easily." This was the woman with whom Vadim eventually collided, and you could not ask for a better, more precise description of her character arc in "Metzengerstein."

How interesting that Fonda would follow the completion of a film that found her enamored of a handsome black steed with a film entitled *They Shoot Horses, Don't They?*—what armchair psychologist could resist the evidence that this decision, made three years before their divorce, embodied a subconscious wish to end their relationship? Adding still more to the coincidence is the fact that her Oscar-nominated performance was scripted by a man named... Poe.[41]

---

[41] Screenwriter James Poe (1921 – 1980), who from 1969 to 1978 was married to British actress Barbara Steele, the Queen of Italian Horror and a member of Marcello's harem in *8 ½*.

William Wilson

by Edgar Allan Poe, 1832

What say of it? what say (of) CONSCIENCE grim, That spectre in my path?

—Chamberlayne's *Pharronida*

LET ME CALL MYSELF, FOR THE PRESENT, William Wilson. The fair page now lying before me need not be sullied with my real appellation. This has been already too much an object for the scorn—or the horror—for the detestation of my race. To the uttermost regions of the globe have not the indignant winds bruited its unparalleled infamy? Oh, outcast of all outcasts most abandoned!—to the earth art thou not forever dead? to its honors, to its flowers, to its golden aspirations?—and a cloud, dense, dismal, and limitless, does it not hang eternally between thy hopes and heaven?

I would not, if I could, here or today, embody a record of my later years of unspeakable misery, and unpardonable crime. This epoch—these later years—took unto themselves a sudden elevation in turpitude, whose origin alone it is my present purpose to assign. Men usually grow base by degrees. From me, in an instant, all virtue dropped bodily as a mantle. From comparatively trivial wickedness I passed, with the stride of a giant, into more than the enormities of an Elah-Gabalus. What chance —what one event brought this evil thing to pass, bear with me while I relate. Death approaches; and the shadow which foreruns him has thrown a softening influence over my spirit. I long, in passing through the dim valley, for the sympathy—I had nearly said for the pity—of my fellow men. I would fain have them believe that I have been, in some measure, the slave of circumstances beyond human control. I would wish them to seek out for me, in the details I am about to give, some little oasis of fatality amid a wilderness of error. I would have them allow—what they cannot refrain from allowing—that, although temptation may have erewhile existed as great, man was never thus, at least, tempted before—certainly, never thus fell. And is it therefore that he has never thus suffered? Have I not indeed been living in a dream? And am I not now dying a victim to the horror and the mystery of the wildest of all sublunary visions?

I am the descendant of a race whose imaginative and easily excitable temperament has at all times rendered them remarkable; and, in my earliest infancy, I gave evidence of having fully inherited the family character. As I advanced in years it was more strongly developed; becoming, for many reasons, a cause of serious disquietude to my friends, and of positive injury to myself. I grew self-willed, addicted to the wildest caprices, and a prey to the most ungovernable passions. Weak-minded, and beset with constitutional infirmities akin to my own, my parents could do but little to check the evil propensities which distinguished me. Some feeble and ill-directed efforts resulted in complete failure on their part, and, of course, in total triumph on mine. Thenceforward my voice was a household law; and at an age when few children have abandoned their leading-strings, I was left to the guidance of my own will, and became, in all but name, the master of my own actions.

My earliest recollections of a school-life, are connected with a large, rambling, Elizabethan house, in a misty-looking village of England, where were a vast number of gigantic and gnarled trees, and where all the houses were excessively ancient. In truth, it was a dream-like and spirit-soothing place, that venerable old town. At this moment, in fancy, I feel the refreshing chilliness of its deeply-shadowed avenues, inhale the fragrance of its thousand shrubberies, and thrill anew with indefinable delight, at the deep hollow note of the church-bell, breaking, each hour, with sullen and sudden roar, upon the stillness of the dusky atmosphere in which the fretted Gothic steeple lay imbedded and asleep.

It gives me, perhaps, as much of pleasure as I can now in any manner experience, to dwell upon minute recollections of the school and its concerns. Steeped in misery as I am—misery, alas! only too real—I shall be pardoned for seeking relief, however slight and temporary, in the weakness of a few rambling details. These, moreover, utterly trivial, and even ridiculous in themselves, assume, to my fancy, adventitious importance, as connected with a period and a locality when and where I recognize the first ambiguous monitions of the destiny which afterwards so fully overshadowed me. Let me then remember.

The house, I have said, was old and irregular. The grounds were extensive, and a high and solid brick wall, topped with a bed of mortar and broken glass, encompassed the whole. This prison-like rampart formed the limit of our domain; beyond it we saw but thrice a week—once every Saturday afternoon, when, attended by two ushers, we were permitted to take brief walks in a body through some of the neighboring fields—and twice during Sunday, when we were paraded in the same formal manner to the morning and evening service in the one church of the village. Of this church the principal of our school was pastor. With how deep a spirit of wonder and perplexity was I wont to regard him from our remote pew in the gallery, as, with step solemn and slow, he ascended the pulpit! This reverend man, with countenance so demurely benign, with robes so glossy and so clerically flowing, with wig so minutely powdered, so rigid and so vast—could this be he who, of late, with sour visage, and in snuffy habiliments, administered, ferule in hand, the Draconian laws of the academy? Oh, gigantic paradox, too utterly monstrous for solution!

At an angle of the ponderous wall frowned a more ponderous gate. It was riveted and studded with iron bolts, and surmounted with jagged iron spikes. What impressions of deep awe did it inspire! It was never opened save for the three periodical egressions and ingressions already mentioned; then, in every creak of its mighty hinges, we found a plenitude of mystery— a world of matter for solemn remark, or for more solemn meditation.

The extensive enclosure was irregular in form, having many capacious recesses. Of these, three or four of the largest constituted the playground. It was level, and covered with fine hard gravel. I well remember it had no trees, nor benches, nor anything similar within it. Of course it was in the rear of the house. In front lay a small parterre, planted with box and other shrubs; but through this sacred division we passed only upon rare occasions indeed—such as a first advent to school or final departure thence, or perhaps, when a parent or friend having called for us, we joyfully took our way home for the Christmas or Midsummer holy-days.

But the house!—how quaint an old building was this!—to me how veritably a palace of enchantment! There was really no end to its windings—to its incomprehensible subdivisions. It was difficult, at any given time, to say with certainty upon which of its two stories one happened to be. From each room to every other there were sure to be found three or four steps either in ascent or descent. Then the lateral branches were innumerable—inconceivable—and so returning in upon themselves, that our most exact ideas in regard to the whole mansion were not very far different from those with which we pondered upon infinity. During the five years of my residence here, I was never able to ascertain with precision, in what remote locality lay the little sleeping apartment assigned to myself and some eighteen or twenty other scholars.

The schoolroom was the largest in the house—I could not help thinking, in the world. It was very long, narrow, and dismally low, with pointed Gothic windows and a ceiling of oak. In a remote and terror-inspiring angle was a square enclosure of eight or ten feet, comprising the sanctum, "during hours," of our principal, the Reverend Dr. Bransby. It was a solid structure, with massy door, sooner than open which in the absence of the "Dominic," we would all have willingly perished by the *peine forte et dure*.[42] In other angles were two other similar boxes, far less reverenced, indeed, but still greatly matters of awe. One of these was the pulpit of the "classical" usher, one of the "English and mathematical." Interspersed about the room, crossing and recrossing in endless irregularity, were innumerable benches and desks, black, ancient, and time-worn, piled desperately with much-bethumbed books, and so beseamed with initial letters, names at full length, grotesque figures, and other multiplied efforts of the knife, as to have entirely lost what little of original form might have been their portion in days long departed. A huge bucket with water stood at one extremity of the room, and a clock of stupendous dimensions at the other.

---

[42] Translation: "... powerful and enduring pain."

Encompassed by the massy walls of this venerable academy, I passed, yet not in tedium or disgust, the years of the third lustrum of my life. The teeming brain of childhood requires no external world of incident to occupy or amuse it; and the apparently dismal monotony of a school was replete with more intense excitement than my riper youth has derived from luxury, or my full manhood from crime. Yet I must believe that my first mental development had in it much of the uncommon—even much of the *outré*. Upon mankind at large the events of very early existence rarely leave in mature age any definite impression. All is gray shadow—a weak and irregular remembrance—an indistinct regathering of feeble pleasures and phantasmagoric pains. With me this is not so. In childhood I must have felt with the energy of a man what I now find stamped upon memory in lines as vivid, as deep, and as durable as the exergues of the Carthaginian medals.

Yet in fact—in the fact of the world's view—how little was there to remember! The morning's awakening, the nightly summons to bed; the connings, the recitations; the periodical half-holidays, and perambulations; the play-ground, with its broils, its pastimes, its intrigues;—these, by a mental sorcery long forgotten, were made to involve a wilderness of sensation, a world of rich incident, an universe of varied emotion, of excitement the most passionate and spirit-stirring. "Oh, le bon temps, que ce siecle de fer!"[43]

In truth, the ardor, the enthusiasm, and the imperiousness of my disposition, soon rendered me a marked character among my schoolmates, and by slow, but natural gradations, gave me an ascendancy over all not greatly older than myself;—over all with a single exception. This exception was found in the person of a scholar, who, although no relation, bore the same Christian and surname as myself;—a circumstance, in fact, little remarkable; for, notwithstanding a noble descent, mine was one of those everyday appellations which seem, by prescriptive right, to have been, time out of mind, the common property of the mob. In this narrative I have therefore designated myself as William Wilson,—a fictitious title not very dissimilar to the real. My namesake alone, of those who in school

---

[43] Translation: "Oh, what good times, this age of iron!" Stephen Peithman identifies this as a quote from Voltaire's *Le Mondaine* (1736). See Peithman, p. 83.

phraseology constituted "our set," presumed to compete with me in the studies of the class—in the sports and broils of the playground—to refuse implicit belief in my assertions, and submission to my will—indeed, to interfere with my arbitrary dictation in any respect whatsoever. If there is on earth a supreme and unqualified despotism, it is the despotism of a mastermind in boyhood over the less energetic spirits of its companions.

Wilson's rebellion was to me a source of the greatest embarrassment;—the more so as, in spite of the bravado with which in public I made a point of treating him and his pretensions, I secretly felt that I feared him, and could not help thinking the equality which he maintained so easily with myself, a proof of his true superiority; since not to be overcome cost me a perpetual struggle. Yet this superiority—even this equality—was in truth acknowledged by no one but myself; our associates, by some unaccountable blindness, seemed not even to suspect it. Indeed, his competition, his resistance, and especially his impertinent and dogged interference with my purposes, were not more pointed than private. He appeared to be destitute alike of the ambition which urged, and of the passionate energy of mind which enabled me to excel. In his rivalry he might have been supposed actuated solely by a whimsical desire to thwart, astonish, or mortify myself; although there were times when I could not help observing, with a feeling made up of wonder, abasement, and pique, that he mingled with his injuries, his insults, or his contradictions, a certain most inappropriate, and assuredly most unwelcome affectionateness of manner. I could only conceive this singular behavior to arise from a consummate self-conceit assuming the vulgar airs of patronage and protection.

Perhaps it was this latter trait in Wilson's conduct, conjoined with our identity of name, and the mere accident of our having entered the school upon the same day, which set afloat the notion that we were brothers, among the senior classes in the academy. These do not usually inquire with much strictness into the affairs of their juniors. I have before said, or should have said, that Wilson was not, in the most remote degree, connected with my family. But assuredly if we had been brothers we must have been twins; for, after leaving Dr. Bransby's, I casually learned that my namesake was born on the nineteenth of January, 1813[44]—and this is a

---

[44] Worth noting as the date of Poe's own birth.

somewhat remarkable coincidence; for the day is precisely that of my own nativity.

It may seem strange that in spite of the continual anxiety occasioned me by the rivalry of Wilson, and his intolerable spirit of contradiction, I could not bring myself to hate him altogether. We had, to be sure, nearly every day a quarrel in which, yielding me publicly the palm of victory, he, in some manner, contrived to make me feel that it was he who had deserved it; yet a sense of pride on my part, and a veritable dignity on his own, kept us always upon what are called "speaking terms," while there were many points of strong congeniality in our tempers, operating to awake me in a sentiment which our position alone, perhaps, prevented from ripening into friendship. It is difficult, indeed, to define, or even to describe, my real feelings towards him. They formed a motley and heterogeneous admixture; —some petulant animosity, which was not yet hatred, some esteem, more respect, much fear, with a world of uneasy curiosity. To the moralist it will be unnecessary to say, in addition, that Wilson and myself were the most inseparable of companions.

It was no doubt the anomalous state of affairs existing between us, which turned all my attacks upon him, (and they were many, either open or covert) into the channel of banter or practical joke (giving pain while assuming the aspect of mere fun) rather than into a more serious and determined hostility. But my endeavors on this head were by no means uniformly successful, even when my plans were the most wittily concocted; for my namesake had much about him, in character, of that unassuming and quiet austerity which, while enjoying the poignancy of its own jokes, has no heel of Achilles in itself, and absolutely refuses to be laughed at. I could find, indeed, but one vulnerable point, and that, lying in a personal peculiarity, arising, perhaps, from constitutional disease, would have been spared by any antagonist less at his wit's end than myself;—my rival had a weakness in the faucal or guttural organs, which precluded him from raising his voice at any time above a very low whisper. Of this defect I did not fail to take what poor advantage lay in my power.

Wilson's retaliations in kind were many; and there was one form of his practical wit that disturbed me beyond measure. How his sagacity first discovered at all that so petty a thing would vex me is a question I never could solve; but, having discovered, he habitually practiced the annoyance. I had always felt aversion to my uncourtly patronymic, and its very common, if not plebeian praenomen. The words were venom in my ears; and when, upon the day of my arrival, a second William Wilson came also to the academy, I felt angry with him for bearing the name, and doubly disgusted with the name because a stranger bore it, who would be the cause of its twofold repetition, who would be constantly in my presence, and whose concerns, in the ordinary routine of the school business, must inevitably, on account of the detestable coincidence, be often confounded with my own.

The feeling of vexation thus engendered grew stronger with every circumstance tending to show resemblance, moral or physical, between my rival and myself. I had not then discovered the remarkable fact that we were of the same age; but I saw that we were of the same height, and I perceived that we were even singularly alike in general contour of person and outline of feature. I was galled, too, by the rumor touching a relationship, which had grown current in the upper forms. In a word, nothing could more seriously disturb me, although I scrupulously concealed such disturbance,) than any allusion to a similarity of mind, person, or condition existing between us. But, in truth, I had no reason to believe that (with the exception of the matter of relationship, and in the case of Wilson himself) this similarity had ever been made a subject of comment, or even observed at all by our schoolfellows. That he observed it in all its bearings, and as fixedly as I, was apparent; but that he could discover in such circumstances so fruitful a field of annoyance, can only be attributed, as I said before, to his more than ordinary penetration.

His cue, which was to perfect an imitation of myself, lay both in words and in actions; and most admirably did he play his part. My dress it was an easy matter to copy; my gait and general manner were, without difficulty, appropriated; in spite of his constitutional defect, even my voice did not escape him. My louder tones were, of course, unattempted, but then the key, it was identical; and his singular whisper, it grew the very echo of my own.

How greatly this most exquisite portraiture harassed me, (for it could not justly be termed a caricature,) I will not now venture to describe. I had but one consolation—in the fact that the imitation, apparently, was noticed by myself alone, and that I had to endure only the knowing and strangely sarcastic smiles of my namesake himself. Satisfied with having produced in my bosom the intended effect, he seemed to chuckle in secret over the sting he had inflicted, and was characteristically disregardful of the public applause which the success of his witty endeavors might have so easily elicited. That the school, indeed, did not feel his design, perceive its accomplishment, and participate in his sneer, was, for many anxious months, a riddle I could not resolve. Perhaps the gradation of his copy rendered it not so readily perceptible; or, more possibly, I owed my security to the master air of the copyist, who, disdaining the letter (which, in a painting, is all the obtuse can see), gave but the full spirit of his original for my individual contemplation and chagrin.

I have already more than once spoken of the disgusting air of patronage which he assumed toward me, and of his frequent officious interference withy my will. This interference often took the ungracious character of advice; advice not openly given, but hinted or insinuated. I received it with a repugnance which gained strength as I grew in years. Yet, at this distant day, let me do him the simple justice to acknowledge that I can recall no occasion when the suggestions of my rival were on the side of those errors or follies so usual to his immature age and seeming inexperience; that his moral sense, at least, if not his general talents and worldly wisdom, was far keener than my own; and that I might, to-day, have been a better, and thus a happier man, had I less frequently rejected the counsels embodied in those meaning whispers which I then but too cordially hated and too bitterly despised.

As it was, I at length grew restive in the extreme under his distasteful supervision, and daily resented more and more openly what I considered his intolerable arrogance. I have said that, in the first years of our connection as schoolmates, my feelings in regard to him might have been easily ripened into friendship: but, in the latter months of my residence at the academy, although the intrusion of his ordinary manner had, beyond doubt, in some measure, abated, my sentiments, in nearly similar proportion, partook very much of positive hatred. Upon one occasion he saw this, I think, and afterwards avoided, or made a show of avoiding me.

SPIRITS OF THE DEAD

It was about the same period, if I remember aright, that, in an altercation of violence with him, in which he was more than usually thrown off his guard, and spoke and acted with an openness of demeanor rather foreign to his nature, I discovered, or fancied I discovered, in his accent, his air, and general appearance, a something which first startled, and then deeply interested me, by bringing to mind dim visions of my earliest infancy—wild, confused and thronging memories of a time when memory herself was yet unborn. I cannot better describe the sensation which oppressed me than by saying that I could with difficulty shake off the belief of my having been acquainted with the being who stood before me, at some epoch very long ago—some point of the past even infinitely remote. The delusion, however, faded rapidly as it came; and I mention it at all but to define the day of the last conversation I there held with my singular namesake.

The huge old house, with its countless subdivisions, had several large chambers communicating with each other, where slept the greater number of the students. There were, however (as must necessarily happen in a building so awkwardly planned), many little nooks or recesses, the odds and ends of the structure; and these the economic ingenuity of Dr. Bransby had also fitted up as dormitories; although, being the merest closets, they were capable of accommodating but a single individual. One of these small apartments was occupied by Wilson.

One night, about the close of my fifth year at the school, and immediately after the altercation just mentioned, finding everyone wrapped in sleep, I arose from bed, and, lamp in hand, stole through a wilderness of narrow passages from my own bedroom to that of my rival. I had long been plotting one of those ill-natured pieces of practical wit at his expense in which I had hitherto been so uniformly unsuccessful. It was my intention, now, to put my scheme in operation, and I resolved to make him feel the whole extent of the malice with which I was imbued. Having reached his closet, I noiselessly entered, leaving the lamp, with a shade over it, on the outside. I advanced a step, and listened to the sound of his tranquil breathing. Assured of his being asleep, I returned, took the light, and with it again approached the bed. Close curtains were around it, which, in the prosecution of my plan, I slowly and quietly withdrew, when the bright rays fell vividly upon the sleeper, and my eyes, at the same moment, upon his countenance. I looked—and a numbness, an iciness of feeling instantly pervaded my frame. My breast heaved, my knees tottered, my whole spirit became possessed with an objectless yet intolerable horror. Gasping for breath, I lowered the lamp in still nearer proximity to the face. Were these—these the lineaments of William Wilson? I saw, indeed, that they were his, but I shook as if with a fit of the ague in fancying they were not. What was there about them to confound me in this manner? I gazed—while my brain reeled with a multitude of incoherent thoughts. Not thus he appeared—assuredly not thus—in the vivacity of his waking hours. The same name! the same contour of person! the same day of arrival at the academy! And then his dogged and meaningless imitation of my gait, my voice, my habits, and my manner! Was it, in truth, within the bounds of human possibility, that what I now saw was the result, merely, of the habitual practice of this sarcastic imitation? Awe-stricken, and with a creeping shudder, I extinguished the lamp, passed silently from the chamber, and left, at once, the halls of that old academy, never to enter them again.

After a lapse of some months, spent at home in mere idleness, I found myself a student at Eton. The brief interval had been sufficient to enfeeble my remembrance of the events at Dr. Bransby's, or at least to effect a material change in the nature of the feelings with which I remembered them. The truth—the tragedy—of the drama was no more. I could now find room to doubt the evidence of my senses; and seldom called up the subject at all but with wonder at extent of human credulity, and a smile at the vivid force of the imagination which I hereditarily possessed. Neither was this species of scepticism likely to be diminished by the character of the life I led at Eton. The vortex of thoughtless folly into which I there so immediately and so recklessly plunged, washed away all but the froth of my past hours, engulfed at once every solid or serious impression, and left to memory only the veriest levities of a former existence.

I do not wish, however, to trace the course of my miserable profligacy here—a profligacy which set at defiance the laws, while it eluded the vigilance of the institution. Three years of folly, passed without profit, had but given me rooted habits of vice, and added, in a somewhat unusual degree, to my bodily stature, when, after a week of soulless dissipation, I invited a small party of the most dissolute students to a secret carousal in my chambers. We met at a late hour of the night; for our debaucheries were to be faithfully protracted until morning. The wine flowed freely, and there were not wanting other and perhaps more dangerous seductions; so that the gray dawn had already faintly appeared in the east, while our delirious extravagance was at its height. Madly flushed with cards and intoxication, I was in the act of insisting upon a toast of more than wonted profanity, when my attention was suddenly diverted by the violent, although partial unclosing of the door of the apartment, and by the eager voice of a servant from without. He said that some person, apparently in great haste, demanded to speak with me in the hall.

Wildly excited with wine, the unexpected interruption rather delighted than surprised me. I staggered forward at once, and a few steps brought me to the vestibule of the building. In this low and small room there hung no lamp; and now no light at all was admitted, save that of the exceedingly feeble dawn which made its way through the semi-circular window. As I put my foot over the threshold, I became aware of the figure of a youth about my own height, and habited in a white kerseymere morning frock, cut in the novel fashion of the one I myself wore at the moment. This, the faint light enabled me to perceive; but the features of his face I could not distinguish. Upon my entering he strode hurriedly up to me, and, seizing me by the arm with a gesture of petulant impatience, whispered the words "William Wilson!" in my ear.

I grew perfectly sober in an instant. There was that in the manner of the stranger, and in the tremulous shake of his uplifted finger, as he held it between my eyes and the light, which filled me with unqualified amazement; but it was not this which had so violently moved me. It was the pregnancy of solemn admonition in the singular, low, hissing utterance; and, above all, it was the character, the tone, the key, of those few, simple, and familiar, yet whispered syllables, which came with a thousand thronging memories of bygone days, and struck upon my soul with the shock of a galvanic battery. Ere I could recover the use of my senses, he was gone.

Although this event failed not of a vivid effect upon my disordered imagination, yet was it evanescent as vivid. For some weeks, indeed, I busied myself in earnest inquiry, or was wrapped in a cloud of morbid speculation. I did not pretend to disguise from my perception the identity of the singular individual who thus perseveringly interfered with my affairs, and harassed me with his insinuated counsel. But who and what was this Wilson?—and whence came he?—and what were his purposes? Upon neither of these points could I be satisfied; merely ascertaining, in regard to him, that a sudden accident in his family had caused his removal from Dr. Bransby's academy on the afternoon of the day in which I myself had eloped. But in a brief period I ceased to think upon the subject; my attention being all absorbed in a contemplated departure for Oxford. Thither I soon went; the uncalculating vanity of my parents furnishing me with an outfit and annual establishment, which would enable me to indulge at will in the luxury already so dear to my heart—to vie in profuseness of expenditure with the haughtiest heirs of the wealthiest earldoms in Great Britain.

Excited by such appliances to vice, my constitutional temperament broke forth with redoubled ardor, and I spurned even the common restraints of decency in the mad infatuation of my revels. But it were absurd to pause in the detail of my extravagance. Let it suffice, that among spendthrifts I out-Heroded Herod, and that, giving name to a multitude of novel follies, I added no brief appendix to the long catalogue of vices then usual in the most dissolute university of Europe.

It could hardly be credited, however, that I had, even here, so utterly fallen from the gentlemanly estate, as to seek acquaintance with the vilest arts of the gambler by profession, and, having become an adept in his despicable science, to practice it habitually as a means of increasing my already enormous income at the expense of the weak-minded among my fellow-collegians. Such, nevertheless, was the fact. And the very enormity of this offence against all manly and honorable sentiment proved, beyond doubt, the main if not the sole reason of the impunity with which it was committed. Who, indeed, among my most abandoned associates, would not rather have disputed the clearest evidence of his senses, than have suspected of such courses, the gay, the frank, the generous William Wilson—the noblest and most commoner at Oxford—him whose follies (said his parasites) were but the follies of youth and unbridled fancy—whose errors but inimitable whim—whose darkest vice but a careless and dashing extravagance?

I had been now two years successfully busied in this way, when there came to the university a young parvenu nobleman, Glendinning—rich, said report, as Herodes Atticus—his riches, too, as easily acquired. I soon found him of weak intellect, and, of course, marked him as a fitting subject for my skill. I frequently engaged him in play, and contrived, with the gambler's usual art, to let him win considerable sums, the more effectually to entangle him in my snares. At length, my schemes being ripe, I met him (with the full intention that this meeting should be final and decisive) at the chambers of a fellow-commoner (Mr. Preston), equally intimate with both, but who, to do him justice, entertained not even a remote suspicion of my design. To give to this a better coloring, I had contrived to assemble a party of some eight or ten, and was solicitously careful that the introduction of cards should appear accidental, and originate in the proposal of my contemplated dupe himself. To be brief upon a vile topic, none of the low finesse was omitted, so customary upon similar occasions that it is a just matter for wonder how any are still found so besotted as to fall its victim.

We had protracted our sitting far into the night, and I had at length effected the maneuver of getting Glendinning as my sole antagonist. The game, too, was my favorite: *Écarte!* The rest of the company, interested in the extent of our play, had abandoned their own cards, and were standing around us as spectators. The parvenu, who had been induced by my artifices in the early part of the evening, to drink deeply, now shuffled, dealt, or played, with a wild nervousness of manner for which his intoxication, I thought, might partially, but could not altogether account. In a very short period he had become my debtor to a large amount, when, having taken a long draught of port, he did precisely what I had been coolly anticipating—he proposed to double our already extravagant stakes. With a well-feigned show of reluctance, and not until after my repeated refusal had seduced him into some angry words which gave a color of pique to my compliance, did I finally comply. The result, of course, did but prove how entirely the prey was in my toils; in less than an hour he had quadrupled his debt. For some time his countenance had been losing the florid tinge lent it by the wine; but now, to my astonishment, I perceived that it had grown to a pallor truly fearful. I say to my astonishment. Glendinning had been represented to my eager inquiries as immeasurably wealthy; and the sums which he had as yet lost, although in themselves vast, could not, I supposed, very seriously annoy, much less so violently affect him. That he was overcome by the wine just swallowed, was the idea which most readily presented itself; and, rather with a view to the preservation of my own character in the eyes of my associates, than from any less interested motive, I was about to insist, peremptorily, upon a discontinuance of the play, when some expressions at my elbow from among the company, and an ejaculation evincing utter despair on the part of Glendinning, gave me to understand that I had effected his total ruin under circumstances which, rendering him an object for the pity of all, should have protected him from the ill offices even of a fiend.

What now might have been my conduct, it is difficult to say. The pitiable condition of my dupe had thrown an air of embarrassed gloom over all; and, for some moments, a profound silence was maintained, during which I could not help feeling my cheeks tingle with the many burning glances of scorn or reproach cast upon me by the less abandoned of the party. I will even own that an intolerable weight of anxiety was for a brief instant lifted from my bosom by the sudden and extraordinary interruption which ensued. The wide, heavy folding doors of the apartment were all at once thrown open, to their full extent, with a vigorous and rushing impetuosity that extinguished, as if by magic, every candle in the room. Their light, in dying, enabled us just to perceive that a stranger had entered, about my own height, and closely muffled in a cloak. The darkness, however, was now total; and we could only feel that he was standing in our midst. Before any one of us could recover from the extreme astonishment into which this rudeness had thrown all, we heard the voice of the intruder.

"Gentlemen," he said, in a low, distinct, and never-to-be-forgotten whisper that thrilled to the very marrow of my bones, "Gentlemen, I make no apology for this behavior, because in thus behaving, I am but fulfilling a duty. You are, beyond doubt, uninformed of the true character of the person who has tonight won at *Écarte* a large sum of money from Lord

Glendinning. I will therefore put you upon an expeditious and decisive plan of obtaining this very necessary information. Please to examine, at your leisure, the inner linings of the cuff of his left sleeve, and the several little packages which may be found in the somewhat capacious pockets of his embroidered morning wrapper."

While he spoke, so profound was the stillness that one might have heard a pin drop upon the floor. In ceasing, he departed at once, and as abruptly as he had entered. Can I —shall I describe my sensations? —must I say that I felt all the horrors of the damned? Most assuredly I had little time given for reflection. Many hands roughly seized me upon the spot, and lights were immediately reprocured. A search ensued. In the lining of my sleeve were found all the court cards essential in ecarte, and, in the pockets of my wrapper, a number of packs, facsimiles of those used at our sittings, with the single exception that mine were of the species called, technically, *arrondées*; the honors being slightly convex at the ends, the lower cards slightly convex at the sides. In this disposition, the dupe who cuts, as customary, at the length of the pack, will invariably find that he cuts his antagonist an honor; while the gambler, cutting at the breadth, will, as certainly, cut nothing for his victim which may count in the records of the game.

Any burst of indignation upon this discovery would have affected me less than the silent contempt, or the sarcastic composure, with which it was received.

"Mr. Wilson," said our host, stooping to remove from beneath his feet an exceedingly luxurious cloak of rare furs, "Mr. Wilson, this is your property." (The weather was cold and, upon quitting my own room, I had thrown a cloak over my dressing wrapper, putting it off upon reaching the scene of play.) "I presume it is supererogatory to seek here (eyeing the folds of the garment with a bitter smile) for any farther evidence of your skill. Indeed, we have had enough. You will see the necessity, I hope, of quitting Oxford—at all events, of quitting instantly my chambers."

Abased, humbled to the dust as I then was, it is probable that I should have resented this galling language by immediate personal violence, had not my whole attention been at the moment arrested by a fact of the most startling character. The cloak which I had worn was of a rare description of fur; how rare, how extravagantly costly, I shall not venture to say. Its fashion, too, was of my own fantastic invention; for I was fastidious to an absurd degree of coxcombry, in matters of this frivolous nature. When, therefore, Mr. Preston reached me that which he had picked up upon the floor, and near the folding doors of the apartment, it was with an astonishment nearly bordering upon terror, that I perceived my own already hanging on my arm (where I had no doubt unwittingly placed it), and that the one presented me was but its exact counterpart in every, in even the minutest possible particular. The singular being, who had so disastrously exposed me, had been muffled, I remembered, in a cloak; and none had been worn at all by any of the members of our party with the exception of myself. Retaining some presence of mind, I took the one offered me by Preston; placed it, unnoticed, over my own; left the apartment with a resolute scowl of defiance; and, next morning ere dawn of day, commenced a hurried journey from Oxford to the continent, in a perfect agony of horror and of shame.

I fled in vain. My evil destiny pursued me as if in exultation, and proved, indeed, that the exercise of its mysterious dominion had as yet only begun. Scarcely had I set foot in Paris ere I had fresh evidence of the detestable interest taken by this Wilson in my concerns. Years flew, while I experienced no relief. Villain!—at Rome, with how untimely, yet with how spectral an officiousness, stepped he in between me and my ambition! At Vienna, too—at Berlin—and at Moscow! Where, in truth, had I not bitter cause to curse him within my heart? From his inscrutable tyranny did I at length flee, panic-stricken, as from a pestilence; and to the very ends of the earth I fled in vain.

And again, and again, in secret communion with my own spirit, would I demand the questions "Who is he?—whence came he?—and what are his objects?" But no answer was there found. And then I scrutinized, with a minute scrutiny, the forms, and the methods, and the leading traits of his impertinent supervision. But even here there was very little upon which to base a conjecture. It was noticeable, indeed, that, in no one of the multiplied instances in which he had of late crossed my path, had he so crossed it except to frustrate those schemes, or to disturb those actions, which, if fully carried out, might have resulted in bitter mischief. Poor justification this, in truth, for an authority so imperiously assumed! Poor indemnity for natural rights of self-agency so pertinaciously, so insultingly denied!

I had also been forced to notice that my tormentor, for a very long period of time, (while scrupulously and with miraculous dexterity maintaining his whim of an identity of apparel with myself,) had so contrived it, in the execution of his varied interference with my will, that I saw not, at any moment, the features of his face. Be Wilson what he might, this, at least, was but the veriest of affectation, or of folly. Could he, for an instant, have supposed that, in my admonisher at Eton—in the destroyer of my honor at Oxford—in him who thwarted my ambition at Rome, my revenge at Paris, my passionate love at Naples, or what he falsely termed my avarice in Egypt—that in this, my arch-enemy and evil genius, could fall to recognize the William Wilson of my school boy days—the namesake, the companion, the rival—the hated and dreaded rival at Dr. Bransby's? Impossible! But let me hasten to the last eventful scene of the drama.

Thus far I had succumbed supinely to this imperious domination. The sentiment of deep awe with which I habitually regarded the elevated character, the majestic wisdom, the apparent omnipresence and omnipotence of Wilson, added to a feeling of even terror, with which certain other traits in his nature and assumptions inspired me, had operated, hitherto, to impress me with an idea of my own utter weakness and helplessness, and to suggest an implicit, although bitterly reluctant submission to his arbitrary will. But, of late days, I had given myself up entirely to wine; and its maddening influence upon my hereditary temper rendered me more and more impatient of control. I began to murmur—to hesitate—to resist. And was it only fancy which induced me to believe that, with the increase of my own firmness, that of my tormentor underwent a proportional diminution? Be this as it may, I now began to feel the inspiration of a burning hope, and at length nurtured in my secret thoughts a stern and desperate resolution that I would submit no longer to be enslaved.

It was at Rome, during the Carnival of 18—, that I attended a masquerade in the palazzo of the Neapolitan Duke Di Broglio. I had indulged more freely than usual in the excesses of the wine-table; and now the suffocating atmosphere of the crowded rooms irritated me beyond endurance. The difficulty, too, of forcing my way through the mazes of the company contributed not a little to the ruffling of my temper; for I was anxiously seeking, (let me not say with what unworthy motive) the young, the gay, the beautiful wife of the aged and doting Di Broglio. With a too unscrupulous confidence she had previously communicated to me the secret of the costume in which she would be habited, and now, having caught a glimpse of her person, I was hurrying to make my way into her presence. At this moment I felt a light hand placed upon my shoulder, and that ever-remembered, low, damnable whisper within my ear.

In an absolute frenzy of wrath, I turned at once upon him who had thus interrupted me, and seized him violently by tile collar. He was attired, as I had expected, in a costume altogether similar to my own; wearing a Spanish cloak of blue velvet, begirt about the waist with a crimson belt sustaining a rapier. A mask of black silk entirely covered his face.

"Scoundrel!" I said, in a voice husky with rage, while every syllable I uttered seemed as new fuel to my fury, "scoundrel! impostor! accursed villain! you shall not—you shall not dog me unto death! Follow me, or I stab you where you stand!"—and I broke my way from the ballroom into a small antechamber adjoining—dragging him unresistingly with me as I went.

Upon entering, I thrust him furiously from me. He staggered against the wall, while I closed the door with an oath, and commanded him to draw. He hesitated but for an instant; then, with a slight sigh, drew in silence, and put himself upon his defense.

The contest was brief indeed. I was frantic with every species of wild excitement, and felt within my single arm the energy and power of a multitude. In a few seconds, I forced him by sheer strength against the wainscoting, and thus, getting him at mercy, plunged my sword, with brute ferocity, repeatedly through and through his bosom.

At that instant some person tried the latch of the door. I hastened to prevent an intrusion, and then immediately returned to my dying antagonist. But what human language can adequately portray that astonishment, that horror which possessed me at the spectacle then presented to view? The brief moment in which I averted my eyes had been sufficient to produce, apparently, a material change in the arrangements at the upper or farther end of the room. A large mirror—so at first it seemed to me in my confusion—now stood where none had been perceptible before; and, as I stepped up to it in extremity of terror, mine own image, but with features all pale and dabbled in blood, advanced to meet me with a feeble and tottering gait.

Thus it appeared, I say, but was not. It was my antagonist—it was Wilson, who then stood before me in the agonies of his dissolution. His mask and cloak lay, where he had thrown them, upon the floor. Not a thread in all his raiment—not a line in all the marked and singular lineaments of his face which was not, even in the most absolute identity, mine own!

It was Wilson; but he spoke no longer in a whisper, and I could have fancied that I myself was speaking while he said:

"You have conquered, and I yield. Yet, henceforward art thou also dead—dead to the World, to Heaven and to Hope! In me didst thou exist—and, in my death, see by this image, which is thine own, how utterly thou hast murdered thyself."

"WILLIAM WILSON" FIRST APPEARED in the pages of the 1840 edition of *The Gift*, a Philadelphia-based publication issued annually in advance of Christmas—therefore, in December 1839. It was the second of Poe's five sales to *The Gift* (where "The Pit and the Pendulum" would make its debut three years later), which then enjoyed a circulation of 7,500 readers.

It is one of Poe's most fully realized and cinematic stories, and it is remarkable that no one filmed it prior to Malle's adaptation. The reason for its neglect is that it became obscure in the profusion of other works it inspired. Oscar Wilde's *The Picture of Dorian Gray* was perhaps the first and remains the most famous of these, first published by *Lippincott's Monthly Magazine* in July 1890, in a version of 13 chapters (later amended to 20 chapters for its subsequent book printing). Everyone knows the novel's central conceit: a handsome young man named Dorian Gray—whose portrait has just been painted—makes the casual wish that he might remain forever young, as he has been captured in oils on canvas. He subsequently embarks on a hedonistic lifestyle in which the quests for beauty and pleasure are paramount, and he eventually discovers that each heart he breaks, every sin of vanity and amorality he commits, lend themselves to the corruption of his hidden portrait while he remains young and beautiful. When he is no longer able to bear the externalized truth of what he has become inside, Gray takes a knife to the painting and is discovered suddenly old and unbeautiful, stabbed to death beside the original portrait.

The Picture of Dorian Gray has been filmed numerous times. The 1945 version directed by Albert Lewin, starring Hurd Hatfield and Angela Lansbury, is considered definitive. This was followed by *Portret Doriana Greya*, a Russian television adaptation in 1968; Massimo Dallamano's sexy modern day version of 1970 with Helmut Berger and Marie Liljedahl; a Dan Curtis-produced 1973 made-for-television retelling with Hammer star Shane Briant, that returned to period; another modern, fairly low-budget 2005 version directed by Dave Rosenbaum (it somehow seems wrong to have Oscar Wilde interpreted by anyone named Dave, much less one who gives us The **Portrait** of Dorian Gray rather than his *Picture*); a 2009 production starring Ben Barnes, directed by Oliver Parker; and a new television series geared to the Young Adult market is said to be in preparation. In the 1950s, an Italian actress born Maria Luisa Mangini adopted the name Dorian Gray and made more than thirty films before her retirement in the late 1960s. Also, in 1976, the Spanish expatriate filmmaker Jesús Franco made a Swiss-funded erotic film entitled *Das Bildnis der Doriana Grey*, which was in effect a remake of his earlier *Vampyros Lesbos* (1970) though it also borrowed from "William Wilson" indirectly via *The Student of Prague* (not to mention Bram Stoker's *Dracula*) in telling its story of twin psychologically bonded sisters—a frigid aristocrat and her identical sister, whose violent sexual insatiability requires that she be restrained in a decorous asylum.

A still more similar satellite of Poe's concept is the frequently remade (and aforementioned) *Der Student von Prag/The Student of Prague*, first filmed in 1913 under the joint direction of Stellan Rye and actor Paul Wegener. Set in 1820 at the University of Prague, it tells the story of Balduin

(Wegener), a penniless but active student known for his talent with the sword. In the course of his exuberant adventures, he happens to save a young woman from drowning and, for him, it is love at first sight—a passion that becomes complicated when she is introduced to him as the Countess Margit Schwarzenberg (Grete Berger), and thus quite far out of his league. In his doldrums, he meets an ominous stranger named Scarpelli (John Gottowt) who tempts him by offering 100,000 gold pieces in exchange for any personal possession of his choosing. Balduin, who has nothing in his room but a bed and a mirror, accepts—and Scapinelli takes possession of the student's mirrored reflection, which steps out of the looking glass and leaves with him. Balduin uses his money to set himself up to pursue his romancing of the Countess, but he is repeatedly thwarted in doing one thing or another by the interference of his double. Another of the Countess' suitors—the Baron Waldis-Schwarzenburg (Fritz Weide-mann), her cousin—resents Balduin's persistence and challenges him to a duel. Margit's father, the Count von Schwarzenberg, aware of Balduin's gifts as a swordsman, explains to him that they are dependent on their cousin's support and that he is last in line to the family fortune; he pleads with him to spare the Baron's life by stepping aside...to which Balduin naturally agrees. However, his mirror image shows up for the duel in his stead and the Baron is killed. When Balduin goes to Margit to declare his love for her, the double also appears, causing the Countess to have a hysterical fit and faint. Upset with the disaster brought upon his life by this taunting shadow self, Balduin shoots his double and drops down, himself, dead.

Over the years, many films—and many different kinds of films—have explored the central idea of, not just twinship, but a relationship between two people and their struggle to confirm a dominant personality, or yield to one: Roy William Neill's *The Black Room* (1935), Robert Siodmak's *The Dark Mirror* (1946), Curtis Bernhardt's *A Stolen Life* (1946), Mario Bava's *La maschera del demonio/Black Sunday* (1960), Joseph Losey's *The Servant* (1964), Donald Cammelll & Nicolas Roeg's *Performance* (1968), Brian De Palma's *Sisters* (1972), David Cronenberg's *Dead Ringers* (1988), John Woo's *Face Off* (1997), and Charlie Kaufman's *Adaptation.* (2002), not to mention the various adaptations of Alexandre Dumas' The Man in the Iron Mask. They all owe something to *William Wilson*.

"William Wilson"
by Louis Malle

SCRIPT by Louis Malle with Clement Biddle Wood, dialogue by Daniel Boulanger.
DIRECTOR OF PHOTOGRAPHY: Tonino Delli Colli.
CAMERA OPERATOR: Sergio Bergamini. Music: Diego Masson.
EDITOR: Franco Arcalli, assisted by Piera Gabutti, Suzanne Baron and Catherine Mazover.
ART DIRECTOR: Ghislain Uhry.
SET DECORATOR: Carlo Leva.
ASSSITANT DIRECTORS: Michel Clément, Vana Caruso.
PRODUCTION SECRETARY: Pierre Caro.
CONTINUITY: Sheyla Rubin.
CAST: Alain Delon (William Wilson), Brigitte Bardot (Giuseppina/Josephine), Renzo Palmer (the priest), Marco Stefanelli (young Wilson), Massimo Ardù (the other Wilson), Umberto D'Orsi (Franz), Daniele Vargas (medical school professor), Katia Christine (the girl), Andrea Esterhazy (officer at casino), John Karlsen (military school instructor).
FILMED in Bergamo, Italy in February-March 1968.
RUNNING TIME: 36:48.

WHILE ROGER VADIM'S "METZENGERSTEIN" is set squarely in the realm of fantasy, a blithely organized daydream wherein a sister and brother imagine themselves as treacherous fairy tale lovers in haunted castles and enchanted woods, Louis Malle's "William Wilson" is a different sort of beast: a coldly realistic, carefully constructed, inescapably logical narrative, filmed with almost documentary-like purity and set in different cities of 19th Century Europe.

And yet, if we look at the two stories closely, they share a great deal in common. "Metzengerstein" and "William Wilson" both tell the story of a young and charismatic sadist whose criminal exploits have attracted a coterie of followers, witnesses and participants. Each of these central characters has lived in life-long opposition to a kind of mirror image of themselves, who exposes them (to others, or to themselves) for who they really are, which makes it necessary for them to be destroyed—an act of murder that leaves the murderer no more room in which to exist. As we will see when we reach the third story, Federico Fellini's "Toby Dammit," it too contains such undeniable shared traits of this obsessively repeated story that the overall shape of *Histoires Extraordinaires* becomes akin to a Cubist painting of the same story, the same subject, depicted three different ways.

As noted earlier, Malle set out to make this film needing a complete break from accustomed procedure. Joining him on the frontlines of production and post-production were two new collaborators, cinematographer Tonino Delli Colli (1922-2005) and editor Franco "Kim" Arcalli (1929-1978), his first-ever experience of working with Italian technicians in such key positions.

Active in features since the end of the war, Delli Colli was one of the most respected and accomplished men in his field; he had been the first Italian cinematographer to shoot a color feature (1952's *Totò in colore/Totò in Color*) and was, at this juncture of his career, the go-to cameraman for both Pier Paolo Pasolini and Sergio Leone. To shoot a short film was probably somewhat beneath Delli Colli at this point in his career, but he was undoubtedly secured for the production by Alberto Grimaldi, who had produced Leone's immensely successful "Dollars" sequels, *For A Few Dollars More* (1965) and *The Good, the Bad, and the Ugly* (1966). In later years, Delli Colli would become Lina Wertmüller's principal cameraman, take over the reins of Fellini's last few features after Giuseppe Rotunno relocated to America, shoot two films for Roman Polanski, and Roberto Begnini's *La vita è bella/Life is Beautiful* (1997). He would also work with Louis Malle once again on one of his key works, 1974's *Lacombe, Lucien*—

which is virtually the story of what might befall a William Wilson without a mirror image, without a proper soul.

Alternately, "William Wilson" came as a great career moment for Franco Arcalli, whose previous experience had been limited to only two directors on a somewhat larger number of films: Giulio Questi (*Amori pericolosi*, 1964; *Si sei vivo spara/Django, Kill...If You Live, Shoot!*, 1967; *La morte ha fatto l'uovo/Death Laid an Egg*, 1968) and Valerio Zurlini (*La soldatesse/The Camp Followers*, 1965; *Seduto alla sua destra/Black Jesus*, 1968). In each of these films, Arcalli had cultivated a cold, hard-hitting, confrontational style of cutting. In years to come, he would apply it to such films as Michelangelo Antonioni's *Zabriskie Point* (1969) and *The Passenger* (1980), Liliana Cavani's *The Night Porter* (1974), and Bernardo Bertolucci's *Last Tango in Paris* (1973) and *Novecento/1900* (1976).

"Metzengerstein" segues into "William Wilson" as the black billowing smoke of the fires that consume Frédérique dissolve into the somber cloudscape that will later be revealed as the protagonist's last sight in life. The clouds then dissolve to a subjective view of someone running through narrow, labyrinthine streets (the view favoring not the path itself, but the walls enclosing the runner)—an image that prophesies the last 10 minutes of Fellini's segment. On the soundtrack we hear the tolling of a heavy, venerable bell and running feet. As the sound of a man's panting breath joins the mix, picking up where the sound of the previous story's heavy-breathing stallion left off, we cut outside his viewpoint to an objective view of a handsome, desperate, brutalized face—first shown in equilateral profile, and then in a more confrontational, facing view.

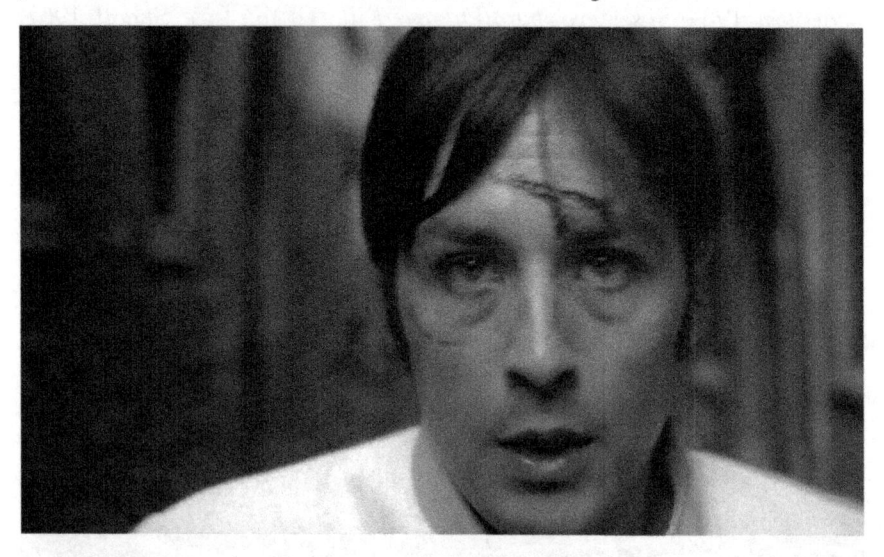

This is William Wilson, played by the great French actor Alain Delon (b. 1935), best-known for his portrayals of amoral characters in such films as Rene Clement's *Plein soleil/Purple Noon* (1960, in which he played "The Talented Mr. Ripley") and Jean-Pierre Melville's *Le samourai* (1967). Though Louis Malle was first approached to become involved in *Histoires Extraordinaires* through Delon's personal invitation, he initially refused—partly because he was wary of the actor's reputation for resisting direction. True to his intuition, they did not collaborate at all comfortably. Malle would later describe Delon as "probably the most difficult actor I ever worked with." The two men experienced a deep psychological conflict, for which Malle allowed that his own state of mind at that time was partly responsible ("I was irritable...basically very uncomfortable. I kept wondering 'What am I doing here?'"), as was Delon's resentment at having to be directed. The result was a consistently argumentative rapport, but it paid off in a gripping central performance.

"William Wilson" by Louis Malle

The first shots of Wilson's handsome face, scarred by two slashes of a sword, quickly lead to dissociative cuts of a man wearing the same uniform plummeting to his death from a great height, the height of the town's central bell tower. Is Wilson running with the intention of preventing this death? When he arrives at the base of the tower, he looks up—no one has yet fallen.

The ancient-looking location was Bergamo, the fourth largest town in the northern Lombardy region of Italy. Bergamo has long been a popular city for filmmakers making historical films, as it was one of the few Italian cities to have survived the second World War mostly intact. The *Campanone* or bell tower is part of the Civic Tower in the Piazza Vecchia and dates back to the 12th century. The church is the Basilica of Santa Maria Maggiore, founded in 1137.

Wilson races inside an adjacent church. Unfamiliar with such places, he quickly searches the interior. He finds the bell-ringer, who pauses in his pulling of the rope to find his palms torn, blistered, streaked with blood.

Wilson sees the confessional and a priest (Renzo Palmer) emerging.[45] Demonstrating no respect for the place, the man or the sanctity of his

---

[45] Palmer (1929-1988), a Milanese actor active in films and television since 1957, had just completed a role as the assistant to Terry-Thomas' Minister in Mario Bava's *Diabolik/Danger: Diabolik* (1968).

office, Wilson demands to confess. The priest demurs; it is time for Mass and others are waiting—but Wilson insists. Once he kneels inside, he confesses that he doesn't know the procedure, that he is not a Catholic. The priest feels confirmed, then, that his needs can wait, at which point Wilson becomes loudly blasphemous. (Like Poe's tale, which is related by a narrator who teasingly admits that "William Wilson" is not his real name, Malle's script predisposes the audience to doubt the veracity of its tale—which is related in the confessional of a Catholic church by an admitted atheist.)

In a more hushed voice, Wilson reveals that he has killed a man, not someone local, but someone he has known for a long time.

At this point, the film cuts to an earlier point in time, to Wilson's childhood at a military school in a wintery castle setting. The location is the Castello del Principe Odescalchi in Bracciano, the episode's only footage shot outside Bergamo. In these boyhood scenes, Wilson is played by child actor Marco Stefanelli. With only two features behind him, Stefanelli does an excellent job of proposing a youthful Wilson—not only sullen and cruel but already bordering on the soulless. Malle took care to shoot all of Stefanelli's scenes last, giving the 12 year-old actor the opportunity to watch Delon at work, allowing his performance to inform the one that the younger Wilson would give later.

Malle himself had attended a Roman Catholic boarding school during the years of the second World War and would later adapt his personal memories into the award-winning film *Au revoir, les enfants* (1987). Of these military school scenes, Malle recalled: "This was the part of the shoot when I felt the most comfortable, on familiar ground." (This may well have been due to the fact that, for the only time during the filming, he was working away from Delon.) "It was easy for me to imagine these scenes and I ad-libbed them, using my personal memories [of boarding school]. The conflicts between the boys and the rough discipline—it was something I'd never dealt with [in a film] before; it was the first time I'd dealt with my childhood."

We see an elderly schoolmaster delivering mail to the uniformed students. He looks on in dismay as the young Wilson tears a letter from his parents into several unread pieces. The schoolmaster in this brief scene is the long-lived New Zealand-born actor John Karlsen (1919-2017). His career in Italian films can be traced back as far as Henry Koster's Hollywood-on-the-Tiber production *The Naked Maja* (1958), and includes work for Fellini (*8½*, *Amarcord* and *Casanova*), Joseph Losey (*Modesty Blaise*) and Roman Polanski (*What?*), yet he is best remembered for his more prominent appearances in such Italian horror classics such as *Lycanthropus/Werewolf in a Girl's Dormitory* (1961), *La cripta e l'incubo/Terror in the Crypt* (1964), and *La sorella di Satana/The She-Beast* (1965). His casting may suggest a once larger part cut down to its present glimpse, or Karlsen may have taken a role somewhat beneath him for the privilege of having a Louis Malle film on his résumé.

When Wilson, along with his fellow students, is instructed in class to open his school notebook, he opens it to a page of handwriting in German that reads *"Louis ist müde er ist müde weill er nicht arbeiten will er will nur schlaffen morgen geht er nach Paris sein sohn Alexander..."* which translates as "Louis is tired, he is tired, he does not want to work, he just wants to sleep, tomorrow he is going to Paris with his son Alexander..." The text, supposedly transcribed from a past lesson, is unrelated to Wilson but seems very much related to the dark ennui being experienced during the filming by Louis Malle.[46] Wilson pours a small pool of red ink onto the

---

[46] Malle, incidentally, had no son named Alexander, however he would in the next few years have an affair with Canadian actress Alexandra Stewart (featured in his previous film *Le feu foullet/The Fire Within*, 1963) that would produce a daughter.

SPIRITS OF THE DEAD

page, steers its flow up and down the page, then closes the book, reopening it to display a Rorschach type blot—an indication of the ways in which Poe's intensely psychological fiction pre-dated the study of human psychology.

A new student is brought into the classroom, greeted by whistles and catcalls. Wilson drops the lid of his desk to initiate a roaring chorus of imitators. When the new boy receives a ripe tomato in the face, he identifies Wilson as the culprit (just introduced to the class, he already knows him by name), which gets him called to the front of the room. There, he takes his punishment from the professor (Franco Arcalli) coolly,

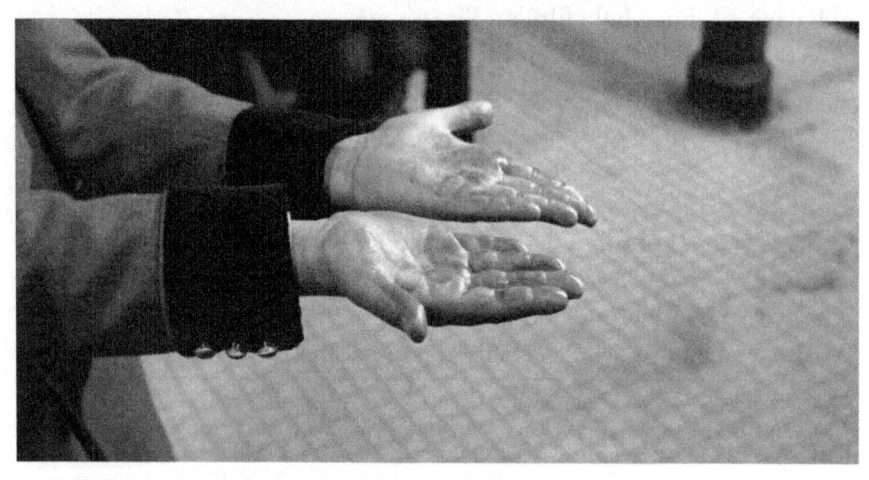

"William Wilson" by Louis Malle

as his hands are slapped raw by a ruler—a visual echo (or indeed premonition) of the bell ringer's bloodied hands.

At this point, the segment cuts to a remarkable, slightly overcranked shot of a snowball fight that recreates the opening image from a sequence in Jean Cocteau's Surrealist short *Le sang d'un poète/Blood of a Poet* (1933).[47] While the other boys are engaged in this malicious sport, Wilson and his compatriots are onto more sadistic pleasures, lowering the new student, bare-legged and hog-tied, into a barrel of squealing rats. Suddenly, a snowball strikes Wilson at the back of the head. He turns blankly to face his attacker—an identically dressed boy who introduces himself as "Wilson, William Wilson." The others laugh at the coincidence, but our

---

[47] It is unlikely that Malle's quotation of the shot was coincidental, as the Cocteau sequence—which has no avowed connection to Poe—continues with the individual torturing of a schoolboy, the killing of a student with a snowball containing a glass snowball orb, and an outdoor card game between an elegantly dressed man and woman! As their game proceeds, a black angel interrupts the scene to attend to the snowball victim lying dead beside the card table, who has become the twin of the student who threw the killing object. In short, this is quite a very astute, thematically loaded quotation on Malle's part – which I believe I'm the first critic to notice. A snowball fight also figures importantly at the outset of Jean-Pierre Melville's film of Cocteau's play *Les enfants terribles* (1950), as a young man named Paul (Edouard Dermithe) is seriously injured when he is struck in the chest by a loaded snowball thrown by Dargelos (Renée Cosima), the object of his homosexual desire. The film goes on to depict the anarchic third personality that exists when this character and his twin sister Elizabeth (Nicole Stéphane) are together, and the deadly consequences that occur when another woman, Agathe (also Cosima) – a ringer for Paul's earlier object of adolescent desire – arrives on the scene, disrupting the balance of the sibling relationship and turning Elizabeth psychotic. It makes for fascinating parallel viewing to "William Wilson."

Wilson is not amused. Back in the confessional, the adult Wilson declares this intrusion as "unacceptable. Power cannot be shared. Suddenly I had a rival." The young Wilson tries to frighten this pretender to his name and authority by holding a rat in front of his face, but the boy stands unphased.

Curiously, Malle chose to have the young Wilson and his double played by different actors; that is, he didn't have Marco Stefanelli play both roles. For the most part, Alain Delon would play both Wilson and his double, except for shots that called for both characters to share the frame. There was no resorting to trick photography.

That night in the dormitory, Wilson gets up from his bed, crosses the floor, and begins to strangle his mirror image—but the professor overhears the attack and breaks it up. In the confessional, Wilson recalls that he and the other boy were *both* expelled as a result of the incident.

Louis Malle had nothing but praise for young Marco Stefanelli, who played the young Wilson in these earliest scenes: "Not only did he have the same eyes as Delon, but also the same shadings of character he had put forward as an actor. It was necessary to show how ugly he could be with the other children who talked with him. And with what courage, on the other hand, he held a live rat by the tail even when, during the fifth or sixth take, the rat turned to bite his fingers. No, really: not even in the childhood scenes, which I filmed last, did I have any trouble maintaining that particular atmosphere, which I had found thanks to Delon."[48]

[48] *Tre passi nel delirio*, pp. 109-110.

"William Wilson" by Louis Malle

As Wilson's story continues, he remembers that his taste for cruelty led him to a medical education. In a scene filmed in the Clinica Patologica amphitheater at the Università degli Studi di Bergamo, we see him attending a lecture about the heart (Daniele Vargas as the professor) and the dissection of an elderly male corpse. Again, there are certain autobiographical parallels here: when Louis Malle was removed from boarding school at the age of 12 (the same age as Marco Stefanelli at the time of filming), it was due to a pre-existing medical condition: a heart murmur that would later lend itself to the title of his film *Le soufflé de coeur/Murmur of the Heart* (1972). When the professor reaches for his cutting blade, to lay bare a human heart, Wilson makes a silent remark to the student next to him, who initially looks back at him with shock but then bursts out with a disruptive laugh just before the surgeon's first incision. The professor knows Wilson must be responsible and calls him out, but then returns to his demonstration— noticing at this moment that the blade of his knife is already dirty with blood. He wipes it clean, explaining that one's instruments should be spotless, even when dealing with a corpse. As the knife slices through the flesh of the corpse's chest, Wilson leans in, fascinated. The close shot of the incision makes use of an actual cadaver, though an elderly live actor with a somewhat distended rib cage was used for the full body shots—in a good print, you can see the actor holding his chest perfectly still by employing shallow abdominal breathing.

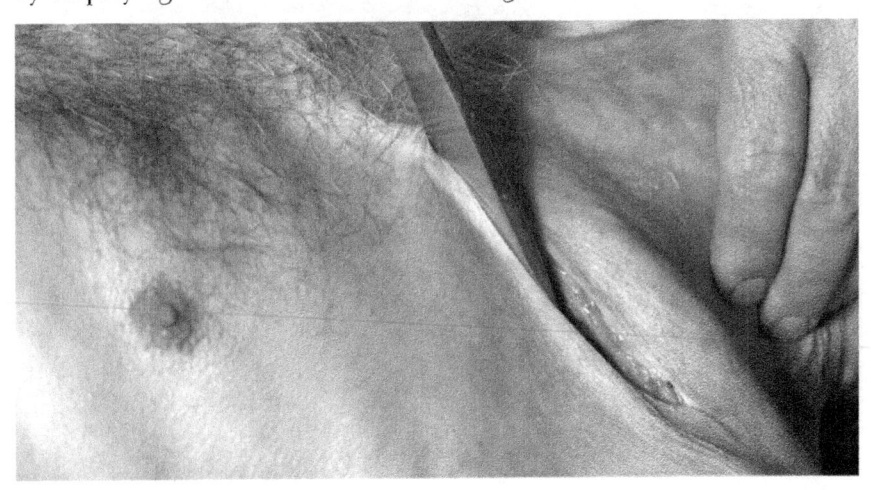

Now it is night and we see a group of the medical students cavorting in the streets. A young, scarved woman (Katia Christine) is making her way home, and cannot avoid them. Wilson, with the others but standing aloof, steals her scarf as she passes. She runs away from him toward the others, who take immediate notice of her blonde beauty and chase her back into his clutches. Wilson covers her mouth and leans in.

The scene cuts to a shot of the same woman's head, now inverted, her expression ecstatic as her long blonde hair tumbles freely. Many, many reviewers of the film have claimed that Brigitte Bardot, like Delon, plays a dual role in the film—this girl, as well as another introduced later—and it is remarkable how much Katia Christine—a Dutch actress (born Christine van Kranenburg) who went on to become the mascot in a series of Italian television commercials for Perugina Baci, an Italian variation on the Hershey's Kiss—resembles Bardot. Wilson's hand plays over an array of gleaming surgical instruments. He takes up the blade used earlier during the dissection. He runs its sharp edge lightly over the woman's body, which we see is nude and tied to a table. Wilson proceeds to quote the earlier lecture, burlesquing the knowledge in the form of a cruel satire. "The heart is the seat of the emotions, the passions..." That Wilson is able to quote the day's lesson with such exactitude shows that he is learning, that he is a good student, but that the evil in him outweighs his own aptitude for good.

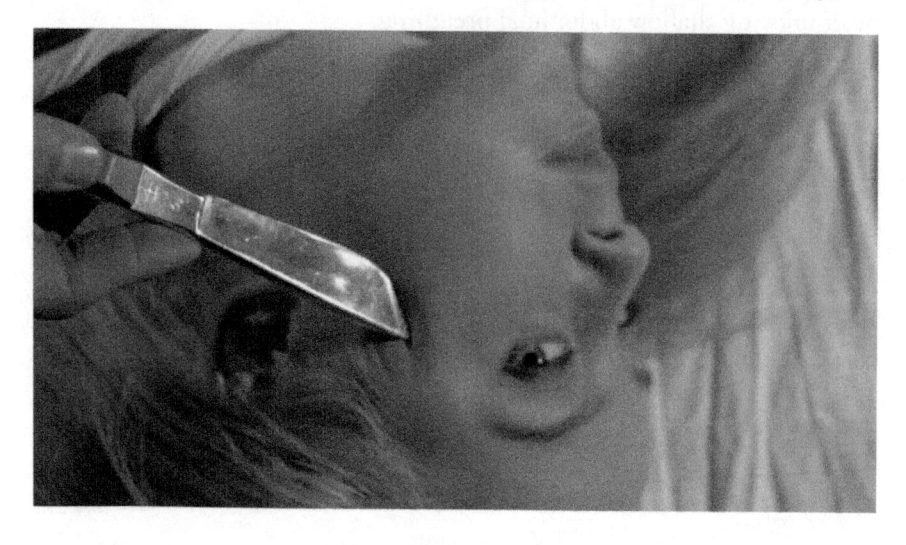

"But experience shows" he proceeds to improvise, "that it is the seat of our cares, our sorrows. It's only generosity lies in the suffering it gives."

Though an overhead shot shows Katia Christine tabled completely nude, with a shadow placing a bar of opacity across her pubic region, a subsequent tracking shot as Delon circuits around the table shows that she was allowed to wear panties during the longer dialogue scenes as a meager concession to her modesty. Even so, it must have been a harrowing day's work.

"Even if your subject is a living person," Wilson cautions the others, tongue in cheek, "make sure that your instrument is clean." At this point, as he prepares to return this young woman to what he calls "her original purity," the other Wilson returns once again to impede his progress into crime. He frees the girl, untying the ropes that bind her. (In this scene only, where it is necessary to make sense of what is about to happen, does Malle unambiguously present Delon as both Wilsons.) The girl sits up, but her mind is so crazed with fear that she cannot differentiate savior from torturer, and the one she instinctively runs toward for protection is holding the blade erect. She screams and there is a zoom into the gaping wound in her abdomen.

This is an ambiguous moment in the film because the choice placed before the girl should be clear to her—one Wilson is her tormenter, the other her rescuer. However, her instinctive (and possibly fatal) embrace of the wrong man echoes many an error made in the throes of disorienting romantic passion, just as it may also speak to the often overriding attraction of the "bad boy"—the choice a lover imagines will be the better protector, the better provider, the more exciting lover, heedless of the danger they propose.

Wilson's narration affords us no solace where the girl is concerned ("The hell with the girl!"), explaining only that he was forced in the wake of this incident to leave the University, which left him only one option: to join the Austrian Army—"to fight, but no one fights anymore." "The twin garrison is infamous," notes the priest. "Thanks to me!" boasts Wilson. The twin garrison, indeed.

Malle later acknowledged that William Wilson might be a far-fetched name for an Austrian Army officer, but he kept an explanation close to hand: "In northern Italy in 1840, there was the Austrian occupation. So I imagined that Wilson was an Austrian officer in an Italian town. But how to explain his English name? I made him the son of a British officer and an Austrian noblewoman. After the death of her husband—perhaps during a campaign, she had a little boy after William's birth—his mother is sleeping with a spice trader, himself an Englishman, who works in India. This character, who in my film is not even mentioned, I can imagine very well: it is John Allan, the stepfather of Poe, and his relationships with his adoptive son are as bad as those of Allan with the young writer. Starting out in India with her new husband, his mother nevertheless gets her son educated in her country of origin, Austria. The college that Wilson attends as a child is one of those places that manufacture military children, very common in the nineteenth century and still found in France today. The letter of the mother, which Wilson tears up at the beginning, is an indication of his isolation from sentiment: a feeling of abandonment which his proud nature transforms into a rejection. It is this sentimental void that he later associates with the faces of women. His sadistic impulses are the other side of his impotence—as is evident when he teases the living girl with the scalpel or when he tries to humiliate Giuseppina."[49]

We cut to Wilson, now a decorated soldier, attending a masquerade party—the thrown confetti recalling the earlier snowballs. On his left

[49] *Tre passi nel delirio*, pp. 107-108.

"William Wilson" by Louis Malle

cheek is the scar left by a fencing sword, suggesting that the climactic duelling scenes were shot first and had left their mark. He brazenly steals the mask from the face of a reveller with the effrontery to bump into him. (Though no such continuity is indicated, this man could easily pass for the adult that the new, abused student at the military school became.) Before going into the casino, he hears the familiar sound of a woman's laughter and intrudes upon her date. Her companion is outraged, but the woman urges him to stand down, saying "It's Wilson."[50] He removes his mask, saying that he is flattered to be recognized: "There were many of us, the other night. It was dark and you were so busy." It's clear that, with just these few words, he has destroyed this woman's only chance for happiness with this man—who slaps her the moment they are left alone.

Wilson ascends a staircase to a gaming salon—filmed at the Villa Chigi di Castelfusano—where he is immediately noticed by Giuseppina (called Josephine in the English version). She is an audacious, voluptuous, panatela-smoking brunette who dares to recognize Wilson with open scorn and to publicly taunt his reputation as a ladies' man. Some who have written about the film have identified Giuseppina as a prostitute, but there is nothing about the character that supports such a presumption. She

[50] The unbilled actress who plays this brief, non-speaking role is the only actor to appear in two of *Histoires Extraordinaire*'s stories. She is also briefly seen, with a different hair color and style, in "Toby Dammit" as the starlet seated beside Miki (Monica Pardo) at the awards ceremony.

doesn't address Wilson like a woman with a personal grievance or even personal experience, nor does he take notice of her with familiarity; it seems more likely that she is a woman of some independence and notoriety, perhaps even a lesbian, who has heard the stories of too many other women who had this misfortune and intends to use her empowerment to give him some of his own back. Were Giuseppina a prostitute, it would mean nothing if she lost all at cards with Wilson.

In fact, permit me to advance an even better explanation. What if the innocent girl whom Wilson killed in his surgical misadventure had her own mirror image? What if her name had been Giuseppina and this Giuseppina was her dark *döppelgänger,* as experienced of men as the other girl was innocent, as darkly vengeful as the other woman's dying embrace had been forgiving?

In Poe's story, Wilson's opponent in the ensuing card game is male, Lord Glendinning—a titled individual, a poor gambler but unable to resist it—whom Wilson victimizes at cards, rather than someone who challenges him. Malle explained his thinking in regard to his reinvention of this character: "The card game I preferred to play with a woman. This would allow me to underscore Wilson's sentimental and erotic difficulties. When I wrote the script, I did not know who the actress was going to be. We were in an advanced stage of the work and still did not know. I wanted an unknown face, somewhat disturbing, tragic. Something similar to Maria Casarès in Cocteau's *Orpheus*—a dark character, who would offer contrast to the vibrant and colorful surroundings, and who in some ways would represent Death.[51] The Death with whom our last game is played. Death with whom one cannot cheat." Malle's original casting suggestion had been rejected by the producers: "Of course, we had to have stars, any stars!" he complained. "I wanted to cast Florinda Bolkan, who was very beautiful, very enigmatic, but hadn't then worked in any films. She was unknown and the producers didn't want her."

It was while dining one evening with his assistant director Ghislain Uhry that the name of Brigitte Bardot first came up. Malle and Bardot had previously worked on the film *Vie privée/A Very Private Affair* (1962); he

---

[51] This association confirms that Malle had the films of Jean Cocteau on his mind as he was preparing the film.

had found her almost as impossible as Delon. Still, Raymond Eger was ecstatic about the idea and even Malle had to admit that "Bardot's presence was one of the few capable of offering a counterbalance to Delon's personality—which is so strong in the film." He was torn, but there are moments on a film set when it is wise for a director to move against his own grain in order to strengthen his bond with his producer, because there are inevitably times when a director may need his producer's indulgence. Malle feigned to be agreeable: "I'd heard that Bardot was away somewhere on a cruise and was so convinced that she wouldn't be available that I said, 'Sure, why not?' However, she'd had a row with her boyfriend [Gunter Sachs, actually her husband] and come back to Paris, and she said, 'Oh, I'd love to work again with Louis and with Alain Delon!' So I was stuck."

The row between Sachs and Bardot had broken out following the release of a new record the actress had made with Serge Gainsbourg, *"Je t'aime...mon non plus."* A sorcerous, hair-raisingly erotic recording, the song (composed by Gainsbourg in tribute to Bardot) captured the sound of a sexual encounter more convincingly than anything else ever heard on record. It was reportedly captured in a two-hour session that, as its engineer William Flageollet would admit, involved a certain amount of "heavy petting." Rumors got back to Sachs, who considered the record a slur against his personal honor; he demanded that his wife have its release suppressed. Bardot consequently pleaded with Gainsbourg to cancel its release and, reluctantly, he agreed to please her. It had already been heard by enough gossips in the French recording industry to become legendary. Two years later, as Bardot's divorce from Sachs was pending, Gainsbourg— perhaps anticipating that she would now begin petitioning him to put the record out—re-recorded the song with British actress Jane Birkin, his co-star in the film *Slogan* (1969). It became an immense hit, but didn't pack half the power of the original recording, which belatedly surfaced with Bardot's approval in 1986.

Sachs accompanied Bardot to the location in Bergamo, perhaps to keep an eye on her and Delon, with whom she had previously starred in another anthology film, Michel Boisrond's *Amours celèbres/Famous Love Affairs* (1961), in which they played Albert III, Duke of Bavaria and his paramour, Agnès Bernauer. Their relationship was to outlast the marriage. In 2015, on the occasion of Delon's 80th birthday, Bardot sent him a well-publicized letter inscribed with a drawing of a rose. It read: "Happy Birthday, my Alain. I love you 80 times... You are the living symbol of the masterpiece that France has produced during this century we have endured together. You are our two-headed eagle, our yin and yang, our best and worst, which makes you inaccessible yet so close, cold and hot. You carry within you the beauty, the courage, the elegance, the power that has made you a huge international star, never equaled nor replaced. You deserve respect and admiration, but also the love, warmth and complicity that I will share with you forever."

As soon as Louis Malle saw Bardot in makeup and wardrobe, he was all the more convinced that his original instincts were correct: "I tried to do what I could—putting her in a dark wig and so on. But it was terrible casting, unforgivable. But somehow the casting of Delon worked—because the anger he had against me served the character—and I made sure I kept him angry all the way through!"

Wilson challenges Giuseppina to a poker game that lasts all night. It is a masterfully staged and edited sequence, and the balanced dramatic weight of the two opposing personalities adds greatly to its élan and suspense. Deliberately, the cutting shows that Wilson is cheating but without drawing undue attention to how. We also must not underestimate the impressions made by its sophisticated control of color, with the green felt of the table contrasting so adroitly with the silver and gold coins and the black and red faces of the playing cards. It is only at the moment just before Giuseppina's eventual loss that Tonino Delli Colli opts to photograph Bardot from a higher angle, permitting the viewer a glimpse down the front of her dress where her labored breathing, valiantly controlled, is suddenly apparent. At the moment of Wilson's artfully arranged victory, the high angle is maintained from a reverse angle over Delon's shoulder — diminishing this brave woman visually.

When the time comes to square accounts, Giuseppina is unable to pay. Wilson (now smoking one of her cigars, thus symbolically reclaiming his masculinity from her) proposes "Double or Nothing" (pun almost certainly intended): if she wins, they will be even; should he win again, he will win her — on whatever terms he may desire. She believes enough in her ability at cards to agree. After briefly permitting Giuseppina an illusion of returning luck to embolden her, he deals the killing card. "Where? When?" she asks. "Here and now," he replies, surprising her. Again, if Giuseppina were a prostitute, this moment would carry far less dramatic weight than it does. The other men in attendance — fellow soldiers, waiters, the casino manager—volunteer to leave, but Wilson halts them: "On the contrary, gentlemen, you're not in my way," he says, inviting them to stay on. Reading the implication of his words loud and clear, Giuseppina rises boldly from the table and prepares to storm out—but Wilson stops her, spins her halfway around, and proceeds to tear off the back of her dress. He flogs her past the point of tears and then proceeds to offer the switch to the majordomo Gino, who doesn't take it from his hand. "Oh? You want something else? I think Gino wants something else, Giuseppina."

At this highly dramatic point, the other Wilson arrives (wearing the same kind of mask Wilson wore as he first entered the casino), extolling that she owes this man nothing. He proceeds to demonstrate the other's surreptitious methods of cheating at cards, showing how the simple act of reaching for his pocket watch could cover a more furtive move. Wilson's subterfuge laid bare, the other Wilson just as suddenly leaves the premises. Unmasked before the others for what he is, Wilson stands slack-jawed as Giuseppina slaps his face several times and the other Army officers confirm his shame by demanding his immediate resignation. Wilson picks up his monogrammed pocket watch from the table only to find an exact duplicate in his vest pocket. Clutching both, he races after his reproachful twin, pulling the saber from his scabbard on the way out. He confronts his

"William Wilson" by Louis Malle

double in the public square below for a duel to the death. The other succeeds in slashing his forehead and disarming him, then calmly walks away. The other's defenses down, Wilson produces a dagger from his uniform and charges his double, slaying him. He unmasks him and sees the fresh scar he was himself dealt there on the brow of the other man. "You shouldn't have killed me," the dying man admonishes him. "Without me, you no longer exist."

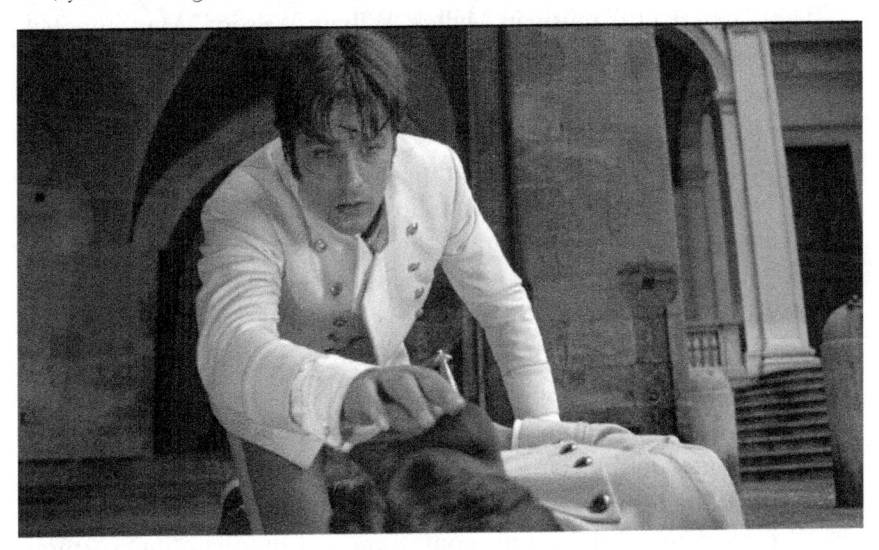

His story now told, Wilson is regarded by his father confessor as a drunkard suffering from nightmares and hallucinations. Wilson damns the priest to Hell and climbs to the heights of the bell tower, leaping to his death. The priest rushes to his side and finds Wilson's hand squeezing the dagger sunk into his abdomen, where Wilson had killed his nemesis.

The musical score for "William Wilson" was the work of Diego Masson (b. 1935), a French conductor, composer and percussionist who, at the time of this project, had just been named the musical director of the Ballet-Théâtre Contemporain of Amiens. The son of French artist André Masson and a former actor (who had appeared in Georges Franju's directorial debut *La Tete contre les Murs/Head Against the Wall*, 1959), Masson was principally a successful conductor of opera and ballet and did very little work as a composer for cinema. "William Wilson" was his first dramatic score; he had previously scored only a short documentary, Monique Lepeuve's *Équivoque 1900* (1966, 13 minutes). Louis Malle was sufficiently pleased with his work to collaborate with him once again on his surrealistic feature *Black Moon* (1975), for which Masson adapted various works of Richard Wagner.

"There is very little music in Malle's 'Wiliam Wilson,'" Masson noted. "Ten minutes in all, out of perhaps thirty minutes. He would have liked to have more, but I wanted to minimize my participation... 'William Wilson' is a rigorous film. It did not lend itself to musical developments. Apart from the vague mazurka theme that accompanies the masked ball, I intervened in only two moments when Wilson follows his impulse to kill his double. The first time in childhood when, in the school dormitory, he rushes him with the intention of strangling him; the second time when he pulls out his sabre to challenge him to a duel to the death. These two explosions of aggression are accompanied by an identical musical theme, somewhat diffused in the younger episode, intense and convulsive in the concluding one. In the instrumentation, the woodwinds prevail even if there are four cellos and one double bass... A discrete musical accompaniment is also heard at the beginning, as Wilson is running toward the streets of the city; it is interrupted during his confession and then continues—more nervously—in the final part, when Wilson leaves the priest to run to the bell tower. This accompaniment consists of the authentic sound of the bells. Bells, bells, bells of all kinds. I had the individual sounds, separate from one another, and I shook and mixed them with an angry rhythm."[52]

Masson's musical emphasis of the natural bell sounds in the Campanone of the Piazza Vecchio, which he combined with additional bell instrumentation, is a marvelous, subtle illustration of the ways in which the secondary contributors to the film's three episodes were able to allude to other dimensions of Poe's writings—in this case, the posthumously published poem "The Bells."

"As you can see," Masson pointed out, "I avoided at all costs what might have been called 'The Double's Theme.' It would have been easy, even

---

[52] *Tre passi nel delirio*, pp. 117-118. All Masson quotes from this source.

suggestive, to underline his every appearance with a recognizable musical motif, but that's exactly what Malle and I did not want. What interested me about 'William Wilson' was the mundane, minimally supernatural aspect of the conscientious objector."

Here, Masson's words are particularly illuminating in that they offer a timely interpretation of the material. The Double is easily interpreted as Wilson's conscience, but this is a superficial reading in contrast to what Malle's film was saying about war in a more timely and contemporary sense. As in his later film *Lacombe, Lucien* (1974, which Tonino Delli Colli would also shoot), Malle delineates this unconscionable personality in a manner that reveals him as later able only to fit into military life, which them redefines the conscientious value of the Double as a Conscientious Objector—a term that, in its oldest and purest sense (dating back to Maximillianus in the year 295) signifies religious objection to war and aggression. The role of religion as the original basis for conscientious objection sheds interesting light on the fact that the story opens with Wilson—an avowed non-believer—taking refuge in a church confessional. He may blaspheme, he may renounce the church and what it represents, but he is there, he has come there voluntarily, and he seeks something from the process of confession no matter how heatedly he denies it. All of this tacitly confirms, even before the story has properly begun, that he and his double are indeed one.

Poe's "William Wilson" is generally regarded as one of the author's great masterpieces, the definitive *döppelgänger* story in the English language. This may well be so; however, from a dramatic perspective, I believe that Louis Malle's "William Wilson" improves upon it in every way.

In Poe's story, Wilson's education begins in a schoolhouse described as a kind of mad labyrinth that might have been designed by M. C. Escher. Malle changes this to a military academy in a snowy, castle-like setting— by the look of it, similar enough to Poe's descriptions—which gives us a psychological grounding for his inclinations to competition, his desire for leadership, and his tendencies to violence. The scenes taking place there suggest the school scenes from François Truffaut's *Les quatre cent coups*/*The 400 Blows* (1959) moved back a century or more in time, with Antoine Doinel's truant and delinquent ways bent in crueler, more aberrant directions.

Similarly, after Wilson is expelled from the academy, we require no explanation of why he next turned up at a medical college; his close attention at the autopsy shows us how the sadism of his youth has become seasoned into a fascination with pain and a more complete emotional detachment from others, without detracting from his ability to attract new followers. The scene in which he mocks his professor's lecture while teasing the naked body of an abducted young woman with a scalpel — and his involvement in her death, which is passive enough so that he would not have been judged responsible for it — lays the groundwork for a traumatic life event that made him still more of an outcast; the implication in both cases of his dismissal, at least from his own psychological perspective, is that the other Wilson who exposes him in both instances assumes the position of leadership from which he is consequently displaced.

The striking resemblance of the actress Katia Christine to the classic blonde image of Brigitte Bardot lays the groundwork for Wilson's psychological response to the later appearance of Giuseppina. It was a masterstroke by Malle to replace the Lord Glendenning of the story with the ultimate affront to Wilson's smug masculinity — a woman who sees through him, who may remind him of the worst of his earlier crimes and thereby embody an avenging angel, who speaks to him publicly as he unconsciously speaks to himself, whose talent with cards forces him to fight back in the only ways he can — as a liar and a cheat and, finally, as a sadist. In claiming Giuseppina's public humiliation as part of his unfairly won spoils, Wilson not only indicts himself but the others in his group, because he welcomes them to stay and take part in her exploitation. Therefore, when the other Wilson appears and lays bare the various techniques his mirror image used to "win," demonstrating his furtive maneuvers with the sort of beautiful gestures one might associate with a professional magician, his fellow soldiers and gamblers have no recourse to their own dignity but to exile him once again. Even Malle's decision to replace the two fur cloaks (used by Poe to confirm the intruder as a genuine double) with monogrammed pocket watches hones the original idea to perfection, associating the bond of the two Wilsons to time and, thus, destiny.

"William Wilson" also has much in common with Malle's later work. The regimentation of the military school scenes would be echoed in *Le soufflé au coeur/Murmur of the Heart* (1971) and *Au Revoir Les Enfants* (1987), and the emotional barrenness of Wilson anticipates the unfeeling, fascistic tendencies of the title character in *Lacombe, Lucien* (1974). What I find most admirable about "William Wilson" is the fact that Malle plays his narrative cards much as Wilson does, with sleight-of-hand. The episode effectively manifests its *döppelgänger* theme without ever resorting to split-screen trickery; in fact, for much of the story, Delon acts opposite his acting double, Massimo Ardù.

The definitive version of "William Wilson" is, without question, the one in French. Though the film was shot in Italy, Alain Delon and Brigitte Bardot gave their performances in French and later recorded their own post-synchronized French dialogue. Neither of them had anything to do with the English soundtrack, which was recorded in Rome with Ted Rusoff (the nephew of AIP's Samuel Z. Arkoff) dubbing Delon.

L OUIS MALLE RECALLED MAKING "William Wilson" when he was "in a strange mood: dark, very dark, suicidal." When the film was finally released, an analyst friend told him, "You are in a period of change, a period of doubt. You had great identity problems, so it's not surprising that you ended up dealing with a story of a man who has a double."

"I recently saw the movie on late-night TV in America, where they show it from time to time," Malle told an interviewer sometime in the 1970s. "I turned it on at one o'clock in the morning, just as the Vadim episode was ending and I watched mine and Fellini's, and realized that I'd put more of myself, on an unconscious level, into that film than I appreciated at the time. There is something about this character, Wilson, that echoes the character in [*Le feu follet/The Fire Within*, 1963] — but in an overly operatic way, which was my mood at that time."

Time magazine allowed that the segment "works some interesting cinematic variations on Poe's classic Doppelganger story, but Alain Delon and Brigitte Bardot seem, to put it gently, out of place. The kinetic opening, with Delon running desperately down the street trying to escape from his own suicide, conjures up a proper air of terror that the rest of the vignette cannot sustain."[53]

Almost a decade later, Alain Delon would star in a similarly themed film, *Monsieur Klein/Mr. Klein* (1976), directed by Joseph Losey — one of the star directors initially named as a participant in *Histoires Extraordinaires*. This script by Franco Solinas and Fernando Morandi, concerns Robert Klein, a prominent Roman Catholic art dealer who, in 1942 Nazi-occupied Paris, took undue advantage of the French Jews who were selling off their art treasures in a panic to leave the country. Klein begins receiving mail clearly intended for a different Robert Klein, mail that appears to incriminate him as a man concealing his true Jewish identity. Klein finds out that a man named Robert Klein, a Jew, is in fact being sought by the

---

[53] *Time*, ibid. The "out of place" description of Delon and Bardot's performances noted by *Time*'s critic was likely due to the fact that the English dub of the film was the version under review. While the English version is quite adequately dubbed, the segment gains authenticity and edge when viewed in French - which, despite its being filmed in Italy, remains its true nationality.

authorities and he goes to the police to report his plight, which they interpret as a possible attempt to anticipate and sidestep their own inevitable deductions. In his attempts to locate the M. Klein responsible for causing him so much trouble, it becomes more important for him to provide his own birth documentation, which cannot arrive before he finds himself pushed aboard a boxcar to Auschwitz with the very Jews he earlier cheated to benefit his business. The film won the 1977 César Awards for Best Picture and Best Director.

Though the three segments of *Histoires Extraordinaires* were made independently and without any of the directors aware of what the other two directors were doing, the closing shots of "William Wilson" curiously echo the imagery of the nightmare disturbing Countess Frédérique at the beginning of "Metzengerstein": a dark-haired man lying dead on stone ground, his forehead bleeding.

Vadim never explains the nightmare; Malle, however, does.

The nightmare from which Vadim's heroine awakens was dreaming Malle's story, whose last spoken words are... "Go to the Devil!"

NEVER BET THE DEVIL YOUR HEAD

"A Tale with a Moral"
by Edgar Allan Poe, 1841

"*C*ON TAL QUE LAS COSTUMBRES DE UN AUTOR," says Don Thomas de las Torres, in the preface to his "Amatory Poems" *"sean puras y castas, importo muy poco que no sean igualmente severas sus obras"* — meaning, in plain English, that, provided the morals of an author are pure personally, it signifies nothing what are the morals of his books. We presume that Don Thomas is now in Purgatory for the assertion. It would be a clever thing, too, in the way of poetical justice, to keep him there until his "Amatory Poems" get out of print, or are laid definitely upon the shelf through lack of readers. Every fiction should have a moral; and, what is more to the purpose, the critics have discovered that every fiction has. Philip Melanchthon, some time ago, wrote a commentary upon the "Batrachomyomachia," and proved that the poet's object was to excite a distaste for sedition. Pierre la Seine, going a step farther, shows that the intention was to recommend to young men temperance in eating and drinking. Just so, too, Jacobus Hugo has satisfied himself that, by Euenis, Homer meant to insinuate John Calvin; by Antinous, Martin Luther; by the Lotophagi, Protestants in general; and, by the Harpies, the Dutch. Our more modern Scholiasts are equally acute. These fellows demonstrate a hidden meaning in "The Antediluvians," a parable in Powhatan," new views in "Cock Robin," and transcendentalism in "Hop O' My Thumb."

In short, it has been shown that no man can sit down to write without a very profound design. Thus to authors in general much trouble is spared. A novelist, for example, need have no care of his moral. It is there—that is to say, it is somewhere—and the moral and the critics can take care of themselves. When the proper time arrives, all that the gentleman intended, and all that he did not intend, will be brought to light, in the "Dial," or the "Down-Easter," together with all that he ought to have intended, and the rest that he clearly meant to intend:- so that it will all come very straight in the end.

There is no just ground, therefore, for the charge brought against me by certain ignoramuses—that I have never written a moral tale, or, in more precise words, a tale with a moral. They are not the critics predestined to bring me out, and develop my morals:—that is the secret. By and by the "North American Quarterly Humdrum" will make them ashamed of their stupidity. In the meantime, by way of staying execution- by way of mitigating the accusations against me—I offer the sad history appended,—a history about whose obvious moral there can be no question whatever, since he who runs may read it in the large capitals which form the title of the tale. I should have credit for this arrangement—a far wiser one than that of La Fontaine and others, who reserve the impression to be conveyed until the last moment, and thus sneak it in at the fag end of their fables.

Defuncti injuria ne afficiantur was a law of the twelve tables, and *De mortuis nil nisi bonum* is an excellent injunction—even if the dead in question be nothing but dead small beer. It is not my design, therefore, to vituperate my deceased friend, Toby Dammit. He was a sad dog, it is true, and a dog's death it was that he died; but he himself was not to blame for his vices. They grew out of a personal defect in his mother. She did her best in the way of flogging him while an infant- for duties to her well- regulated mind were always pleasures, and babies, like tough steaks, or the modern Greek olive trees, are invariably the better for beating—but, poor woman! she had the misfortune to be left-handed, and a child flogged left-handedly had better be left unflogged. The world revolves from right to left. It will not do to whip a baby from left to right. If each blow in the proper direction drives an evil propensity out, it follows that every thump in an opposite one knocks its quota of wickedness in. I was often present at Toby's chastisements, and, even by the way in which he kicked, I could perceive that he was getting worse and worse every day. At last I saw, through the tears in my eyes, that there was no hope of the villain at all, and one day when he had been cuffed until he grew so black in the face that one might have mistaken him for a little African, and no effect had been produced beyond that of making him wriggle himself into a fit, I could stand it no longer, but went down upon my knees forthwith, and, uplifting my voice, made prophecy of his ruin.

The fact is that his precocity in vice was awful. At five months of age he used to get into such passions that he was unable to articulate. At six months, I caught him gnawing a pack of cards. At seven months he was in the constant habit of catching and kissing the female babies. At eight months he peremptorily refused to put his signature to the Temperance pledge. Thus he went on increasing in iniquity, month after month, until, at the close of the first year, he not only insisted upon wearing moustaches, but had contracted a propensity for cursing and swearing, and for backing his assertions by bets.

Through this latter most ungentlemanly practice, the ruin which I had predicted to Toby Dammit overtook him at last.[54] The fashion had "grown with his growth and strengthened with his strength," so that, when he came to be a man, he could scarcely utter a sentence without interlarding it with a proposition to gamble. Not that he actually laid wagers- no. I will do my friend the justice to say that he would as soon have laid eggs. With him the thing was a mere formula—nothing more. His expressions on this head had no meaning attached to them whatever. They were simple if not altogether innocent expletives—imaginative phrases wherewith to round off a sentence. When he said "I'll bet you so and so," nobody ever thought of taking him up; but still I could not help thinking it my duty to put him down. The habit was an immoral one, and so I told him. It was a vulgar

---

[54] The protagonist's name combines "Toby" (a now-antiquated nickname for a person's posterior) with a surname evoking a curse – a combination that pegs him as "a damned ass," if you will. The name was partly inspired by the character of Sir Toby Belch in Shakespeare's "Twelfth Night," for reasons found in my closing notes on the story, and was also meant to impose its pronunciation in the minds or on the tongues of pious moralists who undertook to read it. Today, an American musician and producer (real name: Lawrence Edward Crooke) uses the name Toby Dammit professionally. He has contributed music to many film soundtracks and, in 2011, replaced the late Scott Asheton as the drummer in Iggy and the Stooges.

one — this I begged him to believe. It was discountenanced by society- here I said nothing but the truth. It was forbidden by act of Congress — here I had not the slightest intention of telling a lie. I remonstrated — but to no purpose. I demonstrated — in vain. I entreated — he smiled. I implored — he laughed. I preached — he sneered. I threatened — he swore. I kicked him- he called for the police. I pulled his nose — he blew it, and offered to bet the Devil his head that I would not venture to try that experiment again.

Poverty was another vice which the peculiar physical deficiency of Dammit's mother had entailed upon her son. He was detestably poor, and this was the reason, no doubt, that his expletive expressions about betting, seldom took a pecuniary turn. I will not be bound to say that I ever heard him make use of such a figure of speech as "I'll bet you a dollar." It was usually "I'll bet you what you please," or "I'll bet you what you dare," or "I'll bet you a trifle," or else, more significantly still, "I'll bet the Devil my head."

This latter form seemed to please him best;—perhaps because it involved the least risk; for Dammit had become excessively parsimonious. Had any one taken him up, his head was small, and thus his loss would have been small too. But these are my own reflections and I am by no means sure that I am right in attributing them to him. At all events the phrase in question grew daily in favor, notwithstanding the gross impropriety of a man betting his brains like bank-notes: — but this was a point which my friend's perversity of disposition would not permit him to comprehend. In the end, he abandoned all other forms of wager, and gave himself up to "I'll bet the Devil my head," with a pertinacity and exclusiveness of devotion that displeased not less than it surprised me. I am always displeased by circumstances for which I cannot account. Mysteries force a man to think, and so injure his health. The truth is, there was something in the air with which Mr. Dammit was wont to give utterance to his offensive expression- something in his manner of enunciation- which at first interested, and afterwards made me very uneasy- something which, for want of a more definite term at present, I must be permitted to call queer; but which Mr. Coleridge would have called mystical, Mr. Kant pantheistical, Mr. Carlyle twistical, and Mr. Emerson hyperquizzitistical. I began not to like it at all. Mr. Dammit's soul was in a perilous state. I resolved to bring all my eloquence into play to save it. I vowed to serve him as St. Patrick, in the Irish chronicle, is said to have served the toad,—that is to say, "awaken him to a sense of his situation." I addressed myself to the task forthwith. Once more I betook myself to remonstrance. Again I collected my energies for a final attempt at expostulation.

When I had made an end of my lecture, Mr. Dammit indulged himself in some very equivocal behavior. For some moments he remained silent, merely looking me inquisitively in the face. But presently he threw his head to one side, and elevated his eyebrows to a great extent. Then he spread out the palms of his hands and shrugged up his shoulders. Then he winked with the right eye. Then he repeated the operation with the left. Then he shut them both up very tight. Then he opened them both so very wide that I became seriously alarmed for the consequences. Then, applying his thumb to his nose, he thought proper to make an indescribable movement with the rest of his fingers. Finally, setting his arms akimbo, he condescended to reply.

I can call to mind only the beads of his discourse. He would be obliged to me if I would hold my tongue. He wished none of my advice. He despised all my insinuations. He was old enough to take care of himself. Did I still think him baby Dammit? Did I mean to say any thing against his character? Did I intend to insult him? Was I a fool? Was my maternal parent aware, in a word, of my absence from the domiciliary residence? He would put this latter question to me as to a man of veracity, and he would bind himself to abide by my reply. Once more he would demand explicitly if my mother knew that I was out. My confusion, he said, betrayed me, and he would be willing to bet the Devil his head that she did not.

Mr. Dammit did not pause for my rejoinder. Turning upon his heel, he left my presence with undignified precipitation. It was well for him that he did so. My feelings had been wounded. Even my anger had been aroused. For once I would have taken him up upon his insulting wager. I would have won for the Arch-Enemy Mr. Dammit's little head- for the fact is, my mamma was very well aware of my merely temporary absence from home.

But *Khoda shefa midehed*—Heaven gives relief—as the Mussulmans say when you tread upon their toes. It was in pursuance of my duty that I had been insulted, and I bore the insult like a man. It now seemed to me, however, that I had done all that could be required of me, in the case of this miserable individual, and I resolved to trouble him no longer with my counsel, but to leave him to his conscience and himself. But although I forebore to intrude with my advice, I could not bring myself to give up his society altogether. I even went so far as to humor some of his less reprehensible propensities; and there were times when I found myself lauding his wicked jokes, as epicures do mustard, with tears in my eyes:— so profoundly did it grieve me to hear his evil talk.

One fine day, having strolled out together, arm in arm, our route led us in the direction of a river. There was a bridge, and we resolved to cross it. It was roofed over, by way of protection from the weather, and the archway, having but few windows, was thus very uncomfortably dark. As we entered the passage, the contrast between the external glare and the interior gloom struck heavily upon my spirits. Not so upon those of the unhappy Dammit, who offered to bet the Devil his head that I was hipped. He seemed to be in an unusual good humor. He was excessively lively—so much so that I entertained I know not what of uneasy suspicion. It is not impossible that he was affected with the transcendentals. I am not well enough versed, however, in the diagnosis of this disease to speak with decision upon the point; and unhappily there were none of my friends of the "Dial" present. I suggest the idea, nevertheless, because of a certain species of austere Merry-Andrewism which seemed to beset my poor friend, and caused him to make quite a Tom-Fool of himself. Nothing would serve him but wriggling and skipping about under and over every thing that came in his way; now shouting out, and now lisping out, all manner of odd little and big words, yet preserving the gravest face in the world all the time. I really could not make up my mind whether to kick or to pity him. At length, having passed nearly across the bridge, we approached the termination of the footway, when our progress was impeded by a turnstile of some height. Through this I made my way quietly, pushing it around as usual. But this turn would not serve the turn of Mr. Dammit. He insisted upon leaping the stile, and said he could cut a pigeon-wing over it in the air. Now this, conscientiously speaking, I did not think he could do. The best pigeon-winger over all kinds of style was my friend Mr. Carlyle, and as I knew he could not do it, I would not believe that it could be done by Toby Dammit. I therefore told him, in so many words, that he was a braggadocio, and could not do what he said. For this I had reason to be sorry afterward;—for he straightway offered to bet the Devil his head that he could.

I was about to reply, notwithstanding my previous resolutions, with some remonstrance against his impiety, when I heard, close at my elbow, a slight cough, which sounded very much like the ejaculation "Ahem!" I started, and looked about me in surprise. My glance at length fell into a nook of the framework of the bridge, and upon the figure of a little lame old gentleman of venerable aspect. Nothing could be more reverend than his whole appearance; for he not only had on a full suit of black, but his shirt was perfectly clean and the collar turned very neatly down over a white cravat, while his hair was parted in front like a girl's. His hands were clasped pensively together over his stomach, and his two eyes were carefully rolled up into the top of his head.

Upon observing him more closely, I perceived that he wore a black silk apron over his small-clothes; and this was a thing which I thought very odd. Before I had time to make any remark, however, upon so singular a circumstance, he interrupted me with a second "Ahem!"[55]

To this observation I was not immediately prepared to reply. The fact is, remarks of this laconic nature are nearly unanswerable. I have known a *Quarterly Review* non-plussed by the word "Fudge!" I am not ashamed to say, therefore, that I turned to Mr. Dammit for assistance.

"Dammit," said I, "what are you about? don't you hear?- the gentleman says 'Ahem!'" I looked sternly at my friend while I thus addressed him; for, to say the truth, I felt particularly puzzled, and when a man is particularly puzzled he must knit his brows and look savage, or else he is pretty sure to look like a fool.

"Dammit," observed I—although this sounded very much like an oath, than which nothing was further from my thoughts—"Dammit," I suggested—"the gentleman says 'Ahem!'"

I do not attempt to defend my remark on the score of profundity; I did

---

[55] This word or sound has mutated much over the centuries, from the unavoidable candor of having to clear one's throat to an expression of irony, but is here akin to the literary staple of a vampire being incapable of entering a room without permission. Literally, this Devil cannot exist until his "Ahem!" is returned – that is, until his existence is thereby acknowledged.

not think it profound myself; but I have noticed that the effect of our speeches is not always proportionate with their importance in our own eyes; and if I had shot Mr. D. through and through with a Paixhan bomb, or knocked him in the head with the "Poets and Poetry of America," he could hardly have been more discomfited than when I addressed him with those simple words: "Dammit, what are you about?- don't you hear?—the gentleman says 'Ahem!'"

"You don't say so?" gasped he at length, after turning more colors than a pirate runs up, one after the other, when chased by a man-of-war. "Are you quite sure he said that? Well, at all events I am in for it now, and may as well put a bold face upon the matter. Here goes, then—Ahem!"

At this the little old gentleman seemed pleased—God only knows why. He left his station at the nook of the bridge, limped forward with a gracious air, took Dammit by the hand and shook it cordially, looking all the while straight up in his face with an air of the most unadulterated benignity which it is possible for the mind of man to imagine.

"I am quite sure you will win it, Dammit," said he, with the frankest of all smiles, "but we are obliged to have a trial, you know, for the sake of mere form."

"Ahem!" replied my friend, taking off his coat, with a deep sigh, tying a pocket-handkerchief around his waist, and producing an unaccountable alteration in his countenance by twisting up his eyes and bringing down the corners of his mouth—"ahem!" And "ahem!" said he again, after a pause; and not another word more than "ahem!" did I ever know him to say after that. "Aha!" thought I, without expressing myself aloud—"this is quite a remarkable silence on the part of Toby Dammit, and is no doubt a consequence of his verbosity upon a previous occasion. One extreme induces another. I wonder if he has forgotten the many unanswerable questions which he propounded to me so fluently on the day when I gave him my last lecture? At all events, he is cured of the transcendentals."

"Ahem!" here replied Toby, just as if he had been reading my thoughts, and looking like a very old sheep in a revery.

The old gentleman now took him by the arm, and led him more into the shade of the bridge—a few paces back from the turnstile. "My good fellow," said he, "I make it a point of conscience to allow you this much run. Wait here, till I take my place by the stile, so that I may see whether you go over it handsomely, and transcendentally, and don't omit any flourishes of the pigeon-wing. A mere form, you know. I will say 'one, two, three, and away.' Mind you, start at the word 'away'" Here he took his position by the stile, paused a moment as if in profound reflection, then looked up and, I thought, smiled very slightly, then tightened the strings of his apron, then took a long look at Dammit, and finally gave the word as agreed upon—

One—two—three—and—away!

Punctually at the word "away," my poor friend set off in a strong gallop. The stile was not very high, like Mr. Lord's—nor yet very low, like that of Mr. Lord's reviewers, but upon the whole I made sure that he would clear it. And then what if he did not?—ah, that was the question—what if he did not? "What right," said I, "had the old gentleman to make any other gentleman jump? The little old dot-and-carry-one! who is he? If he asks me to jump, I won't do it, that's flat, and I don't care who the devil he is." The bridge, as I say, was arched and covered in, in a very ridiculous manner, and there was a most uncomfortable echo about it at all times- an echo which I never before so particularly observed as when I uttered the four last words of my remark.

But what I said, or what I thought, or what I heard, occupied only an instant. In less than five seconds from his starting, my poor Toby had taken the leap. I saw him run nimbly, and spring grandly from the floor of the bridge, cutting the most awful flourishes with his legs as he went up. I saw him high in the air, pigeon-winging it to admiration just over the top of the stile; and of course I thought it an unusually singular thing that he did not continue to go over. But the whole leap was the affair of a moment, and, before I had a chance to make any profound reflections, down came Mr. Dammit on the flat of his back, on the same side of the stile from which he had started. At the same instant I saw the old gentleman limping off at the top of his speed, having caught and wrapt up in his apron something that fell heavily into it from the darkness of the arch just over the turnstile. At all this I was much astonished; but I had no leisure to think, for Dammit lay particularly still, and I concluded that his feelings had been hurt, and that he stood in need of my assistance. I hurried up to him and found that he had received what might be termed a serious injury. The truth is, he had been deprived of his head, which after a close search I could not find anywhere; so I determined to take him home and send for the homoeopathists. In the meantime a thought struck me, and I threw open an adjacent window of the bridge, when the sad truth flashed upon me at once. About five feet just above the top of the turnstile, and crossing the arch of the foot-path so as to constitute a brace, there extended a flat iron bar, lying with its breadth horizontally, and forming one of a series that served to strengthen the structure throughout its extent.[56] With the edge of this brace it appeared evident that the neck of my unfortunate friend had come precisely in contact. He did not long survive his terrible loss. The homoeopathists did not give him little enough physic, and what little they did give him he hesitated to take. So in the end he grew worse, and at length died, a lesson to all riotous livers. I bedewed his grave with my tears, worked a bar sinister on his family escutcheon, and, for the general expenses of his funeral, sent in my very moderate bill to the transcendentalists. The scoundrels refused to pay it, so I had Mr. Dammit dug up at once, and sold him for dog's meat.

"NEVER BET THE DEVIL YOUR HEAD" first appeared in *Graham's Magazine*, September 1841. Poe himself referred to it as "an Extravaganza" rather than a "story," which does seem too small a word to contain all that it accomplishes.

It is a remarkable literary achievement: it's a short story that manages to spoof moral storytelling while also keeping the promise inherent in its subtitle; it's an essay that ridicules literary uniformity and literary movements, any grouping that would render a story predictable; and it is also a very specific piece of thinly-veiled revenge against actor and publisher William Burton, whose *Gentleman's Magazine* Poe began editing in 1839.

---

[56] Stephen Peithman offers the amusing and plausible observation that the use of the sinister iron bar as the cause of Toby's decapitation evokes the "bar sinister" of heraldry, an indication of illegitimacy found on coats of arms – and therefore may be Poe's punning way of calling Toby a bastard. It is also interesting to note that the Italian word for iron is *ferro*, the root word in the etymology of the surname Ferrari, which plays a role in the decapitation of Toby Dammit in Federico Fellini's film adaptation.

Burton, who at the time of writing had recently played Sir Toby Belch in a Chamber Street Theater production of Shakespeare's *Twelfth Night* (a character whose fool head is ultimately broken), was highly critical of Poe's story submissions because he found them singularly lacking in moral intent—an idea he sought to bully into him as a necessary wisdom. Poe rejected his unimaginative insistence that the way things were generally done was the only right way to do them, that to write a successful story meant that one had to be fixed and sanctimonious. Besides preferring to remain original, Poe despised the presumption of any writer to know the intentions of God through the supposedly serendipitous design of plot twists they themselves had calculated. As he wrote in his story "Eureka": "...if we cannot comprehend God in his visible works, how then in his inconceivable thoughts, that call the works into being?" Poe also evidently based the description of his Devil on a published likeness of the moralist poet Robert Montgomery (among whose works is included an 1830 poem, "Satan") by Daniel Maclise.[57]

In adapting this story/essay/performance/rant for *Histoires Extraordinaires*, Federico Fellini did so with a radically free hand, yet the extent of his faithfulness to it should not be overlooked. That he would reinvent Toby Dammit (here a stand-in for Poe himself) as an actor proposes some awareness not only of the story but its backstory concerning William Burton. Just as the story concerns itself with the literary trends of its day, Fellini's adaptation concerns itself with the trends of then-contemporary 1960s Italian cinema. Several of the cultists that Poe takes to task—the moralists, the transcendentalists, the zealots—are also manifest in the sprawling landscape of Fellini's story, which brings its central protagonist into contact with members of the Church, the contemporary myth-makers of cinema, gypsy fortune tellers, and television inquisitors. At first glance, it's quite impossible to assimilate all of what the segment absorbs from its 19th century model, but the parallels are as numerous as they are nuanced.

---

[57] The author is indebted to the research of editor Andrew Barger, found in his book *Edgar Allan Poe's Annotated Short Stories* (Bottletree Classics, 2008).

"Toby Dammit"
by Federico Fellini

SCRIPT: Federico Fellini and Bernardino Zapponi.
DIRECTOR OF PHOTOGRAPHY: Giuseppe Rotunno.
CAMERA OPERATOR: Giuseppe Maccari.
MUSIC: Nino Rota. "Ruby" performed by Ray Charles, composed by Heinz Roemheld & Mitchell Parish.
EDITOR: Ruggero Mastroianni, assisted by Wanda Olasio and Adriana Olasio.
ART DIRECTOR: Fabrizio Clerici.
WARDROBE DESIGNER AND SET DECORATOR: Piero Tosi.
ASSISTANTS TO THE DIRECTOR: Eschilo Tarquini, Liliana Betti, and Francesco Aluigi.
SPECIAL EFFECTS: Josef Natanson.
ADDITIONAL EFFECTS PAINTING AND MINIATURES: Renzo Vespignani, Fabrizio Clerici.
PRODUCTION SECRETARY: Tommaso Sagone.
CONTINUITY: Norma Giacchero.
CAST: Terence Stamp (Toby Dammit), Salvo Randone (Father Spagna), Antonia Pietrosi (La Signora), Polidor/Ferdinand Guillaume (blind old actor), Marisa Traversi (Marilù Lollo/English dub: Marisa Traversi), Milena Vukotic (TV interviewer), Mimmo Poli (taxi driver/festival guest), Rick Boyd aka Federico Boido (Toby's double), Campanella (production manager), Alfredo Rizzo (man in traffic), Fabrizio Angeli (Maurizio Manetti, 1st director), Ernesto Colli (Ernestino Manetti, 2nd director), Marina Yaru (The Devil), Aleardo Ward (1st interviewer), Paul Cooper

(2nd interviewer), Anne Tonietti (TV model), Monica Pardo (Miki, young curly-haired actress), Belinda Brown, Brigitte, Letizia Magione, Nella Gambini (Elizabeth), Dakar (black man at airport), Andrea Fantasia (producer), Irina Maleeva (gypsy fortune teller), Ettore Arena (rabbi at airport), Marco Messeri (one Beatle), Giovanni Tarallo (elderly paparazzo), Fides Stagni (herself), and ? as Vicky Rosenthal.
FILMED in 26 days between late October 1967 — early January 1968, in Rome, Italy at Cinecittà, the Centro Sperimentale di Cinematografica, and on location.
RUNNING TIME: 42:38

EARLIER IN THIS BOOK I gave a concise overview of the circumstances that led Federico Fellini to join the making of *Histoires Extraordinaires*. However, there is much more that needs to be detailed about Fellini's life and the state of his physical and mental health before any discussion of "Toby Dammit" can make sense.

Since the completion of *Juliet of the Spirits*, which had proved a critical and commercial failure, Fellini had addressed himself to a nebulous dream project for producer Dino De Laurentiis. *Il viaggio di G. Mastorna/The Journey of G. Mastorna* was conceived as the third part of a loose trilogy begun with *La dolce vita* (1960) and *Otto e mezzo/8½* (1962) and was to chronicle in deceptively concrete, realist terms the astral wanderings of an unexceptional orchestra cellist (played by Marcello Mastroianni, the most apparent connection to the previous two films) after he dies — without his knowledge — in an airline disaster. This nebulous story, co-written with Dino Buzzati and Brunello Rondi, was to follow Mastorna through a fluid procession of encounters with other spirits, all seemingly preparing him for some important but never quite delineated next stage.

When Fellini was in the early stages of this project, he experienced two great losses. The first was the Jungian psychologist Ernst Bernhard, with whom he had been in analysis for several years, who died on June 29, 1965 at age 69. It was Bernhard who had convinced Fellini to keep a dream diary, which he would do for the rest of his life. He recalled that they saw each other often, that his very presence gave him a feeling of peace;

his favorite time to make an appointment to meet in his office was at sunset, when he had noticed the light from his window would strike the settling motes of dust in the air and turn them all golden. (There is a great deal of golden light in Fellini's episode of *Histoires Extraordinaires*.) The second great loss was Gianni di Venanzo, the extraordinary young cameraman of his two most recent films (8½, *Juliet of the Spirits*), who died in February 1966 at the age of only 45. Venanzo had already agreed to photograph the *Mastorna* project. Fellini was devastated by these deaths, and his emotions seemed to permeate his feelings about *Mastorna*, making the material as repellent to him as it was fascinating, and all the harder to fathom.

Even when a script was finally in hand for *Mastorna*, Fellini did not feel ready to embark on the filming. Instead, he felt an insatiable need to better understand it, to objectify it, before proceeding with it, unlike his earlier method, which was to find out what he was doing through the process of doing it, or later still in the editing room. He shared his script with professionals he respected, eager not for their opinion but their analysis. Naturally this drive toward understanding extended to himself and he undertook a new chapter in his Jungian therapy with a new psychologist, Emilio Servadio, under whose earlier supervision he had taken the psychedelic drug LSD-25—an experiment of which Bernhard, his primary therapist, had disapproved. It had turned out to be an experience that Fellini himself had judged as disappointing, agreeing with Servadio's estimation that—as someone already well acquainted with his imaginative plane as an artist, unlike people in other walks of life or people functioning at a less accomplished level—he had less to gain from LSD than those for whom the drug represented a door to consciousness otherwise beyond their reach. He did, however, experience what he called "a great excitation about color." Instead of seeing color as something attached to objects, he began to see "the presence of the color in a detached way."[58]

In the course of interviewing cameramen to replace Gianni di Venanzo, Fellini ultimately hired Giuseppe Rotunno (b. 1923). A former apprentice and assistant to the great cameraman G.R. Aldo, Rotunno was a few years younger than Fellini and his predecessor, yet already a well-established

---

[58] Fellini, BBC Interview, June 1, 1966.

cinematographer and member of both the Italian and American cinematographic unions, much respected for his frequent work with both Luchino Visconti and Vittorio De Sica. After agreeing to work with Fellini on the project, Rotunno worked again with De Sica (and four other directors, including Visconti, Mauro Bolognini, Pier Paolo Pasolini and Franco Rossi) on the anthology film *Le stregha/The Witches* (1967), in a kind of trial run that found him working alongside several other Fellini regulars including production designer Piero Tosi. In the De Sica segment particularly, Rotunno pulls off some exquisitely Felliniesque fantasy sequences and visuals, proving himself ideally suited to the challenges ahead. Indeed, his working relationship with Fellini would endure from 1967 until 1983's *E la nave va/And the Ship Sails On*—after which Rotunno survived the collapse of the Italian film industry by accepting more work in America, which led to later assignments for such directors as Richard Fleischer (*Red Sonja*, 1985), Ivan Passer (*Haunted Summer*, 1988), Terry Gilliam (*The Adventures of Baron Munchausen*, 1988), and Mike Nichols (*Regarding Henry*, 1988; *Wolf*, 1994).

Fellini took note that, as some important friendships were now lost to the past, doors seemed to be opening to new and promising acquaintances and partnerships. One of these was with writer Dino Buzzati, his principal collaborator on the *Mastorna* script—with whom he would attend a séance at the home of Gustavo Adolfo Rol. It was also during this period that he became acquainted with Peter Ammann, a Swiss Jungian psychologist (and, making him still more irresistible, a former cellist) who ended up becoming a personal assistant. According to Ammann, Fellini was very concerned during this period of time with getting outside his own patterns, and experiencing a mounting dread of personal and professional repetition—which sounds very much like the personal crisis being experienced at roughly the same time by Louis Malle.

"With *Mastorna*," Ammann recalled, "his fear of repeating 8 ½ was joined by the upsetting and persistent feeling of entering into a prohibited realm of death, of religion: perhaps he felt overly ambitious and he was terrified of not measuring up to the task. During that period, he felt as if he had lost his vocation as a filmmaker. He suffered from the lengthy months of inactivity. He felt tired, weary; precisely because he had taken a hit in his creativity, he felt incapable of making decisions. Once he told me, 'I'm not making films anymore, I'm losing my profession.'" [59]

In the summer of 1966, construction of the sets for the film began at Dinocittà. By September, Fellini wrote a long and rambling apologetic letter to his producer Dino De Laurentiis, saying that he no longer wished to make the film. Within ten days, De Laurentiis—whose funding of the project was deep and extensive at this point—retaliated by seizing the Fellinis' valuables from their home, putting a lein on their properties and assets, as well as monies owed to Fellini by other companies. It was perhaps the darkest time in Fellini's professional life. Things remained unsettled through the holidays, but in January, Fellini made a settlement with De Laurentiis to continue. The producer promptly hired Ugo Tognazzi to play Mastorna—a move that utterly alienated Fellini from the design of the project, which had always been dependent on the casting of Marcello Mastroianni.

In April, while suffering from bronchitis, Fellini experienced an extreme reaction to an injection given to him by his doctor and collapsed. He was rushed in a disoriented state to the hospital by a doctor in a tuxedo from a neighboring party, whom he overheard describing him as "a dying man" to a policeman bathed in yellow traffic light after their speeding car crashed into another. Once hospitalized, Fellini's complaint was first diagnosed as pleurisy or some other serious respiratory problem. By the time Dino De Laurentiis got to the hospital, fully expecting to discover Fellini up to another of his evasion ploys, the diagnosis had turned to cancer and the producer reportedly broke down in tears. There began a long procession of distinguished visitors. Pope Paul VI, an enemy of *La dolce vita*, sent a conciliatory blessing. Fellini's physical complaint was eventually narrowed down to "acute pleurisy," and he would later claim that no fewer than five of Italy's best surgeons diagnosed his problem as inoperable cancer of the pleura. However, it was an old school friend, also a doctor, who asked to see his charts and deduced from them that his actual problem might be what is now known as Shwachman-Diamond syndrome (a malfunction of

---

[59] Sorge, Giovanni. "Swiss Analyst in Cinecittà: Peter Ammann Speaks of Fellini, Mastorna, Satyricon and Africa," The San Francisco Jung Institute Library Journal, 2006, Vol 24 No. 2, pp. 1-21. All Ammann quotes from this excellent text.

the bone marrow, leading to a shortage of white blood cells, resulting in various bodily infections) that led to his ultimate recovery in summer. When Fellini finally left the hospital, he assured De Laurentiis that he would begin shooting *Mastorna* in August, if his doctors gave their approval.

During his recovery, Fellini was led to another important new acquaintance in the course of his recreational reading, when he discovered a book of macabre short stories called *Gobal*, written by Bernardino Zapponi (1927-2000). As he read the stories, he began to entertain the thought that a dark yet puckish imagination such as Zapponi's might bring a fresh viewpoint to the problems he was experiencing with *Mastorna*. A man who put great faith in tarot cards, palmistry, and seren-dipity, Fellini asked his assistant Liliana Betti to locate the author's contact information and found out that Zapponi made his home in an apartment building directly across the street from where he was sitting, in his office on the Via della Fortuna. It was a sign.

"He rang me at eight thirty in the morning," Zapponi told Fellini biographer Hollis Alpert. "'I read your book,' he told me. 'We have similar tastes. I feel we could be brothers.'"

Zapponi and Fellini became fast friends. They found out that they shared a past as well as a future in common: they had both started out as contributors to the Italian humor publication *Marc'Aurelio*, writing stories and drawing cartoons. Zapponi had also published and edited a short-lived but important cult magazine called *Il delatore*—"The Whistleblower"—which boasted such contributors as Jean Genet, Roland Topor, Jacques Steinberg and Henrí Bergson. It began in Milan in 1958 with an initial run of four issues, each devoted to various interpretations of a given theme: Sadism, Bad Taste In Italy, Women, and Commedia dell'Arte. It then returned in 1964 with a second and final run of five more issues (again starting with Number 1), this time devoted to Madness, a Dictionary of Italian Criminal Jargon, Silence, Death, and Understanding. (The Silence issue consisted entirely of cartoons without text.) According to Italian film historian Roberto Curti, at the time *Il delatore* folded, Zapponi was preparing a further issue that would have been devoted to another of his pet enthusiasms, the films of a director then not taken very seriously in

Italy: Mario Bava. (This will become an important detail.) [60] Zapponi arrived on the scene at a time too inopportune for him to contribute to *Mastorna*, as in August Fellini conceded his defeat to De Laurentiis in a long, rambling, apologetic letter and again withdrew from the project. He agreed to sign a three-picture contract with De Laurentiis in its stead, but none of those pictures would ever be made.

Though Fellini abandoned the project, he would simultaneously plunder it for material that went into his subsequent works and continue to tinker with it well into the late 1970s, by which time he and Zapponi had written several films together, beginning with *Histoires Extraordinaires'* "Toby Dammit" and continuing with *Satyricon* (1969), *Roma* (1972), *Casanova* (1976) and others. Even so, Zapponi shares the byline on the published version of the *Mastorna* script with Fellini, Dino Buzzati and Brunello Rondi, which first appeared from Milan publisher Bompiani in 1995.

"Perhaps I got sick because I didn't feel capable of doing *Mastorna*," Fellini once summarized, adding, "I had the suspicion that the film was going to kill me."

On the night of the very day he wrote to Dino De Laurentiis, admitting his defeat, Fellini had a nightmare that—in a curious way—was a foreshadowing of his next, still undecided project. In it, he was driving a car, a convertible, filled with children whom he had been charged to deliver to safety. In the course of doing so, he sped through a wire stretched across the road and was decapitated. As if disembodied, he saw the sobbing children huddled around his headless body until two disembodied hands entered from the surrounding darkness to take little mourners to shelter. In keeping with the rules of his therapy, he immediately transcribed his bad dream in detail.

As Peter Ammann comments, "Decapitation can represent an immolation of the head, the organ that makes a director, or one who consciously

---

[60] It is not known to what extent Zapponi and Fellini discussed Bava's work. Zapponi would have been interested to learn that Fellini and Bava had been acquaintances since the late 1930s, when they both contributed to short scientific films being made by Roberto Rossellini. More recently, prior to the renting of the Via della Fortuna offices, Fellini had been in daily contact with Bava, as they had offices with a shared corridor at Dinocittà when Fellini was in early-pre-production on *Mastorna* and Bava was planning *Diabolik/Danger: Diabolik* (1968). Bava's son and personal assistant Lamberto remembers his father and Fellini sending each other messages and jokes by writing them on paper and sending them down the hall as the passengers of a radio controlled model car.

decides. At a certain point, Fellini had to let go of his hold; he could no longer make what he wanted, or what he had in his head. It seems to me that his unconscious was suggesting a sort of sacrifice, as if to say, 'You have to give up your head to save the children,' meaning the 'new life.' And that's what he did, acting differently in respect to what he had foreseen. And I must add: with much toil and no lack of resistance... We must remember that *Mastorna* is a story about death, or rather, a story about the loss of identity—which Fellini was, however, incapable of telling. He had to pass over, leave behind him a certain personal identity... I don't mean to say that he had resolved his personal problems, but loosely quoting Jung, 'We do not solve our problems, we get over them.'"

It was at this juncture that Raymond Eger approached Fellini with the invitation to join Ingmar Bergman and Orson Welles in directing an adaptation of Edgar Allan Poe for *Histoires Extraordinaires*.

But which story to adapt? Eger proposed that Fellini tackle "The Tell-Tale Heart," but the idea did not intrigue him. He had his personal assistant Liliana Betti read and synopsize all of Poe's stories, which he then narrowed down a few obscure choices: "The Assignation" (the one that Losey happened to choose), "The Angel of the Odd," and "The Scythe of Time," but he could not think of any way to expand these peculiar sketches into cinematic narratives. Perhaps this is where Zapponi might come in?

The more Fellini's thoughts went back to Zapponi, they returned also to the stories he had collected in *Gobal*, particularly a favorite called "There Is A Voice In My Life." When it turned out to be already optioned by another producer, Fellini considered another of Zapponi's stories, "The Chauffeur," and proposed to Eger that he adapt it instead of one of Poe's tales. Who would know? Who would care? Eger stood firm.

"He wanted to make one of my stories," Zapponi recalled, "and asked me to work with him on the script. But soon he found out this was impossible, that it had to be Poe."[61] As it happens, "The Chauffeur" may have left some trace of itself in the Poe adaptation that would result, as its proto-Ballardian text concerns a driver for a wealthy family who develops a fetish for the family car that finally can only be purged, or perhaps fulfilled, by sending it over the edge of a cliff.

---

[61] Alpert, Hollis. *Fellini* (NY: Atheneum, 1986), p. 196.

"Toby Dammit" by Federico Fellini

After examining Betti's story synopses in greater detail, the two men soon settled on "Never Bet the Devil Your Head"—almost certainly as a result of Fellini sharing with Zapponi the dream of his decapitation. It was part of Fellini's Jungian therapy to recognize that dream and waking reality constituted equal parts of a life, and that dreams were sometimes as informed by events in one's future as by interpretations of what has happened in the past. The dream had simultaneously mirrored Fellini's failure to carry *Mastorna* to term, and the film he would make in its place. And he would write it with the man he had chosen to help him with *Mastorna*, who was much better suited to Poe. Events had unfolded as if written by the hand of the future. They began working at once on a worthy script, turning Poe's macabre 19th century satire of moral tales into a bizarre, acid-tinged, three-ring circus—the closest the cinema has come to bringing Peter Blake's *Sgt. Pepper's Lonely Hearts Club Band* album cover collage to life.

All the while Fellini had been preparing the *Mastorna* project, he had been intent on filming the after-death adventure in black-and-white, in a very realistic and straightforward manner—because what was more inescapably real than death? This was partly in response to the subject matter, but it was also based on the earlier work he had developed with Gianni di Venanzo for 8 ½. This projected turn toward starker realism was also very likely motivated by the critical savaging dealt to the surreal, colorful excesses of *Juliet of the Spirits*.

However, "Toby Dammit" was conceived to be the subjective story of a character that was stoned out of his mind. It had to be hallucinatory; it had to wildly careen over the edge of sensibility and good taste. And when it became apparent that he would be working alongside Roger Vadim rather than Orson Welles—*what did he have to lose?*

"I tried to make fun of myself," Fellini said of his stylistic intentions with the segment. "To throw myself to the sea, destroy myself. To exaggerate the Fellini style until it became parody, grotesque: so there would be no turning back."

SPIRITS OF THE DEAD

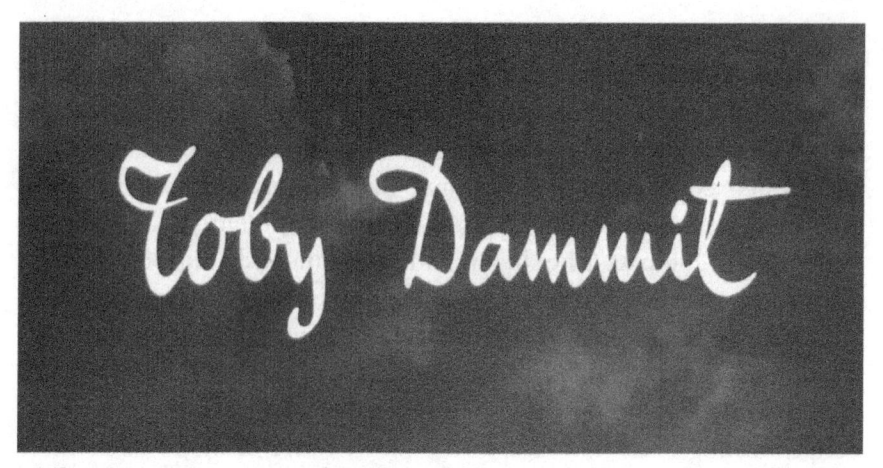

"Toby Dammit" is introduced with a continuation of the billowing cloud/smoke motif that introduces and separated each of the stories: the smoke that opens and concludes "Metzengerstein" segues into "William Wilson," which ends with the title character dying on the ground while gazing up in shock of his own mortality into a cloudy sky. There is a short instance of three dissolving shots—sky into sky into sky—before the calligraphy announcing "Toby Dammit" appears. Whereas the titles of the previous episodes were etched in gold, this one is etched in white—or red, in Italian prints. The same liberality that is applied to the adaptation is applied to the accreditation of the story's title and length: it claims to be based on "the novel 'Don't Wager Your Head to the Devil' by Edgar A.

"Toby Dammit" by Federico Fellini

Poë"—and it is so far afield from Poe's "Never Bet the Devil Your Head," it may well be.

Fellini was the only one of the three directors who saw fit to change the title of his story; however, as a result of his change, the three stories in *Histoires Extraordinaires* become uniform in title, all bearing the names of their decadent, conscience-stricken protagonists—whom, we realize in this stroke, are in some ways all the same character, all stuck in shades of the same dilemma. Much like their three direectors.

Positioned as the third and final story of *Histoires Extraordinaires* (what could possibly follow it?), "Toby Dammit" comes as a shock to the viewer's senses, by this point stabilized by two stories situated in some version of the remote past, as was the custom of nearly all Poe films that came before it.[62] It not only catapults the viewer into a contemporary tense, but an hallucinatory one, as its contemporary tense is palpably that of the comedown following the Summer of Love.

It begins high in orange-hued clouds, as if we are aboard Jefferson Airplane. Like the preceding stories, this one also has a narrator. While the narrator of "Metzengerstein" is, by implication, the story's author and "William Wilson" features the diegetic narration of its protagonist as he recounts his story in a church confessional, "Toby Dammit" is also narrated by its protagonist—but from a place of diegetic impossibility. As Toby dies a hideous death at the end of this story, he could only be looking back on the events he describes as a ghost. This detail is never brought to our attention; we are left to find it for ourselves. He begins speaking to us, in calm measured tones, well before we are out of the clouds. It is worth comparing what he says to us, as the narration is heard in French and English:

French (translation from English subtitles): *The plane kept circling the airport, seemingly unable to decide to land. It was the first time I had been to Rome, and I had the odd feeling that this trip, put off for so long, was to be very significant in my life. For a moment, I even had the absurd hope that the plane wouldn't land, but would take me far from Rome. It was not to be. The airport's invisible nets had already snared the plane.*

---

[62] Rare exceptions to this rule would include Ivan Barnett's *The Fall of the House of Usher* (1950, which includes World War II newsreel footage) and Harold Hoffman's gritty, contemporary take on *The Black Cat* (1966).

English: *The plane continued flying over the airport without deciding to land. It was my first trip to Rome and I had the sensation that this trip, which had taken me so long to decide upon, was very important for me. So much so that, at one point, I had the absurd hope that the plane would turn back and take me far away. No... this was impossible. Already the invisible webs of the airport had captured the plane. They were pulling it, unresisting, to the earth.*

The importance of the English track is immediately apparent. Not only is the English dialogue spoken in recognizable voice of actor Terence Stamp (hence our protagonist), but his choice of words give us immediate insight into the way his character looks at the world around him: he is intuitive, superstitious, dramatic; he is attuned to a kind of supernatural world of invisible webs and miraculous rescues.

We then embark on a dazzling and unsettling sequence depicting Toby's arrival at Fiumicino Airport in Rome—depicted entirely in subjective terms. This involves a lengthy procession of ambitiously composed and choreographed tableaux that overwhelm the viewer with unnatural color, unexpected movement, outrageous artifice, and fascinating faces we will never see again, all of them ripped away from us before we can get our bearings—so that our senses of chronology, dramaturgy and equilibrium continually obliterate and are thus made unreliable.

In the midst of his opening words, we cut from the clouds to a view inside the airplane's cockpit, with the pilot, co-pilot, and navigator (seated behind them) facing away from the camera. The periphery of the windscreen is covered by pleated curtains, the kind found in a cinema, while the view directly ahead shows a hellish horizon, seething like a lava flow. The camera turns slightly to screen left and zooms in to follow a flight attendant—then called a stewardess—as she steps diagonally across the frame, turns (the shadows conceal her eyes, showing only her mouth) and addresses the passengers via public address. In the English version, she speaks in Italian. The English track is sometimes misidentified as the Italian one because there is so much Italian in it. To enjoy "Toby Dammit" fully, it is necessary to experience it as Toby does—without the assistance of subtitles. The bombardment of Italian voices adds immeasurably to Toby's senses of alienation and, ultimately, isolation and paranoia.

"Toby Dammit" by Federico Fellini

Then, a new shot of the cockpit, no flight attendant in view, tighter on three men. The navigator, mostly silhouetted, stands and moves to screen left to adjust some controls, then reseats himself, looking forward as the landing strip draws nearer. Close scrutiny reveals that the landing strip is suggested by nothing more than various white dots and crisscrossing lines painted onto brown bag paper and attached to a large, rotating drum.

As the camera zooms into a close-up, the navigator turns obliquely toward camera—wearing large dark sunglasses and a radio antennae sprouting from the left side of his head, he resembles an insect—and, amid lighting fraught with menace, requests permission from the control tower for the passengers to deplane.

We skip the deplaning. In the next shot, we have a subjective view of an absolutely vacant concourse inside the air terminal, its path extending to infinity, all ashen blue except for the yellow-orange of the windows as a setting sun casts long shadows. It's a travelling matte shot depicting a round television monitor that hangs from one of many exposed ceiling girders; on its screen—as the camera slowly dollies toward it and rises to meet it—is a (deliberately) poorly matted, flickering, black-and-white image of an attractive model conveying information. In English, her voice is deep and Italian, then followed by a lighter, softer, more mellifluous female voice restating the message in comforting English—whereas in the French version, it is French. In the French version, just about everyone speaks French.

The shot cuts to an orange-tinted right angle of what may be the same concourse, or perhaps the one around the next bend. In a waiting area sofa near a departure gate, two men are seated together, holding hands, surrounded by strewn bouquets of flowers. One of them is bearded and wearing a hat while napping in embryo position, while the other is seated upright, and wearing a necktie and a black-and-white cardboard mask of an oversized face, semi-photographic in quality but more likely a charcoal caricature, which slowly turns to continue facing the camera as it dollies past them.

The masked figure comes and goes so quickly that his presence in the montage is impossible to deconstruct on the first pass, making him all the more striking, baffling, and hallucinatory an apparition. For years, I thought it must be a travelling matte effect superimposing an animated face on a stationary figure—I could have sworn it blinked!—until a high-definition version of the film became available.

My friend, the cartoonist, educator and film historian Stephen R. Bissette, tells me that this character was "in many ways, the most haunting after-effect from my first-ever viewing of the film." He also points out that Fellini's use of actors wearing—at more than one point within the film—

"Toby Dammit" by Federico Fellini

black-and-white drawings of dour faces as masks recalls a device used by Bill (later Will) Elder for a multi-part autobiography in comics form (actually written by Harvey Kurtzman) for the 22nd issue of Mad—its "Special ART Issue." In the various chapters of Elder's life ("The Boy!", "The Young Artist!," "The Commercial Artist!," and "The Old Pro!"), whenever Elder himself is represented, the drawn figure wears the same photographic mask, showing the artist looking his most ridiculous. "That little cut-out Will Elder face throughout made me laugh hysterically as a kid," Bissette said. "But seeing something so much like it insidiously folded into the imagery for 'Toby Dammit'... Brrrrr! That chilled me to the marrow! It's a slice of comics history that Fellini was probably familiar with, being a cartoonist and *fumetti* fan and comics reader."[63] Fellini, in fact, was so conversant in the subject that he wrote the introduction for the first volume of Jim Steranko's *The Steranko History of Comics*, published by Supergraphics in 1970.

Histoires Extraordinaires' photographic credit reads "Eastmancolor—Technicolor Roma," which usually means that a film was photographed on Eastmancolor stock and then developed at Technicolor Roma, which had an excellent reputation for striking durable, no-fade prints whose color levels could be adjusted according to the directives of the cinematographer. In this shot, and in most of the remaining shots inside the airport, the imagery is suffused with incredibly rich, orange-based hues ranging from tepid yellow to blood orange, which one may assume were produced on location using color filters. However, close examination of the shot of the two men reveals that the left lower side of the image is not as tinted as the rest of the frame (a bagged bunch of red and white flowers are visible in their actual colors) while the extreme right side of frame shows yellow overlaid with out-of-register (or possibly merely over-amplified and thus distorted) orange shadows, producing a disturbing, shimmering, psychedelic effect.

Indeed, in much of the footage that appears to be shot through colored gels, the attentive eye will note a complete absence of hues from the opposite side of the spectrum—no violets, blues or strong greens—as well as a careful control and separation of yellows, reds and oranges, in which

---

[63] Bissette, Stephen R. Personal correspondence with the author, November 21, 2017.

whites are sometimes seen to remain pure. These anomalies strongly suggest that the color effects on display in this sequence—including manipulating them in and out of register—were created with careful deliberation in post-production at the laboratories of Technicolor Roma.

This oneiric spectacle cuts to another. Viewed to the left of the concourse, through a still darker and richer orange tint, we see we a frieze-like arrangement of nuns, pilots and flight attendants in conversation next to a panoramic picture window. This time, the real concourse is slyly replaced with a layered studio reproduction. Outside the window is the hazy suggestion of a landing strip and a large painted cyclorama suggestive of a heavy fog. As the five nuns begin to move, carrying musical instruments in cases, with a wind from nowhere billowing their habits, the camera dollies along with them, then moves past them—as, outside the window, a miniature jet is shown taxiing along to the sound effect of actual jet turbines. The moving camera briefly comes to rest on two seated Muslims, both facially covered in white, one of them unconscious and seated askew. A handbag and prayer mat lie in front of them on the floor.

Before we can get our bearings, the shot cuts to another right angle, a radically different set-up on the actual airport concourse, brightly tinted yellow. As the camera dollies along, we see in the foreground a black woman in white lipstick wearing a white mackintosh, looking at us shocked, interrupted in the act of drinking a glass of milk. (The idea is that she recognizes the subjective eye, our movie star protagonist.) The camera continues moving forward toward other figures seated or standing immobile in the angled distance—the closest is a woman with her hair full of curlers. The black woman staggers backward in apparent recoil as a thin female, dressed head to toe in black leather and high heels paces with a bag flung over her shoulder.

The left angle is now renewed, a return to the artificial studio environment. Again, there is an intense orange-red tint as four Muslim men are shown kneeling and bowing in prayer before the picture window. Another miniature jet is barely visible as it taxis in behind the glass, moving in precise inversion of the camera dolly, which moves forward then turns slightly to show three older women in hats seated together with handbags and carrying cases in their laps.

The color tinting reverts to yellow with the next right angled shot, in which we see a bearded young man pushing a wheelchair diagonally across the frame; it seats a gabby older woman, garbed in veils and white furs, talking over her shoulder to a caregiver plainly not listening. Their exit reveals two Hasidic Jews standing absolutely still in background, positioned behind a photographic cardboard cutout of a seated man, which occupies the middle distance. The camera then once again moves forward, rising up to reveal another orb-shaped television, showing the black-and-white face of a different woman speaking from inside a square wooden frame. This is the frame of an actual portable television set placed inside the ball-like shell, broadcasting what appears to be (from the roll bars captured on film) a live, closed-circuit video feed.

As the camera approaches the end of the concourse, signaled by two escalators connecting to the next level up, the color filters disappear. A group of rabbis walk toward the down escalator and mount it, going up—one of them (Ettore Arena) robotically follows, walking backwards with a suitcase, turning only at the moment he reaches the escalator. The camera is already in the midst of a lateral pan, right to left, which breezes past various travelers waiting for their flights. We see two well-dressed women in hats in the foreground, more cardboard cutouts of resting passengers arranged behind them. The dolly pulls to a stop in front of a third woman in the act of applying make-up; she is older, somewhat severe in appearance, with very white makeup and very red painted lips, with an arrangement of sleeping cardboard Asians behind her. She glances up as if surprised and about to start a conversation as we cut to...

A orange-tinted camera pan sweeping across a queue of faces in the opposite direction, an assortment of people—pilots, flight attendants, travelers, non sequiturs—arranged in the outer area of an airport bar and restaurant. A series of frieze-like faces turn right in time with the dolly, as if all commonly attracted by the sight of someone passing. A flight attendant paging Captain Edwards walks forward to coincide with the dolly, then turns right to move in parallel to it. She moves out of shot as we arrive at the bar area, where the dolly moves forward to delineate another group of people arranged along the bar front. There is a revolutionary wearing a beret, a blonde woman being affectionately stroked by a burly black man, and a seated man impossible to tell from a cardboard cutout. Someone behind him is facing away.

Before we can get our bearings, there is another cut, this time with a consistent orange tint. It has the look of being part of a continuous shot with the previous one, with the middle bridging material cut out. Here, another revolutionary in beret glowers at us suspiciously as a thick-shouldered man on crutches hobbles toward an exit.

The color filters again disappear as a huge flower arrangement in the form of a mask is pushed across the screen, right to left. A human shadow is cast upon them, and—though we still are not shown his face, Toby

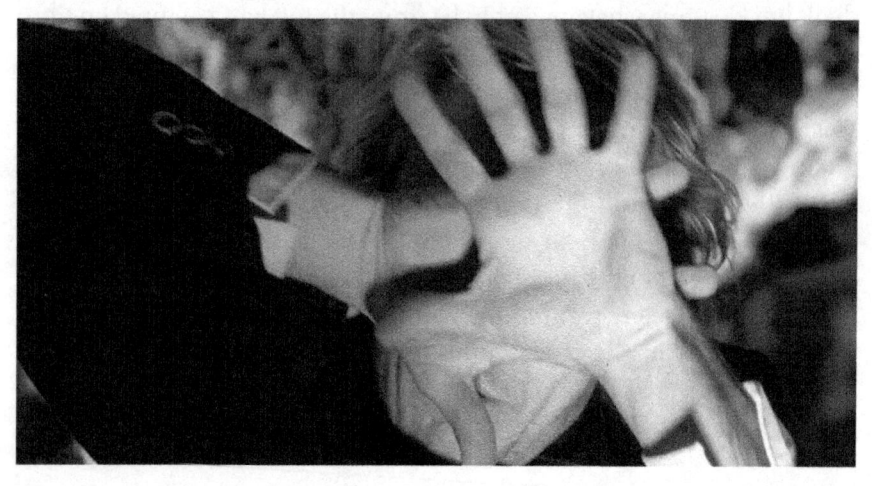

Dammit (lurching, mopping his face with a handkerchief) shambles for the first time into frame, bombarded by the flashbulbs of the paparazzi ("There he is! Toby Dammit!"). All of this is accomplished in slightly less than two minutes of screen time. Traditionally, the protagonist of a story is the character with whom the viewer is meant most to identify. Yet, in this case, before the protagonist is even introduced, the airport scene bombards us with meaningful if glancing contact of more than 50 extras, not counting various background and cardboard characters.

Fellini's first choice to play Toby Dammit was Peter O'Toole, who was pleased to be considered and quite enthusiastic when Fellini first met with him in London. However, when the star of *Lawrence of Arabia* and *Becket* read a translation of the script, he saw perhaps too much similarity to the way his own offscreen behavior was described in the tabloid press and thought that playing such a character, so much like his public self, might tend to expose him to greater scrutiny and criticism. As Tullio Kezich writes: "O'Toole and Fellini end up exchanging insults over the phone: the former shouting 'Fascist!' and the latter responding 'Fuck you!' There is a crisis moment back in the office of P.E.A., the production company on Largo Ponchielli: they need to come up with a replacement—Richard Burton, James Fox, or Terence Stamp.[64] They go with Stamp (b. 1938, nicknaming him *Terenzino Francobollo*... *Terenzino* is a diminutive, Italianized version of Terence, while *francobollo* means 'postage stamp' in Italian."[65]

To better understand why the preceding sequence was constructed in this wild, disorienting way, it is useful to relate Terence Stamp's marvelous anecdote about his first day of shooting. He was standing on the sidelines at the airport, waiting for someone to speak to him, when he sensed that his director was getting very close to calling "*Girà!*" ("Roll 'em")as the Italians do. Feeling a bit disadvantaged, he caught Fellini's eye and called him over.

"*Scusa me, maestro*," he said. "I'm an English actor. I'm here in Rome to make my first Italian film with the great Federico Fellini. This is my first day, first shot. I can't let this moment go by without some direction."

---

[64] According to Hollis Alpert, Richard Burton was discounted because accounts of his drinking binges were equal to O'Toole's. As Fate would have it, Burton would end up playing Toby Dammit, more or less, in the form of a poet named MacPhisto in Christian Marquand's *Candy* (1968) – made directly after "Toby Dammit" at Cinecittà - and photographed by Giuseppe Rotunno.

[65] Kezich, p. 282.

"Fellini didn't miss a beat," Stamp recalled. "He leaned his mouth seductively close to my ear; the aroma of hair lotion and eau-de-cologne wafted across my nostrils.

"*This night, last night, you was at a party. Big party, but really a h'orgy. You come late after your show. You drunk. You drink more, anything, but much whisky, lotta whisky. You smoke hashish, marijuana, sniff cocaine and fuck, much fucking all night. Big woman with big breasts, you fucking her, somebody come fuck you. All night like this. This morning, a mecchina come take you to airport, put you on plane to Rome. But before you get on airplane, your chauffeur drop a big tab of LSD in your mouth. Now you here.*"[66]

According to a 2013 CBC interview with the actor moderated by host George Stroumboulopolous, Stamp glibly shot back, "Got it." However, according to his memoir, the actor claimed, more soberly, "It was the last time I asked my director for direction." With or without Fellini's guidance, Terence Stamp provides everything the character needs and gives what is arguably the most indelible performance of his distinguished and eclectic career. His Toby Dammit is at once himself (Toby), the actor playing him (Stamp), the distilled essence of a besotted and tortured Edgar Allan Poe, and a forerunner of every British punk rocker ever indulged with a television spotlight. He's the Damned—literally. An interesting detail of

[66] Stamp, Terence. *Double Feature* (London: Bloomsbury, 1989), pp. 309-310.

Stamp's makeup is a wild, extended "tail" on his left eyebrow, which in certain lighting gives the impression of a perpetually pained furrow on his brow.

Fellini scholars have noted that the opening airport sequence mirrors the script for *Il viaggio di G. Mastorna*, which opens with passengers aboard a frighteningly turbulent flight that suddenly becomes eerily placid and lands in an otherworldly airport—which makes sense, given Toby's *oltre-tomba* narration.

Blinded by the light, Toby self-defensively—and theatrically—hurls his suitcase at the oldest and frailest of the photographers (Giovanni Tavallo), which causes the others paparazzi to turn against him. They curse him as he stumbles backwards onto an escalator going up, sitting and making his apologies and hiding his face as the mechanized stairwell rides him to a level where the orange light burns brightest. There, at the top, he experiences an inexplicable private moment: his anger at the lights abruptly dissolves; he stands solemn, then seems to cave in upon himself with two mysterious balletic movements. He then seems to alight to something unseen, bowing to a presence in a courtly, genuflecting way. As he lowers himself onto one knee, a brighter light limns the edge of his face. "You swore you'd leave me alone," he mutters in French. In English, he says nothing.

Before his actions can be observed, Toby quickly arises as if nothing has happened, then uses the descending escalator to a group of greeters that has assembled below. They are Father Spagna (a priest played by Salvo Randone, who appears to speak his lines in keeping with the French dialogue), the man in charge of producing Toby's new film, who proceeds to introduce the Manetti brothers, Maurizio (younger, unsmiling) and Ernestino (older, smiling), who will be directing; then his male secretary-driver; and finally Vicky Rosenthal, a severe-looking older woman whom he is told in the French version will serve as his assistant, while the English version (which doesn't assign her a name) introduces her as his translator. In the French version, Vicky notes to Father Spagna, in sinister *sotto voce*, that he is perfect for the part—while in the English version she says this in untranslated Italian, clearly not intending the actor to hear this approval and thus intensifying his isolation. "Let us depart," says Father Spagna in his broken yet elegant (if deathly) English, and they proceed as a group down a corridor toward an orange wall.

The next cut transports the group inside a car driving the Raccondo Anulare toward Rome. We see the backs of three heads, looking out a windscreen toward the orange light of a hellish sunset—an introductory shot inside the company car, meant to mirror the opening shot. The driver and the two directors are up front, Maurizio peering over Ernestino's shoulder. Father Spagna explains to Toby—seated with him in the back seat, beside Vicky—that the film they will be making together is "the first Catholic Western. Christ's return to the bleak desolate prairie..." his hands articulating delicately as he speaks, "...and is this not the secret desire of all men?" In the English version, he babbles in Italian sometimes paraphrased by the translator ("I'm afraid I missed some of that...") as Toby gazes at the movements of the priest's articulate hands with the mesmerized innocence of a child at bedtime.

In the original shooting script, Toby asks to know the title of the film. Father Spagna (identified only as The Priest) tells him, *"Trente dollari"* ("Thirty Dollars")—which draws a blank from the actor, leading to his further explanation *"Giuda...I trenta denari..."* ("Judas...the thirty pieces of silver...")

The line was obviously intended as a good-natured jab at Fellini's

"Toby Dammit" by Federico Fellini

producer Alberto Grimaldi, who was financing this film with dollars earned by the "Dollars" sequels of Sergio Leone. The film that Father Spagna proceeds to describe sounds horribly pretentious. In French, at this point Maurizio Mazetti, the more intense of the two directors, jumps in, describing the film as "syntagmatic, as my friend Roland Barthes would say, something between Dreyer and Pasolini, with a hint of John Ford, of course, as long as it reflects the death throes and decay of our capitalist system." "A Western can claim to be militant—that's what Lukacs says," the secretary chauffeur throws in.

What Mazetti and Father Spagna have been describing, strangely enough, is not at all far afield from some of the more peculiar and aberrant varieties of the so-called Spaghetti Western that were springing up in response to the success of the "Dollars" pictures, nor is it unlike some of the serious criticism such films have attracted. Sergio Corbucci's *Django* (1965), made early in this phenomenon, introduced a protagonist who might possibly be Death or the Resurrection, as he literally dragged a coffin around behind him. Toward the end of Leone's *The Good, the Bad and the Ugly* (1967)—a film that actually takes place before the first two "Dollars" films—Clint Eastwood's character Blondie finds the serape he wears in his earlier adventures in a bombed-out church, a mystical moment of transformation if not resurrection. Twice, American actor Guy Madison played priestly gunfighters in Italian westerns: he was Father Gus Fleming in Osvaldo Civirani's *Il figlio di Django/The Return of Django* (1967) and Reverend Miller in Léon Klimovsky's *Reverendo Colt/Reverend's Colt* (1970). There was also Sabata, the character introduced in Gianfranco Parolini/Frank Kramer's same-titled 1969 film, whose name evokes the Sabbath in the romance languages and returned for several other films, sometimes played by different actors.

Meanwhile, as Vicky Rosenthal primly paraphrases this intellectual banter in the English version, the car passes through a collage of working class situations on the streets and roads of Rome. We see the back end of a butcher's truck, three sides of beef swinging on hooks behind a flapping cover, a young woman in a coat standing outside a magnificent showroom of lamps and chandeliers, a steam roller, a surveyor, cement mixers and pourers, a gigantic spool of steel cable being hoisted aloft, a fashion

SPIRITS OF THE DEAD

photographer grabbing a shot with two models. Stepping through some of these intensely orange shots frame by frame, we can sometimes see objects limned with out-of-register edgings of red, orange and lime green. The steel cable is but one of many foreshadowings of the gruesome finale of the story.

Toby looks out the window at a passing world that may or may not be his own hallucination, the reflected image of a religious parade float gliding along its glass. Now the running commentary is provided, once again, by Mazetti—and subtitled in French: "Thus, our two outlaws represent irresponsibility and anarchy... the busty girl is the illusory escape into the irrational. The film will be in color. Harsh colors, rough costumes to reconcile the holy landscape with the prairie." (In the English version, the translator amusingly offers, "Oh, dear—there was something about bison there, but I didn't get the point.") Disembodied lights pass over the passengers, a car in the next lane seems to float forward in the artificial exterior scenery.

Outside the car, in a choreographed insert filmed on location without color filtering, a young hippie in Sgt. Pepper-like apparel looks at the camera as it passes, turning and walking toward a bombed-out building where other hippies strum or hold instruments. The camera soon surrenders him in favor of another hippie, wearing a backpack and walking

"Toby Dammit" by Federico Fellini

past other musicians toward a hole in the wall, which he passes through.

Toby urgently leans forward, wanting to know more about the Ferrari he was promised as part of his salary for doing the film—as another car floats forward, beeping its horn, in the left-side lane. The line serves to show that Toby has not come to Rome in pursuit of his art, but in search of escape.

The Ferrari is another of the film's inside jokes, one that likely came to Fellini's attention from his cameraman Giuseppe Rotunno or another member of his principal crew, as they all came to this project after completing a film for Dino De Laurentiis entitled *Le streghe/The Witches* (1967), an anthology film consisting of five stories, all starring Silvana Mangano, the wife of De Laurentiis. The producer wanted to assemble the best possible support for her, and hired such directors as Visconti, Pasolini and Vittorio de Sica to present her in the best possible light. He also surrounded her with actors with whom she had enjoyed the biggest of her past successes—people like Alberto Sordi, Annie Girardot, and the Neopolitan comic Totò. But he also wanted to obtain for her the biggest name in the present Italian box office: Clint Eastwood. De Laurentiis flew Eastwood to New York City, first class, put him up in one of the city's finest hotels, all in exchange for one hour of his time. During that hour he made him not one, but two offers—in exchange for playing the leading man in one of five stories, a film of no more than 30 minutes, he would pay him $250,000... or, if he preferred, $200,000 and the latest model Ferrari, tax free. He further sweetened the deal by impressing upon Eastwood that, in the event of his refusal, he would extend the same offer to only one other actor: Sean Connery, then the biggest star in the world. The Leone films had yet to be released in America, and to an actor then closer to 40 than 30 and still known in America only as the star of TV's *Rawhide*, this was heady bargaining. Eastwood savvily accepted the lesser figure and the car, which to him represented a gift from which his agent would not be able to claim his customary percentage. Clint's Ferrari was even briefly immortalized in the main titles of *Le streghe*, designed by the animator Pino Zac (Giuseppe Zaccaria).

With this story in mind, it is easier to understand why the production company would have lured an actor like Toby Dammit to star in their Western—as scripted, he would have been analogous to Clint Eastwood.

SPIRITS OF THE DEAD

As it happens, Terence Stamp came to this project *after* starring in an American Western shot in different areas in the state of Utah: *Blue* (1968), directed by Silvio Narizzano—an Italian-American born in Quebec.

At this point there is a fascinating if anachronistic night exterior of the Coliseum amphitheater in Rome, encircled by heavy, turning traffic. It is another traveling matte shot: in the left background is a highly artificial, stylized backdrop of a sunset sky with mauve clouds looming over a gnarled silhouette of huddled buildings, steeples, even the *"Il Fungo"* or Mushroom tower in the EUR district. At one point, the camera responsible for the documentary component slips slightly, and the rock steadiness of the artificial component matted-in exposes the illusion.

Credited with the short's special effects is Joseph Nathanson—in fact, Jozef Paweł Natanson (1909-2003), a Polish-born, Louvre-educated Surrealist painter who began working in films on Michael Powell and Emeric Pressburger's *The Red Shoes* (1948)—specifically as a combination art director and set designer for the film's celebrated "Red Shoes" fantasy dance sequence. For this, Natanson painted backgrounds as well as glass foregrounds lending dimension to the oneiric scenery. It was his invention with glass painting that was recognized by others around him, and photographs exist showing him at work on unidentified projects at Shepperton through the early 1950s. (He had become a British citizen in 1949.) His accredited trail as a matte painter continues in Italy, where he lived for most of his life, with such assignments as Carmine Gallone's *Puccini* and *Casta diva* (1953 and 1954, the latter a biography of Bellini), Augusto Genina's *Maddalena* (1954), Guido Brignone's *Le schiave di Cartagine/The Sword and the Cross* (1956), Robert Wise's *Helen of Troy* (1956), Giacomo Gentilomo's *Sigfrido/Dragon's Blood* (1958, on which he worked with Eugenio Bava in the special effects department), Vittorio de Sica's *I ciociara/Two Women* (1960), Michael Curtiz' *Francis of Assisi* (1961) and Joseph L. Mankiewicz's epic *Cleopatra* (1963). Between these prestigious assignments, he also labored on some notable genre fare during Rome's "Hollywood on the Tiber" period, including Viktor Tourjansky's *Erode il grande/Herod the Great* (1959), Pietro Francisci's *L'assedio di Siracusa/Siege of Syracuse* (1960), Umberto Scarpelli's eye-*popping Il giganta di Metropolis/Giant of the Metropolis*

"Toby Dammit" by Federico Fellini

(1961), and Edgar G. Ulmer's final film *The Cavern* (1964). He worked with Mario Bava on his episode of the *Odissea/Adventures of Ulysses* miniseries produced by Dino De Laurentiis in 1968, and with Fellini once again on *Satyricon* (1969). All told, it is said that he worked on more than 80 films, often uncredited. A Museology graduate of the Louvre, Natanson published two volumes on Gothic Ivories in the early 1950s, and eventually penned an autobiography—*Zgrzyt otwieraj cej si bramy* ("The Opening of the Gates")—published only in Warsaw in 2003, shortly before his death.

Natanson's responsibilities on "Toby Dammit" extended to the painting of backdrops, such as those seen at the airport and in matte shots like this, as well as the painting of figures onto cardboard to populate the backgrounds of certain shots.

The story now embarks on various *tableaux vivant* of Roman traffic: someone trying to speak to Toby from another vehicle, a driver yawning, character actor Alfredo Rizzo—perhaps best remembered as the business manager Lucas in Piero Regnoli's *L'amante del vampire/The Playgirls and the Vampire* (1960)—driving into frame to lambaste a slow driver (we can briefly see Rotunno's camera reflected in his backseat window as he pulls away), a headlight moving forward. A bus releases its passengers as two men step into the foreground, walking towards one another, butting foreheads in a cartoonish traffic dispute. The camera pans to the left, across various concerned onlookers, to arrive at a man looking under the hood of his stalled car. A harsh orange tint is added for the continuation of the scene, as we push forward through other rubberneckers to an overturned motorcycle (the tinting makes it impossible to identify the pool on the ground as blood or gasoline), as a crash scene is being measured and administered by police, an injured man seated on the bumper of another vehicle. (More foreshadowing.) We cut to an unfiltered shot of a car carrying two nuns—actually two men dressed as nuns, with sunglasses—approaching and braking in front of the camera. Toby and Vicky in the back seat, a primitive mural of cops and robbers, then a painted glamorous face, passing over their window in reflection.

Two gypsy women from an encampment run forward, eager to read palms for loose cash. Everyone in the car gets good news until Toby eagerly

SPIRITS OF THE DEAD

proffers his own hand, which the suddenly woeful palmist (Irina Maleeva) solemnly folds into a closed position. (Might the second gypsy woman — shown reading the driver's palm in a single shot in front of a dissociated, salmon-colored backdrop — be Claudia Cardinale, having a spot of fun by playing an insignificant part?) Father Spagna has a marvelous expression here, impressed by the apparent magnitude of his actor's damnation. Toby, however, exults in the fortune teller's findings, hugging his fist close to him like a prized possession. Vicky: "I'm a coward. I'd rather not know."

"Toby Dammit" by Federico Fellini

This was Maleeva's first speaking part, and it was promptly followed by a role as a handmaiden in Fellini's *Satyricon*. After playing a few other roles in Italian co-productions, including Antonio Margheriti's *Nella stretta morsa del ragno/Web of the Spider* (1971—a remake of Margheriti's earlier *Danza macabre/Castle of Blood*, 1964, in which she plays Silvia Sorrente's former role as a honeymooning bride), she relocated to America in the mid-1970s, where she has worked more commonly in television (*The Gilmore Girls, The Bold and the Beautiful, Six Feet Under*) than in films (*The Yum Yum Girls, Union City, Hard Drive*).

A subjective shot follows a vehicle carrying various painted cardboard figures, then cuts to a car driving along with no apparent passengers. Then, a shot of the three backseat passengers, the camera zooming slowly into one of the segment's definitive portraits of Toby Dammit, slumped in his seat, looking recessed into reality as his mind wanders back—through Father Spagna's cigarette smoke—to readdress some important information postponed until this moment. His narration voice returns:

French: *I had seen her once again. She was waiting for me at the airport... with her big, silent ball.*

English: *Once again, I had seen her. She had been waiting for me at the airport—with her white, silent ball.*

The next shot leaves us with no question as to where and when we are, as the camera places us at Toby's exact vantage point at the top of the airport escalator. However, now we are seeing an additional element not shown to us in our prior, objective viewpoint: a large white ball (looking for all the world like a bubble filled with smoke) bounces up the retreating stairs in slow motion, toward the top. As the earlier scene proves, this right-hand escalator was moving up, not down; therefore, this shot was achieved by filming it in reverse, as the ball was bounced *down* the stairs. Its arrival cuts perfectly to the objective shot of Toby alighting with an outstretched hand.

Next we see an obliquely composed shot of a little girl with long blonde hair (the same color as Toby's) obliquely approaching—dressed in white, with white stockings and black Mary Jane shoes. There is something crab-like, even arachnoid, about the unnatural positioning of her limbs. The film grain shows it is a motion image, yet the figure stands absolutely still, posed.

French: *I told her to go away, but she kept coming back.*
English: *I kept telling her to go away, but she always came back. She seemed to know that, sooner or later, I would join in her game. But when?*

The camera zooms out from the luminous ball as the girl pulls it toward her, her head downcast to hide her face as she hunkers down on the still escalator, the ball clutched in both hands, their nails painted blood-red. A one-sided conversation ensues:

"Toby Dammit" by Federico Fellini

Toby (in close-up): *But you told me you'd leave me alone.*

In the reverse shot, the camera has now zoomed in closer, so that we see one stair on the escalator rather than three. *La bambina diavola*, as Fellini termed her, is now looking up with bright surprise, her fingers nearly interlacing around the ball. The camera framing moves forward in two short jerks before she lowers her head, shaking it violently in stubborn, childish denial.

Fellini was unresponsive to the Devil as he was described in Poe's morality tale; however, one detail in his description proved useful: "his hair parted in front like a girl's." The more Fellini considered his dissolute protagonist, and his Devil, he came to the conclusion that "His devil must be his own immaturity, hence, a child." When Fellini mentioned this to his writing partner Bernardino Zapponi, he—being the Mario Bava fan that he was—thought immediately of Melissa Graps, the little girl's ghost in Mario Bava's then-still-obscure film *Operazione paura/Kill, Baby...Kill!* (1966), which he had seen in Rome when it opened in the month of August, considered the dead zone of Italian film distribution because most people were then away on vacation to escape the overbearing heat. In Bava's film, scripted by Romano Migliorini and Roberto Natale, Melissa was the vengeful ghost of a little girl, the daughter of a noble family in a superstitious village who was trampled to death by horses after chasing her ball into their path, as the villagers stood by and did nothing. In the final act, it is revealed that Melissa is not a self-motivated ghost, but rather a violent demiurge summoned forth by her mediumistic mother's refusal to forgive those who watched her child die.

This ball-bouncing spectre, an inversion of traditional images of fright, has been related to assorted cinematic and literary forebears by critics and historians determined to identify her peculiar resonance: I see antecedents for Melissa and the *bambina diavola* in the bouncing ball child murder of Fritz Lang's *M* (1930), as well as the little girl ghost inhabiting the spectral underground train in Georges Franju's short film *La prémière nuit* (1953, a film whose slow-motion train also surely inspired Bava's ghostly horse-drawn carriage in *La maschera del demonio/Black Sunday*, 1960); Richard Harland Smith pointed out to me the image of such a character peering through a transparent curtain in Fellini's *Giulietta degli spiriti*, which predated *Operazione paura*; Kimberly Lindbergs found just such a ghost—named Jessica—in a 1953 teleplay by Richard Lortz entitled "The Others," first broadcast on the program *Suspense* and later adapted into a play called "Voices" that ran successfully in London and was later filmed under that title in 1973—to name only a few.

Bernardino Zapponi, in the book he later wrote about Fellini, tried to separate the *bambina diavola* from *Operazione paura* as much as he could, explaining, "Fellini liked contrasts. The devil's ugly? Let's make it beautiful. Is he hideous and evil? We will make it attractive and innocent.

"Toby Dammit" by Federico Fellini

It will be a boy—better yet, a girl!"[67] However, in a story about the world of Italian cinema, that makes such knowing references to the likes of Marilù Tolo and Tomas Milian and Clint Eastwood's Ferrari, a quotation from the universe of Mario Bava seems perfectly native and at home. Indeed, thanks in no small part to the starting shot of Fellini's *bambina diavola*, Melissa Graps has gone on to become arguably the most imitated of all monsters originating in 20th century cinema with her offspring appearing in such varied films as Lamberto Bava's *La casa con la scala nel buio*/*A Blade in the Dark* (1983), Martin Scorsese's *The Last Temptation of Christ* (1988), Umberto Lenzi's *La casa 3*/*Ghosthouse* (1988), William Malone's *Feardotcom* (2002), Joe Dante's *The Hole* (2012), and Guillermo del Toro's *Crimson Peak* (2015).

In casting the part, Fellini would experience the same difficulties that Bava had gone through before him. In both cases, hundreds of little girls were auditioned and found to be unacceptable; they did not have the specific, uncanny quality that was needed. Bava had ended up casting *a boy*, the son of his concierge, in the role. This was not a generally known detail at the time, and it was not the solution found by Fellini, who—according to his assistant Liliana Betti—ended up casting two people: "In the end, Toby Dammit's terrorizing presentiment of death would have the flaxen head, the mysterious ghostly face, of a twenty-two-year-old Russian girl and the wiry little body of a pupil in a dance school."[68] The latter can be seen dancing with her ball on the edge of the collapsed bridge at the end of the film, before Toby makes his jump, and the other was used for close-ups. Only one name is credited, likely that of the Russian girl: Marina Yaru, a name attached to no other film. Though the Yaru surname is Slavic in origin, the Internet claims her to be an Italian actress, probably an assumption based on the patrimony of the film. The most commonly reproduced photo of *la bambina diavola* gives us our only close look at the tiny dancer's face; it is not the same face that we see in this sequence—the girl in the photo is much younger, charming, pretty, soft-featured, full-lipped, without a hint of perversity or menace. She is

---

[67] Quoted in Curti, Roberto. *Italian Gothic Horror Films, 1957-1969* (Jefferson, NC: McFarland & Company), p. 188.

[68] Betti, Liliana. *Fellini: An Intimate Portrait*, p. 152.

anything but frightening. The *bambina diavola* shown in these close-ups is clearly older, thin-lipped, with more prominent teeth and the bonier hands of a woman in her twenties. The coloring of her eyebrows and the almost Van Gogh-like yellow of her long straight hair suggest to me that she was not a natural blonde. Although Liliana Betti mentions only two *bambini diavola*, as many as two others also appear. I will mention them when we get to them.

Mario Bava had taken particular pride in *Operazione paura*, a film made for very little money and, ultimately, for even less than that — the budget ran out during production and the cast and crew volunteered to continue working for no salary out of their devotion to the story and its director. The film's star Erika Blanc told me that Luchino Visconti gave the film a standing ovation at its first screening. After the release of *Tre passi nel delirio* — as *Histoires Extraordinaires* was called in Italy — rumors of the... (shall we say "quotation"?)... got back to Bava, who went to see the film for himself. "I saw Fellini's 'Toby Dammit,' with that little ghost playing ball," Bava later told Luigi Cozzi. "It was the same character I had in my film — exactly the same! I told this to [Fellini's wife] Giulietta Masina, and she just shrugged her shoulders and said, smiling, 'You know how Federico is...'"

Toby keeps the memory of the *bambina diavola* at bay with a deep swig from his silver hip flask. He looks very nearly embalmed with alcohol, but this is the first time we see his response to drink, which is to wince and crumple over ("I'm alright, I'm alright, I'm alright...") as if his liver, stomach and kidneys are already well on their way to being eroded from within. Behind his head, the rear window of the vehicle is lined with pleated red silk, like the lining of a coffin. He is comforted by the hand of his interpreter on his arm, her fingernails painted red like those of you-know-who.

Though Fellini and Zapponi seem to be veering wildly away from Poe's original story, satire is at the very heart of "Toby Dammit." Instead of satirizing so-called "morality tales" and the boorish critics who considered morals to be *de rigeur* in storytelling, Fellini uses his segment to satirize the world of Italian cinema (which was his own literary milieu, if you will), as well as French intellectualism, the impact of American showmanship on

European culture, and much else besides. The film has already touched on the personalities found behind the scenes of filmmaking and the increasingly baroque mutations taking place in Italian Westerns, but now—in its most straightforward comic passage—it proceeds to deflate the absurd pretenses of the television interview.

In the pensive electrical hum of a TV studio, Toby sits silently as the room prepares for broadcast, swinging a boom mic into place as a team of interviewers pace or sit studiously or sullenly. Toby indulges in another drink, again recoiling from the pain that follows each swallow. He sees the program's hostess (Anne Tonietti) preparing for her close-up by licking her lips and indulging in a series of ridiculous facial exercises. As her camera flashes the word "PRONTI," she snaps into position. The studio's three cameras point at Toby, who smilingly holds up both arms like a man under arrest. "PRONTI" switches to "ONDA" and the hostess launches into her introduction (in unsubtitled Italian in the English version), walking past a mural of various images of the actor till she finally sits beside him and gives his name. A jaunty, pre-recorded fanfare is played—a tape activated by two bored-looking, middle-aged technicians in lab coats, working from a mezzanine sound booth.

"What the—? Are you serious?" Toby reacts.

As the music dies down, the hostess—now off-camera—dips down and crawls below camera across the floor beside Toby's legs. He can't believe what he's seeing, and the questions that follow are no more believable. The interviewers are, in order of their questioning, Aleardo Ward, Paul Cooper and the wonderful Milena Vukotic, who previously played Giulietta's maid in *Juliet of the Spirits*. A favorite of Luís Buñuel, Vukotic would be prominently featured in *Le charme discret de la bourgeoisie/The Discreet Charm of the Bourgeoisie* (1972), *Le fantôme de la liberté/The Phantom of Liberty* (1974), and *Cet obscure objet du desire/That Obscure Object of Desire* (1977). Horror devotees surely recall the fine performances she gave as the plain sister Esmeralda in Paul Morrissey's *Blood for Dracula/Andy Warhol's Dracula* (1974) and the severe-looking psychiatrist in Carlo Lizzani's *La casa del tappeto giallo/The House of the Yellow Carpet* (1983).

AW: *Have you ever been in Italy before?*
No.[69]
PC: *Why did you come now?*
The Ferrari they're giving me.
Canned applause.
AW: *Do you use LSD or other drugs?*
Always!

---

[69] In French, he is asked if this is his first time in Rome, which he answers in the affirmative.

AW: *Why?*
When I want to return to normal. (If you read Stamp's lips, he says "Because I like them.")
PC: *What do you like most in life?*
I don't know...
PC: *What do you dislike most?*
My public!
MV: *Some say you no longer have a public, Mr. Dammit.*
He blows a raspberry.
[The interviewer giggles and applauds adoringly.]
PC: *How do you explain the success your "Hamlet" had with the critics?*
Obviously, they didn't understand it.
MV: *Mr. Dammit, was your childhood very sad?*
No. My mother was very gay when she beat me. Maybe she was drunk.
PC: *They say, Mr. Dammit, that your temperament is violent and angry. Is it true?*
Say that again and I'll punch you on the nose.

It's a scene that the young John Lydon must have studied very closely before giving any interviews as Johnny Rotten. Toby's public demeanor foreshadows the entire punk movement and its relationship to the press. Just before he answers this last question, he looks over his shoulder to the preparations for another show taking place on an adjacent set that is part kitchen, part dining room. A beautiful brunette is there, dancing amid the workers and technicians preparing for the broadcast. She wears a black *haute couture* dress, matching high heels and pearls—and an apron. As he continues to look, she strikes a mannequin-like pose. She's what would later become known as a Stepford Wife. After answering the question, he turns again to feast his eyes on this robotic creature. In a voice that's barely a whisper, he asks her "Will you marry me?" Fellini doesn't linger on the point, but what this woman and her surroundings embody is a child's interpretation of the perfect mother more than a mature male's ideal of the perfect wife. She is glamorous and model-like, with an apron to underscore her domestic functions as a provider and caregiver, but the image she projects is all but completely desexualized.

The questions renew.

MV: *Do you consider yourself neurotic?*
It's my only quality.
MV: *Can you tell us what is wrong with your life, Signor Dammit?*
Nothing! I'm desperately happy! (At this, the studio lights become blinding to his eyes. He shows signs of beginning to fall apart.)
MV: *Is it true that you've had many jobs—even of an undignified kind?*
Yes...yes...but...*never*...a TV interviewer.
The two lab technicians look at each other, confused. They shrug their shoulders and play the canned applause.
The clever banter continues a bit longer, but then a seriously aimed question pierces the artifice.
AW: *Do you believe in God?*
No. (Toby's reply sounds almost regretful.)
MV: *What about the Devil?*
Yes! In the Devil, yes!
MV: *Oh, how exciting! What is he like? Have you seen him?*
Yes, I've seen him.
MV: *What does he look like? A black cat or a goat or a bat?*
Oh, no. I'm English...not Catholic. To me, the Devil is...cheerful, agile.

"Toby Dammit" by Federico Fellini

At this point, we are shown an image later revealed to be a moment from the end of Toby's life, as the *bambina diavola* raises her lowered head upward to gaze into camera, the long blonde fall of her hair exposing only one eye. As we see the shot now, it places her at screen left—it is a *flipped* version of the image from later in the film, with some of the road from the bridge site visible behind her. The face in this shot, peering through a blonde wig that is now wavy, is not the same shown to us in the flashbacks from the airport—this woman's eyes are a brilliant blue. Nor does she appear to be the same actress shown in the studio photograph of the character, as her lips are not so full. This shot of the evil child—or rather its later reversal to its correct position—is perhaps the most disturbing look at the *bambina diavola*, a kind of Western inversion of the eerie imagery found in such Japanese ghost films as Nobuo Nakagawa's *Yotsuya Kaidan/The Ghost of Yotsuya* (1959) and Masaki Kobayashi's *Kaidan/Kwaidan* (1964).

Back in the studio, Toby has dropped all his defenses. He says: "She looks like a little girl."

At this point in the film, the action cuts to the evening of the Italian Oscars, where Toby is an honored guest. However, according to Fellini scholar Tullio Kezich, "During the edit [of "Toby Dammit"], the director completely cut a fifteen-minute episode of a Western-style film set that had been fun to shoot but ultimately was superfluous."[70] This episode would have shown Toby at work on the set of his Catholic Western *Trente dollari* and would most likely have been placed between the interview and award ceremony sequences, if retained. The disruption that such placement would have provoked is easily imagined, but we must remember that this material was Fellini's only contribution to the Italian Western—if the edited footage still exists, its recovery would be priceless, and certainly well worth including as an extra on any future Blu-ray release of *Histoires Extraordinaires*. Alas, the only known surviving remnant of the *Trente dollari* filming is slightly less than two minutes of behind-the-scenes footage included in the 12-part documentary *La Fellinia*, which is among the supplementary features found in the Infinity Arthouse Collection (UK/Region 2) DVD box set of Fellini's *Orchestra Rehearsal, And the Ship Sailed On,* and *Ginger and Fred*. It can be found in the seventh episode "Il mestiere dal genio" ("The Work of a Genius") on the bonus disc of *And the Ship Sailed On*, beginning at time code 26:25. Unfortunately, the footage offers no glimpse of Terence Stamp in character, but we do get a couple of shots of American actor Van Heflin among the rather more obscure supporting players. It's just a glimpse of what might have been, but the existence of this fragment suggests that more such documentation

[70] Kezich, Tullio. *Federico Fellini: His Life and Times* (Farrar Straus & Giroux, 2007), p. 284.

"Toby Dammit" by Federico Fellini

is likely stored away in a vault somewhere. If you are reading this and in a position to do something about it, I would urge you to locate this footage (Fellini's *Trente dollari* or the documentation of its filming) and interest its owners in sharing it with the rest of us.

Credited as the film's art director (his only screen credit) is the painter Fabrizio Clerici, who—according to Fellini's assistant Liliana Betti—

created a great deal for the film that was ultimately never used. The actual production designer of "Toby Dammit" was its wardrobe designer, Piero Tosi—a frequent collaborator with Luchino Visconti, like Giuseppe Rotunno. Between them, Tosi and Fellini created a lagoon-like setting for the Italian Oscars ceremony that is emphatically purgatorial yet tiered like Dante's vision of Hell. The room itself is immense and hollow, like an airplane hanger—which suggests it was perhaps shot on the legendary Stage 5 at Cinecittà, which had and would house so many sets from so many Fellini films, and eventually play host to the public viewing of Fellini's own coffin in 1993. The walls are rocky and tiered, suggesting the different levels of Hell; there is a surprisingly bare and rudimentary stage, with an unidentified five-piece rock band off to one side, pretending to play Nino Rota's score; a row of stage lights arrayed in front of the stage, while another will be shown looking over Toby's shoulder like yet another luminous white ball; and there's a pool under an undulating cover of smoke, with various round and rectangular tables set about.

But, most of all, there are faces—as many different types as Fellini could find. We are shown approximately thirteen caricatures of other guests before we see Toby seated, looking pensive, gripping and drinking deeply from a tall tumbler of Johnny Walker Red. The woman shown in the next shot is identified as Brigitte in the *Tre passi nel delirio* book (it's important to identify them whenever possible), and the grinning yet somewhat dangerous-looking man with white hair at the end of this brief camera pan is, by implication, the producer of Toby's Western (Andrea Fantasia). Toby drains his glass and looks nervously around, as if ashamed of his alcoholism; Fellini cuts to an arrangement of statuesque brunettes, each with her own way of conveying flirtatious interest—one toasts him, one winks, one closes her eyes and shakes her head as if wallowing in the mere thought of him, one chews her finger, the last raises an eyebrow. Toby smiles at them, hunched over, then sits erect to drink in his companions at table—a smiling middle aged man with none of Toby's style, a sour judgmental-looking woman with white hair, a bosomy actress later identified as "Marilù Lollo" (Marina Traversi) displays her cleavage in a proud arcing gesture, a dour youth, a daydreaming redhead, a face-pulling comedian who is famous for being so ugly.

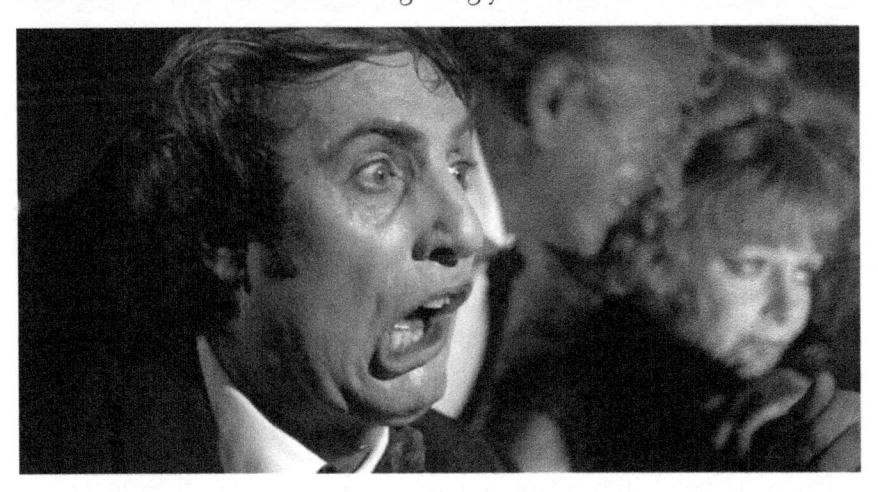

As the Master of Ceremonies makes his opening remarks, a man whispers something to the white-haired man that turns his expression brutal. Toby takes the opportunity to toast his producer. Toby is accosted by a tear-faced clown admirer and a persistent impressionist who calls himself D'Artagnan, who has to be pushed away by a bouncer. A bespectacled woman (I don't know the actress's name, but she can be seen in a fantasy sequence in the De Sica episode of *Le streghe,* calling to her husband as he joins a crowd shadowing the irresistible Silvana Mangano through the streets of a Felliniesque dream city) pushes her teenage daughter Elizabeth (Nella Gambini)—"an exceptional child"—in front of Toby, who asks *"Il è vergine?"* ("Is she a virgin?") It's a joke to him, but the woman crosses her heart and offers her earnest assurances. "She is just a child!" A perspiring, anxious man forever combing his hair (Campanella) identifies himself as Lombardi, Toby's assistant producer. In broken English, he asks Toby to follow the fashion show presentation with a speech of some sort, perhaps a recital from Shakespeare—to which the menacing, dead-faced producer adds "Keep it snappy." Lombardi helpfully explains that, if Shakespeare goes on too long, it becomes boring. The producer then stands and raises a champagne glass to Father Spagna, the two directors, and Vicky Rosenthal, all seated at a table on the next highest tier of the amphitheater.

Up to this point, Toby Dammit has been described by others as a great actor, an important star of the British cinema, but when he is asked to recite some lines of Shakespeare, he is being more specifically allied with the generation of British film actors who achieved their initial success on the London stage in one or more of the great roles of Shakespeare. Peter O'Toole, the actor whom Fellini and Zapponi originally had in mind for the part, had attended the Royal Academy of Dramatic Art and was first recognized for his stage interpretations of Shakespeare at the Bristol Old Vic and with the English Stage Company, well before he began making films. Terence Stamp had done some of this as a student at the Webber

"Toby Dammit" by Federico Fellini

Douglas Academy of Dramatic Art in London, but made his breakthrough as a film actor, scoring an Oscar® nomination for his screen debut in *Billy Budd* (1962). Toby does indeed later recite some lines from the Bard and, in so doing, links himself to the other two protagonists of *Histoires Extraordinaires*, who, as Poe wrote in his original tales, "out-Heroded Herod"—a phrase purloined from Shakespeare's *Hamlet*, Act 3, Scene 2. As with Fellini's decision to change the story's title to the name of its protagonist, the idea to recast Toby Dammit as a Shakespearean actor was thus a unifying masterstroke.

The fashion show is introduced with the wavy reflection of two models crossing the stage, inverted on the surface of the pool separating the audience from the stage like an ersatz River Styx. The camera tilts up to show the stage area, where various models take or hold their positions in front of a table of judges. There is a technician standing on a raised platform, manning a Klieg light. The MC announces models wearing different fashion designs we do not see—"The Queen of Sheba," "Nicht Plus Ultra," both named during a remarkable cutaway to Toby, sunk in his seat behind waves of smoke and looking his most Poe-like as he surveys the abounding show business vampires with alcoholic loathing—and then see two models introduced as "Flux Within Flux," stepping into a Helmut Newton-like two-shot, one of them striking her pose with an aghast facial expression. The models keep coming: "Humiliation," "Lady Hamilton." Lombardi tells Toby it's time for him to go on—just as a man (Federico Boido) rides up on a black horse, dismounting and approaching Toby proudly in a silver shirt, black vest and blue scarf, a huge silver-encrusted sombrero worn around his neck. This is Toby's double in the Western, and he grabs a photo opportunity with the star that Marilù Lollo happily crashes in a mad grab for publicity. The double—who boasts that he has also doubled Tomas Milian, and whom Lombardi addresses as "Robert" in the French version—orders 20 copies for himself. With the explosion of each flashbulb, we know the pictures are going to look ghastly; both Toby and his double look like Death's heads. In this particular block of vignettes, Fellini appears to be satirizing the other two stories in *Histoires Extraordinaires*—the horse and the procession of Jacques Fontenay fashions from "Metzengerstein" and the double from "William Wilson."

SPIRITS OF THE DEAD

As soon as the pictures are taken, Marilù and the double promptly ignore Toby, who is moved to a chair out of the way until he is introduced. His order of another drink is not humored. The ditzy, curly-haired starlet sitting next to him (Monica Pardo, later addressed by the MC as "Miki") suggests that he shouldn't drink so much and he shows her all the sides of his tongue. Sitting to this girl's left is the once-busy woman met by William Wilson outside his fateful casino, now a peroxide blonde. An elderly woman in a glittering gown breaks in, introducing herself: "I am the painter, Stagni. I won an award for a screenplay I wrote. Have you ever seen *What Did You Do With Your Corpse?*[71] Have you seen it? No? Oh well, welcome to Rome. So pleased to meet you..." This small part is in fact played by the painter Stagni, Fides Stagni (1904-2002), who had made a name for herself during the Fascist era as a major artist of the *secondo futurismo* movement. To the best of my knowledge, she never wrote a screenplay, much less an award-winning one, but she acted on occasion — first in Pier Paolo Pasolini's *Uccellacci e uccellini/The Hawks and the Sparrows* (1966), and several other Fellini films, including *Roma, Amarcord, Casanova* and *E la nave va/And the Ship Sails On* (1983).

---

[71] In the French version of the film, the title of this prize-winning screenplay translates as "Take Your Carcass Home," but the title offered by the English track seems to make a more pointed reference to the English title of Raymond Eger's earlier production, Jean Girault's *Les Bricoleurs* (1963), which was also known as *Who Stole the Body?*.

"Toby Dammit" by Federico Fellini

The camera drifts back, with this woman's polite withdrawal, to reveal a short blind man arriving on the arm of a tall woman hatted, scarfed and cuffed in white ostrich feathers. His entrance coincides with Nino Rota's quotation of Julius Fucik's "Entrance of the Gladiators" as part of the score, a musical element never released as part of the film's official soundtrack. The blind man, who is later explained as a legendary Chaplin-like comic who is there to receive a Lifetime Achievement Award, is played by Ferdinand Guillaume (1887-1997), who was one of the first Italian screen comics, if not the first—having begun his career with approximately 100 shorts in which he played the character Tontolini, all made within the space of a few years, followed by an even greater number of shorts in which he played the character Polidor, made between 1912 and 1919. Guillaume also played Pinocchio in the first film version of Carlo Collodi's classic story (1911). Fellini began using him in his own films with *Le notte di Cabiria/The Nights of Cabiria* (1957), in which be played a friar, followed by bit parts in *La dolce vita, Boccaccio 70, 8 ½*, and this—his final work onscreen.

Toby is next accosted by a puppy-nuzzling neurotic who identifies himself as a the publisher of a magazine who is preparing a special issue devoted to the ancient pagan gods—indicating that Fellini was having fun with Zapponi's past history with *Il Delatore*, as well. He wants Toby to pose for eight large photos, "almost completely naked." The actor fields the proposal half-hiding, half-flirting behind the veil of his black silk scarf. Though Terence Stamp was never publicly allied with anyone other than glamorous women, a certain sexual ambiguity was often noted in his early film performances, beginning with Billy Budd, and teased further here; it would be a vital quality in his casting as the mysterious pansexual visitor in Pasolini's *Teorema* (1968, also designed by Piero Tosi) and his much later performance as "Bernadette" in Stephan Elliott's *The Adventures of Priscilla, Queen of the Desert* (1994).

Two slapstick comedians finish their act and leave the stage, one of them walking like a chimp, and the MC[72] announces the Moment of Truth—but first extends his thanks to the judges. The Golden She Wolf Awards are then presented to Marilù Lollo (the camera zooms past her face directly into her

---

[72] This important, uncredited role is played by a handsome, white-haired actor who looks remarkably like the famous Mexican actor Claudio Brook, who was in fact active in French-Italian co-productions at the time; however, a difference in earlobe formations negates this theory.

bosom)[73], the comedy duo Lyon and Tiger (another double act!), then a procession of actresses—including Miki—who repeat the same acceptance speech, and then "the most warmly human of our actresses," Annie Ravel, introduced and dismissed with a single close shot of her voluptuous derrière bumping from side to side as she ambles toward the stage. Finally, Polidor is led onstage by his female companion to tumultuous applause; he is so famous that his name is never mentioned. In French, he jokes that he has a cat's eye ("I only sleep with one eye, with the other, I catch mice"), while in the English version he says, in broken English, "I'm very happy, but you haven't got the right equipment, I need a trapeze"—followed by shots of Toby in the hazy audience, laughing himself sick.

These last several minutes, beginning with Polidor's arrival, were cut from the American International version released as *Spirits of the Dead*. It was the opinion of AIP's Samuel Z. Arkoff that Fellini's spoofing of the Italian Oscars went on too long— too long *in the context of a horror picture*, which is how the film would be viewed in America. He also felt that this footage was disrespectful to the film industry in ways that would not be understood or appreciated in America—and which he, personally, did not appreciate. While I personally enjoy this material, it was not part of my original experience of the picture and I must say the episode feels tighter and more focused without it.

As Toby doubles over in hilarity, the scene drastically shifts gears as the ballad "Ruby"—performed by another blind man, Ray Charles—fades in on the soundtrack. A tall and enigmatic young woman in furs (Antonia Pietrosi, identified in the *Tre passi nel delirio* book as "La Signora") emerges from the shadows to sit beside the actor, a row of spotlights receding into the darkness behind her. When her face hits the light, with her exaggerated eye makeup and ornate hairstyle, she is virtually a living *anime* character of an Italian fashion model. Everything about her looks cold, yet her message to Toby is warm. What she tells him in the French and English versions is essentially the same, yet the wording of the English dialogue differs in revealing ways:

---

[73] This scene was cut from the original US theatrical version; however, in the complete English version now available on DVD and Blu-ray, when the Master of Ceremonies introduces this actress and summons her to the stage in Italian, he calls her "Marilù Traversi."

"Toby Dammit" by Federico Fellini

French (translated from subtitles): *Don't be afraid anymore. I'll take care of you. Always. Yes, always. I understand you. I know you. I've always known you. You won't be alone anymore, because I'll be with you always. Whenever you put out your hand, you'll find mine. You are no longer shipwrecked, no longer a fugitive. No more loneliness. No more selfishness. We will share a life of serenity and devotion. The one you and I were waiting for. You had no faith but you trusted and found me. I am the one you were waiting for. And I am here with you. For ever.*

English: *Don't worry. I will look after you. I understand you, I already know you. I've always known you. From this moment, you will never be alone anymore. I will always be next to you. You'll never have to feel abandoned again. Every time you put out your hand, you'll find mine to hold. You won't have to try and escape anymore. At last, you can stop running. Your loneliness is over. We will have a perfect life, the one we've always been looking for. I know that you have been searching, and now that you have found me, you won't have to search anymore. I am the one you have always been waiting for, and now I am here. With you. For ever.*

This nameless starlet could be an ordinary narcissist who is spinning a romantic yarn of fulfilling Toby's every need in the hope of hitching her wagon to his stardom. However, in the English dialogue, she doesn't mention his solitude; she mentions his *abandonment*. She also mentions his past attempts at *escape*, a life spent *running*. She speaks to him as only the *bambina diavola* would know him, or perhaps only as he would know himself. Her personal presentation also asserts her eyes, which gaze at him through fur—much as the eyes of the *bambina diavola* did through the cascade of her hair. With this in mind, the rack of receding spotlights behind her evoke animated drawings of the approaching bounce of the devil girl's white, silent ball.

Toby listens to her pitch with great calm and appears to be completely seduced by her vision of their mutual happiness. Then, having spun her bliss, she falls silent and recedes back into the shadows, leaving him slumped like a broken doll on his little chair in the dark. Then his name is called from the stage... a spotlight illuminates his crumpled form... it's Showtime!

The actor in this human wreckage kicks in and Toby stands erect with the most hideous forced smile, alcohol all but squirting from his pores. In this moment, Stamp projects not only Toby's pounding headache, his stiffened joints, and his vertigo, but also his inner child, his shattered dreams, and also the last ragged remnants of his professional pride—his desire to give his public what they want, insomuch as it is still within his power to give it. He gains the stage with difficulty and the camera cuts to his subjective viewpoint as he is flung onstage into its tumult of its artifice. There are the MC, the Golden She Wolf winners, and three decorative matrons who look more like ancient caryatids than human beings. As the announcers praise Toby's contributions to British cinema, a young girl with long brown hair snaps his photograph, her bulb flashing a white ball at him; there is a fleeting resemblance. Much of the applause and congratulations footage was also trimmed from the AIP version, which cut directly from his arrival onstage to his speech.

Toby chooses Macbeth's speech from Act V, Scene V of Shakespeare's Scottish play, whose title is considered bad luck to be spoken by actors under the roofs of theaters, so its selection is another way in which Toby seems to be inviting his own doom:

All our yesterdays have lighted fools
The way to dusty death. Out, out, brief candle!
Life's but a walking shadow, a poor player
That struts and frets his hour upon the stage
And then is heard no more. It is a tale
Told by an idiot, full of sound and fury...

Might this one moment have been recorded with live sound? If Terence Stamp post-synchronized this speech to his onscreen lip movements, it is a masterful achievement. By the same token, this moment, dubbed by a different actor in English, is the most painful moment in the film's entire French soundtrack.

Our "poor player" neither begins nor ends his speech properly, as it begins in progress and ends when he makes the sudden decision to turn the stage into a confessional: "But it's not true, I'm a great actor. No. I'm not a great actor. I could have been. I haven't worked for a year. My last director complained because he said I was drunk. I don't know why I'm telling you this. Why did you make me come here? *What do you want from me?*" His attack on the audience suddenly shifts gears to an affectionate reverie about the woman who spoke to him earlier with promises of their future ("She asked me to marry her," he tenderly misremembers—a misstatement that recalls his own proposal to the model at the television station) which builds to digression on alcohol and finally a schizophrenic attack on her, ending in English with "What rubbish!" and in French with "You give me the shits!" As Toby runs offstage, the spotlights suspended in the dark look like so many bouncing balls pursuing him.

Outside, other balls of light surround the Ferrari that's awaiting him in the custody of a man who looks like he was sent there by the mob. It's golden in color, like the She Wolf Award he left behind on the stage—license number 74844 P4. Toby's Ferrari was not really "the latest model," but it was one-of-a-kind: a 1964 Ferrari 330 Fantuzzi Spyder, chassis number 4381SA. Built in 1963 with a V12 engine and a 5-speed manual transmission, the 2100-lbs vehicle had previously been used as a racing car at LeMans and at the Sebring International Raceway in Florida. According

"Toby Dammit" by Federico Fellini

to Nick D, writing for the Supercars.net blog on April 17, 2016, the chassis of 4381SA was rebodied for use in the Fellini film at Carrozzeria Fantuzzi in Modena, "where it was given a new Spyder body, loosely modeled after the 1964 Ferrari 275 P with a similar roll hoop and front end. At the front, the body work was rather crudely riveted around the front grill. The same treatment was done around the rear Kamm tail."

Toby grabs the keys and drops into the driver's seat, caressing the steering wheel with its famous "Prancing Horse" insignia—another connection to "Metzengerstein." This emblem was intended by Enzo Ferrari as a tribute to the fallen Italian World War I fighter pilot Francesco Baracca, who died in 1918 at the age of 30 after flying 34 victorious raids, one of the outstanding achievements of all Allied aviators during the Great War. The Prancing Horse was painted on his plane. Baracca finally flew one too many times, but he was never taken; his body was found shot in the head and it is believed that he took his own life rather than crash or be taken hostage. When Ferrari met Baracca's mother, the Countess Paulina, at a racing event, she suggested that he use the emblem as it would bring him good luck—and it did.

Peter Ammann, who was present on the set of "Toby Dammit," has described it as "a goodbye story, taken from Edgar Allan Poe; we could say, a sort of suicide." He believed that the jaundice informing the satire of the piece—which occasionally extends to literal piss-colored tinting—was very much Fellini's own bile. "Something struck me distinctly during the filming of 'Toby Dammit,'" Amman said. "Fellini gave the impression of feeling a sort of antipathy or even contempt for the world, and especially the film world. Whereas, during *Satyricon*, I found him much more relaxed, untroubled: his face, as well as the atmosphere on the set. The sensation of disgust that emanated from 'Toby Dammit' had disappeared. Indeed, that film seemed to reflect his state of mind: an actor wins an award and receives a sports car; nauseated, he leaves the ceremony, racing in the car towards the abyss of death."

As representatives from the ceremony emerge from the studio to chase Toby, he revs up the Ferrari and speeds off into the night. Fellini's original script covers the remaining 15 minutes of the film in three extremely sketchy pages, indicating that he filmed and assembled the sequence largely on the spot, and to some extent without Stamp's participation, following the actor's departure. The film now embarks on a harrowing acceleration into the labyrinth of Rome after dark, largely divided between shots of Terence Stamp at the wheel in a controlled studio environment and overcranked subjective shots of headlights barreling along actual country roads, down narrow alleys, into culs-de-sac. He soon arrives at an empty plaza where an equestrian statue, printed or painted on cardboard, leans flatly against whatever monument was actually there. The light

"Toby Dammit" by Federico Fellini

source illuminating the area is wobbly, causing Toby to stop and look around: he sees two similarly painted cardboard dogs looking eagerly in the same direction. He follows their line of sight to a small group of workmen using a high ladder and cherry picker to lower a suspended light, which spins down in its descent like a flying saucer.

As Roberto Curti has noted, this image may be another of the film's *hommages* to Mario Bava, as it evokes a moment in his own seminal Italian horror anthology—"*La goccia d'acqua*"/"The Drop of Water" in *I tre volti della paura/Black Sabbath* (1963)—in which a ceiling lamp of similar design repeatedly lowers on a faulty electrical cord, causing its exposed bulb to burn a dress laid out for a dead woman's burial.

Toby revs his motor and speeds in the lamp's direction, driving directly below it as the workers curse him. He drives down a steep road into another area where we see a life-sized painted cardboard figure of a chef stirring a pot, and another figure positioned in the distance. He speeds down the road, through more country, arriving at another small village where an actual man in waiter's clothes stands posed like a cardboard figure. Amused, Toby continues on, taking the road to Frascati and quickly passing a male mannequin in a white tuxedo. At some further roaring distance, he stops the car and allows the scene to grow quiet. He looks lost, uncertain where to go. He pierces the night with yells and screams, sounding like an animal in pain—live sound recording. Then he revs the motor to a level equal to his frustration and speeds off again.

After hellblazing along a few more twists and turns, Toby finds himself in a clearing where two men can be seen sleeping, slumped over an outdoor table next to a herd of sheep penned in by a rope partition. All but one of the sheep are artificial. A drunk stumbles out of the shadows. Toby calls out to him, "How do I get to... Roma?" The addle-pated man smiles back, saying nothing.

Toby's question clearly alludes ironically to the saying "All roads lead to Rome," which dates back to the days of the Roman Empire, when all roads to outlying territories literally radiated outward from central Rome. There is also the Medieval Latin phrase, "*Mille vie ducunt hominem per secula Romam*," which means "A thousand roads lead a man forever towards Rome," which in the context of this scene suggests that Toby is locked into the fate to which he was damned, no matter how he may contrive to escape it.

The roar of the motor tells us that Toby has sped off again. He follows a curving road with an outer wall painted with arrows, urging him on—but these lead to barricades. Turning around, he sees a baker (a real man) standing perfectly still at the side of the road, holding a tray of baked goods. Darting evil glances side to side, Toby races forward, his Ferrari clipping the baker and knocking him over. He speeds away down a road overhung with festive Art Nouveau lighting, possibly *luci natalizie* (Christmas lights), and there is a beautiful shot showing each of these lights serially combing the car's shiny surface front to back as it cruises beneath them. Seeing the film for the first time, I had never felt as gripped by a movie as I felt at this moment, having no idea where this journey was going to take Toby—or me. The road leads to more turns, more culs-de-sac, even an off-kilter street where a poster for Walt Disney's *Mary Poppins* is displayed.

A ghost-like sheet, hung on an outdoor line to dry, overhangs a street where Toby pauses to stretch his legs and call out for assistance. He dampens his face with water from a trough and walks past a donkey, tearing off his jacket as a church bell tolls. After the fourth toll, he exits frame and we're back on the road. He accelerates through an open tollgate, through a service station, faster, faster, onto a new road—where, before he has a chance to see it, he soon crashes through a roadblock, sending the Ferrari spinning out of control.

The entire Ferrari by night sequence strongly recalls a similar one in Vincente Minnelli's film *Two Weeks in Another Town* (1962), and it is unlikely that the resemblance was accidental as the two films tell a similar story. In Minnelli's film, based on a novel by Irwin Shaw, Kirk Douglas plays Jack Andrus, a once-successful filmmaker who succumbed to alcoholism and a nervous breakdown in the wake of a romantic betrayal, who is summoned to Rome to assist his former mentor, the great but aging director Maurice Kruger (Edward G. Robinson). Seeing Kruger's project as an opportunity to rebuild his own life and career, Andrus accepts and seems poised for even greater opportunity when Kruger suffers a non-fatal heart attack and recommends him to take over as director. Andrus seems to be doing well, until a chance encounter with Carlotta (Cyd Charisse)—

"Toby Dammit" by Federico Fellini

the woman who once destroyed him—endangers his equilibrium. The film culminates in an hysterically-pitched scene where Jack speeds off in a car with Carlotta, very much in artificial process shot mode, pushing her to the edge of a madness to regain his authority and self-control. Though very much a soap opera, *Two Weeks in Another Town* was shot on location in Rome and includes some marvelous inside references and mementos of the time period for viewers familiar with the "Hollywood on the Tiber" era, including a hotel room party where the young actors are playing records like Bruno Martino's "Dracula Cha Cha Cha," heard in the film *Tempi duri per I vampire/Uncle Was a Vampire* (1959).

When Toby climbs out of his car, into a barren landscape of darkness and overturned pylons, his first response to having cheated death is to giggle, which prompts the voices of some concerned onlookers to shout from the surrounding dark. A silhouetted figure calls out to him from a tin-roofed shack on the side of the road, telling him in Italian that the bridge is out, that he will have to take the detour. On the opposite side of the road, another Italian voice confirms this. Toby peers into the dark from whence the voices came and sees a small campfire and a man kneeling on all fours inside a tent. He's like the figure briefly seen at the airport, wearing a false face in black-and-white. The face, held to his head with a cloth bandage, looks like a drawing in charcoal.

In the French version of the film, these characters call out their warnings to Toby in French—and, as we have seen him speaking in French earlier, it makes no sense that he is subsequently shocked by his discovery of the bridge's collapse. In the English version, these warnings are addressed to him in Italian, so his obliviousness is more understandable. He saunters forward and stumbles over a large oil drum. He sends it rolling with an annoyed kick, then turns back—in the distance, we see (as he does) that only one headlight of the Ferrari seems to be working now, so the car appears to be winking at him, or taunting him like the eye of the *bambina diavola* through a veil of hair—only to spin around once again as he hears the reverberant sound of the drum falling over the lip of the impasse, its crash far below resounding through the night. It is only at this point that he understands. He steps tentatively forward through the darkness, and sees the white stripe down the middle of the road suddenly interrupted by a large gap where the bridge has collapsed.

Poe's original story concludes with Toby Dammit decapitated by an iron bar used to support a bridge. While developing the film script, Bernardino Zapponi read a news item about the Ariccia Bridge, in the Castelli Romani quarter outside Rome, which had collapsed. According to *Wikipedia*, they visited the location one night and "were deeply impressed by the bridge's ruined splendor." However, the bridge seen in the film is a painting by

"Toby Dammit" by Federico Fellini

Josef Nathanson, given an illusion of depth by photographing it through a live veil of smoke. Toby stares at the impressive sight, his expression of terror melting into one of tender delight, as we suddenly see his little Devil dancing with her ball on the lip of the bridge's other side. (This would be the dance school pupil mentioned by Liliana Betti, whose face is only seen in the film's official still of the character.) He boasts to men in the dark: "I am going to get across!" (The French version offers the far weaker "Wait— the car!") Toby once again smiles across the gap in the road, and we cut to an off-centered shot of the *bambina diavola* clutching her ball, seeming to issue him a challenge as both her eyes gaze around a loose, descendent curl of hair. It may be an illusion of her makeup, but this does not appear to be the same actress seen in either of the character's earlier appearances; she looks older than both, with darker, more piercing eyes and a cleft in her chin, clearly wearing a different wig with slight curls. In Liliana Betti's book, it is a photograph of this actress that is identified as Marina Yaru.

Toby laughs, hops back into the Ferrari and accelerates it in reverse to the bridge's entrance. There, as the *bambina diavola* waits, he sits calmly as the car's chassis sucks the smoke on the road up into its bowels. Looking like a ravaged Saint, Toby makes peace with his destiny and, laughing maniacally to find his courage, speeds once more into the dark. There is no sound of a crash. As the camera slowly penetrates the dark to approach the other side of the collapsed bridge—a scale model created by the painter Renzo Vespignani, replacing the painting—we begin to hear a weak, indefinable sound that is gradually revealed as the *squeak squeak squeak* of a steel wire plucked as if by an unseen hand. It was strung as a barrier across the opposing edge of the pit. As we move inexorably forward, we see a neck-wide portion of the wire that is dripping with fresh blood. The wire appears to be a thin but hollow tube, allowing a continual flow of stage blood to trickle out from pre-drilled holes. It is a shot that Zapponi would paraphrase when he wrote the climax of his script for Dario Argento's *Profondo rosso/Deep Red* (1975). On my first viewing, I had never experienced a moment so exquisitely terrifying and neither its power or its chilling delicacy has ever diminished for me.

Presumably the car made the jump successfully—perhaps it (and its decapitated pilot) made it all the way to Roma, but there is no sign of it. Goodbye the Ferrari, but Toby's severed head is shown lying on the road. I believe the head to have been one of numerous uncredited special makeup effects props created during the 1960s by Carlo Rambaldi. The luminous ball bounces in out of the darkness onto the striped road, then rolls toward the prize it has come to claim. In a print reversal of the earlier shot used to identify her during the television interview, the *bambina diavola* reappears, one eye peering through the fall of her golden hair. We see the lap of her dress of white lace, one hand at rest on her ball as the other reaches out of shot and returns clutching the head by its hair.

The last shot of the film shows a third version of the bridge, this one a more ambitious scale model that includes a series of arcing street lamps and encompasses some depth to the road beyond. Viewed behind a sheet of glass that has been painted to include the nearest broken lip of road, the other side is a different model with a thinner surface of road. It is built in front of a cyclorama showing some vaguely delineated hills and a cloudy sky, and the whole blooms into view as stage lights are faded up. The end credits roll over a portrait of Poe that is tinted red in the version presently available on Blu-ray, though I remember it being sepia-toned when it played at my local theater and in TV syndication.

ONE OF THE MOST IMPORTANT ELEMENTS of "Toby Dammit" is its score, composed by Fellini's longtime collaborator Nino Rota (1911-1979), and arranged and conducted by Carlo Savina (1919-2002). It is the only music from *Histoires Extraordinaires* to have had an official release, but that official release took many years to materialize.

Rota's score, as heard in the film, relies on recurrences and subtle reworkings of two basic themes—one for Toby, one for the *bambina diavola*—as well as brief, incidental themes for the talk show and awards ceremony; no more than that. However, as heard in the score's fullest expression as a recording, the main cues amount to just under 26 minutes, which would cover a good deal more of the film than one might imagine.

Rota's main theme is a virtuosic study in contrasts: at its foundation, it's a straight 2/4 rhythm played by acoustic guitar (in a jaunty, 1920s jazz manner) and a double bass, over which an impressively dextrous, Django Reinhardt-style theme is played—not on guitar, but rather on keyboard in eighth note triplets, initially on piano, followed by a response of softer *staccato* chords played on electric organ. After two statements of the main theme in this mode, the two keyboard instruments trade parts for a third statement (that is, Hammond on the main theme, followed by piano staccato), before the piece segues into a hazy, jazzy, minor key refrain—too short for a bridge, and not quite a chorus—with a lead clarinet, its part mirrored on electric keyboard, which encompasses a brief quotation from the song "Ruby." The piece ends with keyboard and clarinet trading off the tricky lead part, and building to a kind of frenzied arrival at synchronicity and an abrupt end. The piece conjures a remarkable cartoon image of a stumbling imp on the loose in fashionable high society.

The "Demon Child Theme," as it's called in English, is fairly minimalistic, taking in drama from the available space around its alternating keyboard notes played over a suspended note played on electronic keyboard or strings.

In music for the awards ceremony that Fellini did not use, Rota introduced a blithe "Tea for Two" shuffle, based on the song by Vincent Youmans and Irving Caesar introduced in the 1925 musical *No, No, Nanette*. Interestingly, the play—like Poe's story—was based on a bet, in the former's case, a woman's bet that she could say "no" to everything for a full two days. The play was filmed by director David Butler in 1950 under the title *Tea For Two*.

To gain a musicologist's insight into the score, I approached David Huckvale, the author of several books on film music as well as one on adaptations of Edgar Allan Poe's works to film. In the latter, he writes about

"Toby Dammit" by Federico Fellini

Spirits of the Dead but makes no specific remarks about its score. "What stuck me about [Rota's] music as a whole," he told me, "is that it is largely monothematic, the piano subjecting the main theme to variations, and this lends a unity to the otherwise kaleidoscopic imagery of the piece. The use of piano is interesting, not only lending the kind of sophistication that Fellini is obviously after, but also signaling the film's subversion of moviemaking as a whole: this is obviously quite the opposite approach of a mainstream Hollywood symphonic style. Though there is a theme for the girl with the ball, as a whole it's not what one would call a fully synchronized score. Instead, it follows its own structure, playing through the various scenes to provide continuity to Fellini's deliberately disjointed, surrealistic approach, which is, of course, expressive of Dammit's exhausted and increasingly deranged state of mind. Also, though the music can easily be removed from the film and enjoyed as a kind of Jazz Suite, the way it works in the film is to provide a kind of aural glue to the disorientating and exaggerated sound effects, particularly at the beginning of the film when Terence Stamp arrives in the airport and is then driven through the streets. The sound effects are a kind of *musique concrète*, which the formal logic of the music helps to co-ordinate. Indeed, the final scene with the car uses no music, relying almost entirely on sound effects, until the end, when the girl with the ball returns. Rota also picks up on the fairground quality of Fellini's overall approach, quoting Julius Fucik's 'Entrance of the Gladiators' at one point, along with the use of a fairground 'steam-organ' instrumentation. The jazz idiom of course suits the decadent sophistication of the Fellini *demimonde*, but in itself it seems fairly straightforward to me—though it's no less effective and enjoyable for that."

Rota's score also incorporates melodic passages from the song "Ruby," composed by Heinz Eric Roemheld (music) for King Vidor's 1952 film *Ruby Gentry*, starring Jennifer Jones and Charlton Heston. This contradicts the sometimes repeated story that AIP was responsible for including the song in the Fellini segment—as Sam Arkoff himself repeats in his autobiography! Roemheld's powerful melody spawned successful instrumental covers by Richard Hayman, Victor Young and his Orchestra, and also Les Baxter (who subsequently enjoyed great success as AIP's house composer, writing music for most of Roger Corman's Poe films!), whose recording featured the harmonica stylings of Danny Welton. Ray Charles recorded the song, singing lyrics by Mitchell Parish over a lush orchestral arrangement by Marty Paich, for a 1960 single release on the ABC-Paramount label, which subsequently appeared on his 1961 album *Dedicated To You* and many Greatest Hits compilations thereafter:

They say, Ruby you're like a dream
Not always what you seem
And though my heart may break when I awake
Let it be so
I only know, Ruby, it's you
They say, Ruby you're like a song
You don't know right from wrong
And in your eyes I see heart aches for me
But from the start, who stole my heart?
Ruby, it's you
I hear your voice and I must come to you
I have no choice what else can I do?
They say, Ruby you're like a flame
Into my life you came
And though I should beware
Still I don't care you thrill me so.
Ruby, it's you.
Chorus: She's not a dream.

Parish's lyrics—intended to reflect the doomed love of Ruby Gentry and Boake Tackman in Vidor's film, which claims lives outside as well as within the relationship they deny themselves—provide an intriguing touchstone for Toby Dammit, as they can also be taken as relating not only to the *bambina diavola* ("you're like a dream, not always what you seem... I hear your voice, and I must come to you... you're like a flame, into my life you came") but to some ruinous heartbreak that we never learn about ("but from the start, who stole my heart?"). This song, as much as anything written by Rota, suffuses the film with a bleak, gut-wrenching nostalgia that represents the other broken bridge in Toby's life—the one between himself and an irrecoverable past.

The brevity of the music heard in the film may have been responsible

"Toby Dammit" by Federico Fellini

for it being unavailable for so long on record. A promotional single of Ray Charles' "Ruby" (originally recorded in 1960!) was issued at the time of the film's release on the EMI label (QSS 1116); however, cues from Rota's actual score took years to materialize. The first nibble was "Toby Dammit/I Clowns"—a single, shared 3:00 cue!—released in 1974 on an Italian Nino Rota compendium *Tutti I Film di Fellini* (CAM SAG 9053), subsequently issued in France as *Toutes Les Musiques De Film De Fellini* ("All the Music of Fellini Films"; Polydor 2393 084). In 2002, a somewhat more satisfying 7:32 suite of music from the film was included on a promotional Digitmovies CD (CDDM 001). Later that same year, a full score was finally issued by Quartet on CD as *Fellini/Rota: Three Original Soundtracks*, along with the scores for *Satyricon* and *Roma*. In 2005, ten cues from the film were included on another Rota compilation entitled *LSD Roma*, this one originating from the UK on the ÉI label (ACMEM 61CD), along with additional cues from Fellini's *Roma*, Eduardo De Filippo's *Spara Forte Più Forte...Non Capisco/Shoot Loud, Louder...I Don't Understand* (1966) and Lina Wertmuller's *Film d'amore e d'anarchia/Love & Anarchy* (1973). In 2015, Quartet Records issued the complete Rota soundtrack on CD (QR 194): 20 cues in all, including four bonus tracks—two alternate takes of the Awards music (including "Tea for Two" variations, the aforementioned 7:37 suite, and a 2:19 fly-on-the-wall excerpt from the original recording sessions including dialogue from Rota and Fellini. This release was followed a year later by a vinyl pressing of the main score, including 17 cues along with—for the first time ever—the Ray Charles track, from the British label Bella Casa (CASA17LP). Unfortunately, the latter was indifferently pressed and mastered—worth acquiring only as a conversation piece.

When Fellini turned in the completed "Toby Dammit" to his producers, Eger and Grimaldi were deeply impressed—so much so that the future of *Histoires Extraordinaires* was temporarily endangered. The producers believed, accurately, that Fellini's segment would overwhelm the other two, so badly that it might be in the best interests of all concerned to hire another director to complete *Histoires Extraordinaires* and have Fellini shoot another Poe story that could be sent out, *en suite*, with "Toby Dammit." As it happened, Fellini himself was not against the idea. He was drawn to another Poe story that he knew under the title "The Scythe of Time," which may have suggested itself as it was written in the form of a diptych. It was originally published in *The Baltimore American Museum*, September 1838, under the title "The Psyche Zenobia." It is now most commonly reprinted under the bifurcated title "How To Write A Blackwood Article/A Predicament." Fellini was interested in the story within the story, "A Predicament."

As Tullio Kezich wrote, "Federico imagines setting it in Piazza del Campo in Siena, where an elderly English tourist goes up into the Torre del Mangia to watch the horse race. There's a little opening under the big clock and, when the woman sticks her head through it, the minute hand would catch her neck and slice off her head. In Poe's story, Fellini had been particularly taken with the moment in which the horrible pressure of the minute hand pressing onto the woman's neck makes her eyes pop out of their sockets one after the other. They could roll to the foot of the tower and watch the rest of the scene from there."[74]

Fellini met with English actress Dame Margaret Rutherford, who had most recently starred in four popular comic mysteries as Agatha Christie's heroine Miss Marple, and she was quite agreeable to his pitch. But when Fellini came back to his producers with the good news, they had experienced a change of heart—perhaps after breaking the news to Vadim and Malle, who would have been understandably upset about losing the biggest name on their banner.

"Toby Dammit" would win a separate existence from its two fellows, eventually. In 1977, Alberto Grimaldi's company PEA created a double bill that paired the short (identified on posters as *Non scommettere la testa con il diavolo*—an accurate translation of the title of Poe's moral tale—and now featuring "*la participazione straordinaria di*" Salvo Randone) with a slightly retooled version of Fellini's fictional memoir *I clowns/The Clowns* (1971), newly redubbed to replace Fellini's original narration with that of actor Gigi Proietti. The package was sold to Italian audiences as *2 Fellini 2*.

---

[74] Kezich, pp. 285-286.

"Toby Dammit" by Federico Fellini

Time magazine praised the Fellini episode as "a 40-minute excursion across the surreal landscape of his boundless imagination... Indeed, there is almost too much in ["Toby Dammit"] for a short film. Fellini's sometimes prodigal genius threatens to overwhelm the story, which he apparently agreed to do only on the advice of his astrologer. But even to such journeyman projects, Fellini brings the kind of stylistic prestidigitation that has made him one of the world's greatest film makers."

In a curious footnote to this adventure: two years after the completion of "Toby Dammit," during his 50th year, Federico Fellini was involved in a minor traffic accident in Rimini, the town of his birth. From that moment on, he refused to drive a car ever again.

Premiere and Distribution

RAYMOND EGER ARRANGED FOR *Histoires Extraordinaires* to have its World Premiere at the 21st Cannes Film Festival in May 1968, where it had the unscheduled distinction of closing the festival. It was thereafter decided to discontinue the festivities in acknowledgement of the violent political protests then taking place in the streets of Paris. It was screened "out of competition," one of only two films given such consideration that year—the other being a retrospective 30th Anniversary screening of Victor Fleming's *Gone With the Wind* (1939). "William Wilson" director Louis Malle was chosen to be one of the jurors appointed to select the year's best films, along with Monica Vitti, Roman Polanski and Terence Young—but ultimately, no such prizes were ever awarded. One of the films scheduled to be shown in competition that year was Jack Cardiff's *The Girl on a Motorcycle*, also starring Alain Delon, an adaptation of André Pieyre de Mandiargues' novel *Le Motorcyclette*, which had been inspired by "Metzengerstein."

Tullio Kezich describes the scene: "There is so much noise from people disliking the Poe movie that it's almost impossible to hear the positive reactions. The audience doesn't like Vadim's 'Metzengerstein'... Jane Fonda is miscast—and they don't like Malle's 'William Wilson'... Fellini's piece is welcomed with some appreciation, to be echoed in later reviews. When the movie opens the following season in Italy, Fellini's episode again garners favorable reviews. Some people see it as just an occasion to show off technical virtuosity in relation to formal perfectionism, but others detect new elements in the piece, a shift in stylistic approach... 'Toby Dammit' looks like an episode from *La dolce vita*, but without the tenderness or the exuberance. This narrative comes out of a darker vision of life... Fellini expresses his emotions of the moment, the crisis of a man in middle age, as well as his amazement at being a survivor, still standing next to a camera."

Present in that otherwise dissenting crowd was at least one unabashed admirer: Michael Sarne, who was at the festival to present his own first feature, *Joanna* (1968). He was so captivated by the "Toby Dammit" segment in particular that he subsequently penned a valentine to the picture for the November 1972 issue of *Films and Filming*, which may have helped to bring about the film's belated release in the UK as *Tales of Mystery and Imagination* in April 1973. Sarne rhapsodized about the film as a celluloid tonic to which he returned time and again to escape depression and infuse himself with renewed inspiration.

"When I get in this mood, I close the shutters of my oak-lined drawing room," Sarne wrote. "I haul out the projector and lace up the only film I have, a print of 'Toby Dammit.' It is the only piece of film I have ever possessed, the only one I ever wanted. It was made by Fellini and he was good enough to give me a copy for myself because I love it so much. I've never met him. I'm not sure if I want to. But he talks to me very frequently. It is the same conversation. And yet it is never the same. He made this film for me, and I watch it and watch it and watch it. I have been watching it for years, ever since I first saw it at Cannes when I was there with *Joanna*. It was showing in Hollywood in its package of a short by Vadim and another by Louis Malle. It doesn't last long, perhaps fifty minutes, and during the shooting of *Myra Breckinridge*, I would see the film every night, taking careful note to miss both Vadim's and Louis Malle's. So I must have seen 'Toby Dammit' hundreds of times."

"The movie is a dream," Sarne enthused. "Suddenly I am no longer depressed. I giggle and jump about like a child at Saturday morning pictures."

The Hollywood showings mentioned by Sarne were made possible by another receptive viewer in the audience that fateful evening: American International Pictures president Samuel Z. Arkoff. However, according to his autobiography, Arkoff's expression of interest was met with immediate condescension: "'This is a high-class picture,' one of [the producers] said.'We can get more money from someone other than AIP.'"[75]

Arkoff promptly offered $200,000 for the US and Canadian distribution rights to the picture, telling Eger and Grimaldi, "My money is just as green as MGM or 20th Century Fox's."

Arkoff continues: "Their ears seemed to perk up and they saw no problem when I suggested retitling the picture. But then I mentioned, 'I'll want Fellini to re-edit some of his part of the film. There's a scene that spoofs the Academy Awards, and it seems like a private joke on Fellini's part. It just doesn't fit in the midst of a horror picture. The movie's a little too long, too.'

"They were shocked. The thought of asking an *auteur* like Fellini to doctor his movie was more than they could handle. The deal was dead."

Histoires Extraordinaires opened in Paris the following month, where it counted close to 950,000 admissions during its release at a fairly troubled time. The film then opened the following September as *Tre passi nel delirio* in cities throughout Italy, where it earned 512,000,000 Italian *lire* — the equivalent of $2,212,587.04 in contemporary dollars. Considering that Roger Corman's Poe films were made on budgets of roughly $250,000, *Histoires'* total budget is unlikely to have exceeded $500,000 (=$3.5 million in today's money), even with its all-star cast and list of top directors, so it must have done reasonable business overseas, perhaps breaking even before it was sold to English-speaking territories, the greater share of the world market. Those sales took awhile longer to come.

Arkoff bided his time: "The next year, I was back at Cannes. Even by this time, however, *Histoires Extraordinaires* still hadn't found an American distributor. I again contacted the same producers and made them the same offer. After a full year of struggling to sell their picture, and disappointing box office grosses in Europe, they were more receptive to AIP."

Eger and Grimaldi were still hesitant to approach Fellini about cutting "Toby Dammit" and finally left the matter in Arkoff's hands. Arkoff had a conference with the director by telephone. "Fellini was very gracious," he recalled. "'Sure, I understand,' he said, in his broken English. 'I'm a realist,

---

[75] Arkoff, Samuel Z., with Richard Trubo. *Flying Through Hollywood by the Seat of My Pants* (New York: Birch Lane Press), *p. 145. All Arkoff quotes taken from this source.*

I'd like this film to be seen by American audiences, even if it means cutting a few minutes out of it.' In less than a month, Fellini delivered his portion of the film, cutting out the unnecessary scene and thus editing the picture down to the length we wanted."

AIP not only enforced the cuts that Fellini made to his segment, they made some slight additions to the internegative of *Tales of Mystery and Imagination* they were sent.

Someone at AIP had the inspired idea to retitle the film *Spirits of the Dead*, the title of a poem that Edgar Allan Poe had written in 1827, when he was only 18 years of age — the same age as AIP's current target audience.

SPIRITS OF THE DEAD

Thy soul shall find itself alone
'Mid dark thoughts of the grey tomb-stone;
Not one, of all the crowd, to pry
Into thine hour of secrecy.

Be silent in that solitude,
Which is not loneliness — for then
The spirits of the dead, who stood
In life before thee, are again
In death around thee, and their will
Shall overshadow thee; be still.

The night, though clear, shall frown,
And the stars shall not look down
From their high thrones in the Heaven
With light like hope to mortals given,
But their red orbs, without beam,
To thy weariness shall seem
As a burning and a fever
Which would cling to thee for ever.

Now are thoughts thou shalt not banish,
Now are visions ne'er to vanish;
From thy spirit shall they pass
No more, like dew-drop from the grass.

The breeze, the breath of God, is still,
And the mist upon the hill
Shadowy, shadowy, yet unbroken,
Is a symbol and a token.
How it hangs upon the trees,
A mystery of mysteries!

To present an illusion of continuity with their earlier Poe releases, AIP hired an uncredited but instantly recognizable Vincent Price to read the poem's opening and closing stanzas under black screens appended to the main and end titles.

Ultimately, roughly four minutes of footage was cut from AIP's version of the film, eventually retitled *Spirits of the Dead*, which ran 117:34. It is interesting to note that it was the satirical elements of the Fellini episode, not the sado-erotic elements of its companion stories, that posed a problem for the company. Since AIP's founding in 1955, originally as American Releasing Corporation, they had always marketed horror films as juvenile entertainment; throughout the early 1960s, they were forever meddling with the violent and erotic content of their European acquisitions. In the mid-to-late '60s, however, AIP's target audience began to mature, and in an effort to retain their custom, AIP's product did its best to mature with them, producing pictures like *The Wild Angels*, *Wild in the Streets*, *Psych-Out* and *The Trip*.

Spirits of the Dead premiered in Los Angeles on July 23, 1969—one week before "opening wide" across the country. Its New York City release was inexplicably delayed until the film opened at the Rivoli and Pacific East Theaters on September 3, 1969. A New York wire service story reported that "the color film deals with death, horror and supernatural forces, emphasizing neurotic, if not necrophilic, character obsessions which act as a spur to self destruction."[76] *Spirits* had the distinction of being the first American horror release to carry an R rating ("RESTRICTED—Persons Under 16 Not Admitted, Unless Accompanied by Parent or Adult Guardian"). AIP's print ads for *Spirits* were openly decadent and lascivious, heralding "Edgar Allan Poe's Ultimate Orgy of Evil!" with images of nubile women being bound, gagged, and teased with scalpel blades. Meaningfully, the film's nation-wide release coincided with that of John Schlesinger's *Midnight Cowboy* through United Artists, the first X-rated film to be released by a major studio. In retrospect, the *Spirits* campaign looks like a dry run for AIP's first X-rated release, Cy Endfield's *De Sade*, starring Keir Dullea, John Huston and Lilli Palmer, which was released one month later on August 27.

After completing these initial playdates, *Spirits* returned to select drive-in theaters on November 25, in support of *Witchcraft '70*, with the 1961 film *Burn Witch Burn* (now inexplicably rated R) booked as the "3rd hit." There was one last drive-in tour in late March, early April 1972 when the film played in support of Michael Armstrong's *Mark of the Devil* (1970), with Robert Kelljan's *Count Yorga, Vampire* (1970) third on the bill.

In Arkoff's final estimation, the film was "a satisfactory grosser, particularly in view of the small price we paid. It was the most expensive of the Poe pictures (although we bore only a small portion of the costs), but it wasn't the type of Poe picture our audiences were used to. It had more of a European flavor to it, which didn't have the same broad domestic appeal that our own Poe pictures had." *De Sade*, on the other hand, turned out to be a dismal box office failure—despite an original script by Richard Matheson that AIP's line producer Louis M. "Deke" Heyward once described to me as the finest screenplay he had ever read.

Spirits of the Dead would be followed by other Poe pictures from AIP, but not one of them—*The Oblong Box* (1970), *Cry of the Banshee* (1971), *The Murders in the Rue Morgue* (1972)—had anything to do with Poe beyond the title. In 1970, the company distributed to television an independently-made, one-hour production on videotape from Kenneth Johnson Productions, *An Evening with Edgar Allan Poe*. It starred Vincent

---

[76] Unsigned. *The Cincinnati Enquirer*, 31 August 1969, p. 49.

Price in four one-man vignettes based on the stories "The Tell-Tale Heart," "The Sphinx", "The Cask of Amontillado" and "The Pit and the Pendulum." That same year, Roger Corman directed a tongue-in-cheek teenage apocalypse film called *Gas-s-s-s! Or, It Became Necessary To Destroy The World In Order To Save It* (1970), whose sprawling Dramatis Personae included a Victorian biker named Edgar Allan (Bruce Karcher) with a pet raven clamped onto his shoulder. Poe and Mandiargues, reconciled at last. It was Corman's final film for AIP, who made editorial changes to the picture that angered him.

In 2011, I had the honor of interviewing Roger Corman over two nights at the St. Louis Film Festival's "Vincentennial" celebration. It was while discussing with him his own revered "Poe Cycle" that it occurred to me to ask if he had ever seen *Spirits of the Dead*. To my surprise, at a distance of more than 40 years, he had not. This surprised me because I knew Corman to be a great devotee of Fellini who had once gone against his own corporate grain to distribute *Amarcord* through his production/distribution company, New World Pictures. Without pausing to understand, I eagerly recommended it to him, and could see at once in his expression that it mightn't have been a casual oversight at all—that the film may well represent to him—on some level—an intrusion into a trail he had blazed and another of AIP's many thoughtless mishandlings of a once flourishing and mutually beneficial partnership.

AFTERLIFE

OF COURSE, THE YOUNG MAN who stood in the cold for those long, painful hours under the marquee of the Plaza Theater, longing to see *Spirits of the Dead* once again, went on to see it many, many more times — and in many, many different formats.

Archival newspaper listings show that *Spirits of the Dead* had its first local television broadcast in October 1973 — a time when I had neither a television nor exposure to TV listings. However, beginning in February 1976 — by which time I was two years married and with television — it began airing frequently on Cincinnati's independent station, WXIX-TV, Channel 19 — and I do mean frequently. The record shows that the film played that year no fewer than five times, in that year alone, on February 29, March 6, March 7, August 15, and August 22. I must have caught them all. I was still catching broadcasts into the early 1980s, when I acquired my first videocassette recorder and had the pleasure of capturing it on Beta cassette. My recording, with the commercials meticulously removed, was subsequently clocked at 115:25 — a loss of two minutes and nine seconds from AIP's theatrical cut.

While I cannot offer a world tour of the various releases of *Histoires Extraordinaires* on home video, I can at least offer a concise list of those releases I consider important — either as ideals, or as aberrations.

1985

In this year, *Histoires Extraordinaires* was released on Japanese laserdisc (#SF098-0069) by Pioneer Electronic Corporation, in French with Japanese subtitles. The two-disc set was unchaptered and presented each story in CAV on a separate platter side, allowing the film to be examined frame-by-frame with reasonable clarity. The transfer was letterboxed a little tightly at approximately 1.80:1, but looked quite handsome for its time, with strong colors and decent monaural sound. That said, there was some distortion about the color as the surfaces of the casino gaming tables in "William Wilson" were blue rather than green. The subtitles appeared on the image and were not removable.

1987

In the United Kingdom, Xtasy Video LTD released a bizarre and, one suspects, unauthorized version of the film on VHS under the title *Powers of Evil*, which was granted a 15 certificate. Running only 77 minutes, it not only omitted the Louis Malle segment in its entirety but also rearranged the order of the Fellini and Vadim episodes. The box copy reports: "The first stars the legendary TERENCE STAMP in DON'T BET HEADS, directed by FEDERICO FELLINI, a wild and weird story of power and intrigue. The second, METZENGERSTEIN, stars the delectable JANE FONDA in a drama of low morals and high drama. Directed by ROGER VADIM, the erotic content is suitably enacted by the half clad starlet, JANE FONDA, in what must be without doubt her sexiest role in front of the cameras. A film not to be missed."

1995

Water Bearer Films' letterboxed videocassette release of *Histoires Extraordinaires* marks the US debut of the film in its unexpurgated form — and the end of *Spirits of the Dead* as the official US version. However, it is an unauthorized, meddled-with version and should be avoided.

The cassette is letterboxed at 1.85:1, with a slightly taller aperture than Pioneer's Japanese disc. Unfortunately, the colors are muted and the transfer is also brighter than it should be, washing-out some cinematographic detail. The mono sound quality is excellent and boldly detailed, lending an appreciable resonance to the orchestral depths of Jean Prodomides' "Metzengerstein" score.

Water Bearer's source materials originated on tape from the Australian television network SBS, in the 25 frames-per-second PAL format. Therefore, while the compression is not discernible to the naked eye, the 24 f.p.s. film runs 5:03 shorter than it actually is.

More importantly, rather than subtitle the original French narration of "Metzengerstein"—which was certainly possible, considering that it never interfered with actual dialogue—SBS opted to record new, English-language narration over the French soundtrack, which sounds distinctly out-of-place and runs roughshod over the delicate atmosphere of the episode. Narration was also laid over scenes that did not originally make use of it, such as the scene of Frédérique entertaining her stallion with a lute. This new narration also compares badly with the English- dubbed narration heard in the version distributed by AIP.

AIP: *At 22 years of age, Frédérique, Countess of Metzengerstein, became heir to a vast family fortune. Seldom had a noble of her land possessed an estate of such magnificence. She ruled capriciously; day was night, night was day—according to her fancy. That morning, haunted by the nightmare of the dawn, she decided to take her guests to the castle where she had spent her childhood.*

SBS: *At the age of 22, Frédérique, Countess of Metzengerstein, inherited the entire family fortune. Rarely had a noble of this land ever come into such a legacy. She ruled over it capriciously, both night and day, according to her whims. That morning, still haunted by her dawn nightmares, she decided to take her guests to the castle where she had spent her childhood.*

1996

Water Bearer Films subsequently licensed the film to Image Entertainment for release on LaserDisc (#D3561WB). Hearing that this release was imminent, I phoned Image and explained to them that the Fellini episode needed to be presented in English to make proper sense. They had no access to such materials, so I offered to make my homemade Beta cassette available. I sent it to them, they agreed with my findings, and decided to use the English tracks for all three stories as an analog track option. I was honored to receive credit for my service on the back cover, the first public acknowledgement of my love for the film. It is my understanding that the disc was later withdrawn from circulation because the film rights had not been properly cleared. That said, this variant can still be found on eBay.

2008

A new restoration of "Toby Dammit"—supervised by its cinematographer, Giuseppe Rotunno—was presented at the Tribeca Film Festival in New York City by actress Ornella Muti and Sergio Toffetti, director of the CinetecaNazionale in Rome, who financed the project together. As the festival notes mentioned, "The invaluable contribution of the Ornella Muti Network to this project marks the first time an Italian actor has invested in the preservation of a classic Italian film." Attendees acclaimed the film as a lost masterpiece.

2010

The definitive release of the film to date is the Arrow Academy Blu-ray, first issued in the UK and now available in the US as well. Its first printing included a deluxe illustrated softcover booklet that included the three relevant Poe tales and also my in-depth article about the film—originally published in *Video Watchdog* #33 (May/June 1996) and, I am sorry to say, the piece is guilty of several errors which have been corrected in the book you are holding now.

The presentation of the film is breathtaking with authentic Technicolor color values. English, French and Italian audio options are included for all three stories, as well as English subtitles. The Vincent Price recitations from the AIP release are also present, though of necessity bracketed as separate bonus items.

DEAD RECKONING

WITH THE PUBLICATION of this book in 2018, *Histoires Extraordinaires* will mark the 50th anniversary of its release. Given that five decades have now passed, I have a better idea now of why it had the once-in-a-lifetime effect that it had on me, and why it has taken so long for the film to receive its fair due.

Point One: It appears to be a horror picture.

Point Two: It is not a horror picture.

Spirits of the Dead was sold as a horror film, but it is more correctly *fantastique*—a French expression that both means the same, yet encompasses so much more. If one approaches it as a genre piece, it falls short—not short of its goal but of uninformed audience expectations. There isn't much in the film that is designed to frighten—the first and second stories are more interested in darkly titillating the viewer; the film's only monsters are a horse, a man's "good" double, and a little girl with a bouncing ball. There is no clear supernatural element. Each of the stories, however, engages with the metaphysical, the inexplicable—at the same time, as in Poe, a counterbalance is provided by allusions to character psychology; in Poe's time, a terrain still uncharted, still undefined.

If it must be considered as a horror film, it is also an unheard-of occasion in cinema when a group of artists pooled their talents to raise the bar of this critically maligned genre. I cannot help but think that this attempt had something to do with the film's vicious critical reception, at least in my own country. It is interesting to note that this film, which embraced Poe not as a horror writer but as a literary genius, was released in the same year as the first book-length history of the genre in English, *An Illustrated History of the Horror Film* by Carlos Clarens.

For AIP to slip some Vincent Price into it was, I can now see, purely opportunistic on their part—an attempt to incorporate a maverick film with big names attached into their corporate harness and continuity, to ally it with other films with which it had little in common. Nevertheless, I went to see it—and when I heard Price's voice issue from the screen, I was happy; I was comfortable—only to have the rug pulled out from under me most joyously. Others, it seems, were not so pleased.

Point Three: It does not give us the Edgar Allan Poe known to most people.

Point Four: It gives us Edgar Allan Poe—as he existed in the minds and hearts of three distinctive filmmakers, all of whom had read and processed his work to give it back, newly invested with something of themselves. It not only gives us Poe, but his transmigration into the works of other artists—more importantly, European artists.

Edgar Allan Poe was an American author, but—beloved as he was by many—there is much about his writing that works against the American grain. As you have seen, his work was criticized and even condemned by some who considered his work dense and pretentious, unwholesome, and without moral value. The critic in Poe was often at war with his storytelling side, as we can see in the flaunting of his use of archaic and polysyllabic words and foreign phrases, which served only to distance his work from the, ahem, common man. I always take exception when I hear people say that Bram Stoker's *Dracula* is no longer read anymore, because I know perfectly well that it remains a cracking good read; on the other hand, I don't object so much if someone suggests that Poe is a writer now known chiefly through the filmed adaptations of his works. If Poe's writings were as familiar to people as the ancestral portraits in Roger Corman's Poe pictures, *Spirits of the Dead* might have found a stronger foothold in 1968. But "Metzengerstein"? "William Wilson"? "Never Bet the Devil Your Head"? Who had heard of those?

It is generally agreed that Poe found his most enthusiastic readers abroad. He was an American writer but fundamentally European in spirit, as we can see from the subtitle of his very first published story: "A Tale In

Imitation of the German." In a sense, most of what Poe left behind are imitations of lives lived and sold and ruined well outside his home base in Baltimore. Poe more palpably exists in the beleaguered Paris of "The Murders in the Rue Morgue," in the ornate Venice of "The Assignation," in the Spanish dungeons of "The Pit and the Pendulum," in the festive Italy of "The Cask of Amontillado," in the colorful Orient of "The Thousand and Second Tale of Scheherazade," and where the farthest edge of the sea meets another dimension in "Ms. Found In a Bottle."

Did Poe ever dream, as he wrote such works, that they might make their way around the world in his untraveled stead? Did he think these lands real enough to have readers who might read and respond to his stories and poems? Had he ever pondered such a thing—how the world outside his world might respond to his fever dreams—he might have frozen up, worried that all those worldly eyes might see through his landlocked prose and never raise his pen again to relieve his wool-gathering. But the people of those distant lands did read his work, and they found great value in its transmigration into other languages—and what they saw in his writing might well have included things he would never have recognized as coming from himself. *Histoires Extraordinaires'* greatest collective value lies in its embodiment and reflection of the European response to the genius of Poe. As I mentioned at the outset of this book, the film brings to the screen something it did not have before—a sense of the Baudelaire in Poe. It allows us to feel the contribution of this translator to his legend, to his very signature.

Try this metaphor. American rock and roll had to inspire Liverpool's own Beatles to raise that musical form to its next level. While the Beatles' popularity throughout the United Kingdom was of course formidable, it took their arrival in America for them to explode. And if more than 50 years as a Beatles listener and reader have taught me anything, it is that I and my fellow Americans never had the slightest idea of who or what the Beatles were, as they were happening. For us, they were a blast of glad AM tidings in the wake of a Presidential assassination, and those of us who loved them were prepared to follow them anywhere, including down many of the stranger rabbit holes of the 1960s. It is the same thing with Edgar Allan Poe: his work had been influenced by European literature and it needed to return to its inspirational home in its transmogrified form before Poe could—in Toby Dammit's words—"get across."

To me, *Spirits of the Dead* is not only that occasion of homecoming—the occasion of art returning to its birthplace in a necessarily evolved form—but an advancement of the Poe film comparable to the Beatles' summit of artistic expression with *Sergeant Pepper's Lonely Hearts Club Band*. The music from that album, first released in June 1967, was influencing the arts across the board at the time *Histoires Extraordinaires* was in production—as can be seen in the "Rocking Horse People" of "Metzengerstein," the "Within You Without You" of "William Wilson," and in "Toby Dammit," who "blew his mind out in a car."

Not everyone was ready for this shift into third gear. For some reason, the profession of "film critic" seemed especially ill-suited to its evaluation:

"The credentials are impressive. Federico Fellini, Louis Malle and Roger Vadim, each directing a brace of international superstars... but the ads have something else in mind. 'Edgar Allan Poe's ultimate orgy and unbearable horror!' Obviously the distributors were afraid of something—probably the spooks that *Spirits of the Dead* promises but never actually delivers."—*Time* Magazine

"The Vadim is overdecorated and shrill as a drag ball, but still quite fun, and the Malle, based on one of Poe's best stories, is simply tedious... The last hours in Toby Dammit's life become a typical Fellini fantasmagoria, a descent into a maelstrom of grotesque settings, props and faces... From the lip movements, it's apparent that when they were photographed, the actors were speaking everything from English to French, Italian and perhaps even Esperanto."—Vincent Canby

"Vadim's 'Metzengerstein' was made apparently because he had some kinky costumes left over from *Barbarella* and an undaunted desire to continue his campaign of publicly degrading his wife, Jane Fonda."—Richard Schickel

"The only real accomplishment of this shoddy trilogy... is to make Roger Corman's Poe pictures look awfully good in comparison. The contributions of Malle and Vadim, those New Wave pioneers, are silly beyond redemption. Not surprisingly, Fellini's is easily the best, yet it is but a variation on everything he's done for the past decade and has the worst dubbing of all, destroying the film's one potentially satisfying performance (from Terence Stamp). Tedium throughout is definitely the dominant note." — Kevin Thomas, *Los Angeles Times*

Man, you should have seen them kicking Edgar Allan Poe.

A notable exception to this rule was the review by Tony Rayns that appeared in the April 1973 edition of *The Monthly Film Bulletin*. He wrote: "Given that the usual audience for Vadim, Malle and Fellini is not, by and large, the horror film audience, it is not entirely surprising that these adaptations of relatively little known Poe short stories should (with Fellini's notable and characteristic exception) tend to soft-pedal the genre conventions. The predictable disparity between episodes is this time adequately camouflaged by the producers' arrangement of the material in ascending order of interest. Vadim's episode relegates the narrative to a voice-over commentary which makes the film's feeble visual construction (all unsteady zooms and distorted wide angles) all too apparent... Malle films 'William Wilson' in his best *Voleur* manner: a clean, functional shooting style and excellent production design. But despite the use of flashbacks to telescope the narrative, his episode suffers from its brevity... the marathon card game [...] is shot with expert precision... Fellini clearly felt no constraint in adapting Poe... The theme of a *fin-de-siècle* decadent who plays Faust from sheer ennui rather than any spirit of quest still runs through this episode... Terence Stamp's extraordinary androgynous performance... Fellini constructs his episode as two journeys separated by a morbid stasis. The opening touchdown at the airport and journey into Rome... the relationship between these two journeys is possibly the most potent dialectic in all Fellini's work and makes 'Toby Dammit' an indispensible bridge between the private madness of *Juliet of the Spirits* and the public fresco of *Satyricon*."

I appreciate particularly that Rayns isolated a theme — that *fin-de-siècle* decadence — shared by the three stories. Therein lies the Baudelaire. I would like to see the film more often discussed as a trilogy, which requires only that a viewer look past the obvious to everything else that awaits discovery. Fellini's episode gets all the attention as a "liberal" adaptation, but if one knows anything about the original stories, it becomes more apparent how deeply and originally Poe's work was felt by each of its contributors. Every segment in the film is not only representative of the man who made it, but also representative of their collective filmographies—which suggests that Poe had influenced each of them on some level, some elemental level, before they began making films—as he had done with Raymond Eger, looking back on his childhood reading from his recovery bed.

Speaking of childhood, isn't it interesting how all three episodes touch on unresolved disturbances rooted in childhood? The Countess Frédérique of Metzengerstein starts down the slippery slope of her story by choosing to return to the castle where she spent her childhood; William Wilson's story begins in childhood and Louis Malle himself said that filming this story was the first time he had dealt with his own childhood in films (which would subsequently become one of his major topics); and Toby Dammit responds to a question about his childhood with a comic quip about the corporal punishments doled out by a drunken mother—which goes some way toward explaining why the female characters in his highly subjective story are predatory, suspect, at least vaguely demonic in character, all hoping to use him as a pawn in some kind of game.

Spirits of the Dead is a film, I fear, that most people revisit only in part, which not only cheats the film as a whole but prevents its individual parts from striking full chords. As I hope I have shown here, it should be approached as a complete unit, as the three segments venture surprising comment on one another and amount to an interesting, coherent, and surprisingly faithful whole. If the episodes seem (or are) disproportionate in impact, they relate to one another and function together in the way a successful narrative should: a provocative opening, followed by a psychologically resonant middle, culminating in a powerful climax and finale... but this in itself should not cause a boy of fourteen to stand outdoors for two hours on a cold night on the exceedingly slim chance that he might be shown to an indoor seat and forgiven the price of a ticket.

Looking back, I can begin to see, in the spectacle I was willing to make of myself that night, a similarity to the proud demonstrations sometimes made by the young when they "love with a love that is more than love," as Poe wrote in his "Annabel Lee." In making this grand gesture, was I perhaps allying myself with Frédérique, with William Wilson, with Toby

Dammit—all of whom had accepted the gamble that one heroic gesture (a horseback ride to Hell, an armed charge against one's own image, driving a Ferrari across a terrifying chasm) might be all that was separating them from what they most desired?

What had so strongly appealed to me about *Spirits of the Dead* was something I had actually seen before in other films without recognizing it: its fusion of grindhouse and art house cinema, which I've come to consider the headiest aphrodisiac to be found at the movies. It was a profoundly European exercise in the *fantastique*, a more cultured and substantial alternative to American horror films; provocative, adult, avant-garde, as well as some things (the sadistic, druggy things) I wouldn't begin to understand for years to come; it offered me a guidebook to new forms of fear, excitement and titillation. It also connected with my earlier viewing of Mario Bava's *Kill, Baby... Kill!*, with which it interlocked like two pieces of a Borgesian puzzle that would ultimately produce the likeness of my own face. Similar artistic qualities had been present in Val Lewton's RKO productions of the 1940s, which I had seen on television, and in Georges Franju's *Les yeux sans visage* (1960), which I had seen—partly through my fingers—under the title *The Horror Chamber of Dr. Faustus* on a 1963 triple bill with *Corridors of Blood* (1958) and *The Astounding She Monster* (1959-62). What was different about this film was at least partly due to a dawning difference in me, a nascent maturity that was beginning to change the way I looked at everything.

As I walked home that night, I understood on some level that my life had dramatically changed, that somehow it had been given definition. I had been armed with some of the questions I would need to meet my future.

In 1971, I published my first fanzine and became the film and music critic for my high school newspaper. In April 1972, my best friend was found dead in the apartment he shared with his mother—an apparent suicide. I spent the subsequent two weeks out of school, in a form of shock that turned out to be a kind of chrysalis. It was during those two weeks that I did something my friend had once encouraged me to do: I wrote some reviews that I sent to the editor of a recently discovered, favorite magazine called *Cinefantastique*. Within a month or so, a letter came back accepting one of my shorter pieces, and apologizing for not being able to accept my most ambitious submission, a review of Stanley Kubrick's *A Clockwork Orange*, as that title had been promised to another contributor. I was fifteen years old, and I had written something that was going to be read all over the world.

In June of the following year, my increasingly volatile homelife came to an abrupt end. I was forced to leave home and my formal education not long after my sixteenth birthday, losing most of my personal belongings in the process; I was able to take with me only as much as a friend and I could carry out of my apartment in a single trip. My only real prospects were a year or so of writing experience and whatever I had managed to learn about movies. The road of my life had fallen out from under me, but — thanks to a few people who cared whether I lived or died, none of them actual family — I was able to make it across. I — who was born a Gemini (and thus a kind of double) to a widow whose family name was Wilson.

As Fate would have it, waiting for me on the other side was a little girl with long blonde hair. Seventeen and just over five feet tall, she was the box office cashier at the first theater I attended after leaving home. I had called the theater earlier that day to request a pass, but it had not been left at the box office. She remembered transferring my call and allowed my friend and I to go in. As I watched *Theater of Blood* and *Everything You Wanted To Know About Sex (But Were Afraid To Ask)*, the memory of this simple kindness kept coming back to me and I resolved to thank her on the way out. However, by the time we left, the box office had closed, and she was gone. The next day, I got her name from the theater's assistant manager and I sent her a thank you note, care of the theater. My thank you inspired its own thank you, and something about the personality I found in her reply led to a daily mutual correspondence written on butterfly stationery, paper towels and coffee shop napkins. A year later, I proposed to her on the spot where, earlier that night, we had discovered a dead dog.

We married in December 1974 and somehow, with mutual hard work, we were able to make something of ourselves. In the years since, she and I have travelled together to strange and wonderful places; we started a magazine that found readers all over the world; we have been interviewed on television and invited to film sets; and we have walked through applause and popping flashbulbs to step onstage and receive awards of our own.Having crashed one or two cars in my time, I leave all the driving to her.

So when I look now at *Spirits of the Dead*, I see more than the objective facts and subjective opinions I have presented here. I also marvel at the possibilities that it somehow mysteriously proposed to the young and not entirely conscious boy I was—not just possibilities, but a promise as well: a promise of some of the blessings that would come to pass, that I would recognize as they came to greet me, if I took the step of inviting cinema deeper into my heart; a promise that was actually kept.

Select Bibliography

Alpert, Hollis. *Fellini* (New York, NY: Simon & Schuster, 2000).

Betti, Liliana (trans: Joaquin Neugroshel). *Fellini: An Intimate Portrait* (Boston, MA: Little Brown & Company, 1979).

Bosworth, Patricia. *Jane Fonda: The Private Life of a Public Woman* (New York, NY: Houghton Mifflin Harcourt).

Curti, Roberto. *Italian Gothic Horror Films 1957-1969* (Jefferson, NC, McFarland & Company, 2015)

De Mandiargues, André Pieyre (trans: Richard Howard). *The Motorcycle* (New York, NY: Grove Press, 1965).

Fellini, F.; Malle L.; Vadim R. *Tre passi nel delirio* (Bologna: Capelli editore).

Fonda, Peter. *Don't Tell Dad: A Memoir* (New York, NY: Hyperion, 1998).

French, Philip (ed.). *Malle on Malle* (London: Faber & Faber, 1993).

Hardy, Phil (ed.). *The Overlook Film Encyclopedia: Horror* (Woodstock, NY: The Overlook Press, 1995).

Kezich, Tullio. *Federico Fellini: His Life and Work* (Farrar Strauss Giroux, 2007).

Lawrenson, Helen. *Latins Are Still Lousy Lovers* (Hawthorn Books, 1968).

Lucas, Tim. "*Spirits of the Dead* Revisited" in *Video Watchdog* 33 (Cincinnati, OH: Video Watchdog.

Peithman, Stephen. *The Annotated Tales of Edgar Allan Poe* (Garden City, NY: Doubleday & Company, 1981)

Poppi, R. Pecorari, M. *Dizionario del Cinema Italiano I Film vol. 3, dal 1960 al 1969* (Roma ITALY: Gremese editore s.r.l., 1992).

Rayns, Tony. "Histoires Extraordinaires (Tales of Mystery)" reviewed in *The Monthly Film Bulletin*, April 1973.

Sarne, Michael. "Mike Sarne on Fellini's Toby Dammit," *Films and Filming*, November 1972.

Stamp, Terence. *Double Feature* (London: Bloomsbury, 1989).